CROSSED UP
GRAND SLAM LOVE
BOOK 2

HOLLY CRAWFORD

CONTENTS

Trigger Warnings	7
Playlist	9
Prologue	13
Chapter 1	25
Chapter 2	34
Chapter 3	40
Chapter 4	48
Chapter 5	58
Chapter 6	68
Chapter 7	79
Chapter 8	90
Chapter 9	102
Chapter 10	111
Chapter 11	120
Chapter 12	129
Chapter 13	135
Chapter 14	143
Chapter 15	150
Chapter 16	160
Chapter 17	169
Chapter 18	181
Chapter 19	191
Chapter 20	202
Chapter 21	213
Chapter 22	224
Chapter 23	232
Chapter 24	239
Chapter 25	247
Chapter 26	255
Chapter 27	264

Chapter 28	273
Chapter 29	281
Chapter 30	293
Chapter 31	303
Epilogue: Part 1	314
Epilogue: Part 2	323
Acknowledgments	331
About the Author	333

Copyright 2024 Holly Crawford

All rights reserved.

No part of this book may be used or reproduced in any form or by any means, electronic or mechanical, including photocopying, recording, or by any information storage and retrieval system without prior written consent of the author except where permitted by law.

The characters and events depicted in this book are fictitious. Any similarity to real persons, living or dead, is coincidental and not intended by the author.

Published by Crawfish Publishing, LLC.

Edited by Cassidy Hudspeth Edits

Illustrated Cover by Chelsea Kemp Art

Discreet Cover by Disturbed Valkyrie Designs

Trigger Warnings

This book does not necessarily read as a dark book, but does tackle many darker themes throughout. **<u>Trigger warnings in this book include but are not limited to:</u>**

- Domestic violence/abuse **(on page)**
- Child abandonment, pregnancy **(brief mention on page for a side character)**
- Drug and alcohol use during pregnancy resulting in premature birth **(mentioned but not shown on page)**
- Sudden and traumatic loss of a parent **(on page)**
- Child neglect **(described on page but not graphic)**
- Drunk driving
- Forced food regulation **(in past reference, not seen directly on page)**
- Mentions of past disordered eating
- PTSD/Panic attacks **(on page)**
- Breeding kink
- Mild Daddy kink **(NO age play)**

There will be pregnancy and birth depicted on page in second epilogue, but there is NO pregnancy in the main story itself.

Please note this may not be a complete list of triggers. Proceed with caution

✦ Crossed Up @authorhollycrawford

AidanLyla Playlist
Better Together
Luke Combs   3:39

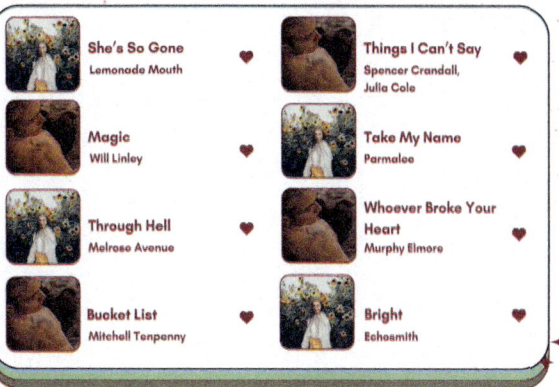

She's So Gone
Lemonade Mouth

Things I Can't Say
Spencer Crandall, Julia Cole

Magic
Will Linley

Take My Name
Parmalee

Through Hell
Melrose Avenue

Whoever Broke Your Heart
Murphy Elmore

Bucket List
Mitchell Tenpenny

Bright
Echosmith

*If you find somewhere to belong; a place that sets your soul on fire,
carve out a space just for you and become the candle in their jack-o-lantern.*

PROLOGUE

Thundering footsteps sound on the stairs leading from the garage to the kitchen and the dish I had been washing slips from my shaking hands into the soapy hot water. Shit. *Why is he home so early? It's not even five o'clock yet, so I don't have dinner started or the house tidied up from where the kids were playing all day.*

"Little bunny, I'm hooome!" Sebastian's grating voice is full of faux cheer and rings out through the large kitchen, sending ice through my veins. I carefully slip off my pink rubber gloves, the material catching on the obnoxious diamond ring on my left hand. The stone is so large the thin silver band barely supports it, but I'm not allowed to take it off, even to do chores.

I'm so lost in my anxiety I don't notice him slipping up behind me until it's too late, my body stiffening when his lips hit the back of my neck with accuracy earned from pulling this same move every day for nearly two years. He must feel me tense up because he bites down on the side of my neck in some bullshit Alpha male bid for my submis-

sion. *The bite is too hard, enough to break the skin, making me cry out.*

His dark chuckle sends a terrified shiver down my spine, and I brace myself for the barrage of insults. Right on cue, his attention wanders to the living room, visible from our position in the kitchen. "Lyla," *he says calmly.* "Why is the house such a disaster, bunny?"

I start to bite my fingernails, one of my nervous habits, and stutter in my haste to appease him. "I-I'm so sorry, Bas. Your sister's kids were here a-all day and I-I haven't had a chance to clean up after our activities yet." *Deep down beneath my terror, I feel anger simmering, and I worry one day soon it will boil over and I'll explode.*

How did I let it get this bad?

The glint in his eyes promises I'll be spending some quality time with the first aid kit later, and the anger starts to boil as I feel myself subconsciously bracing for the hit. Rather than dole out the blow I'm expecting, he sighs a heavy breath through his nose before pasting on a sarcastic little smile that makes his unnaturally angled jaw stand out more than usual.

"Right," *he drawls.* "I'm sure your day babysitting my sister's three kids was...taxing. Meanwhile my twelve-hour day at my real job that pays for this house that you live in for free, was just so terribly easy."

My body goes unnaturally still in response to Sebastian's tone, knowing my chances of making it out without a trip to the hospital this time will be practically nonexistent if I give him the reaction I know he wants, so I do what I have to do to distract him. Swallowing back the bile threatening to ruin my fiancé's expensive suit as I once again play my part of the dutiful fiancée, I rearrange my expres-

sion into one I hope is more sex-kitten and less cornered possum.

"Bas," I purr seductively, running my hands up his chest. "Why don't I make your favorite dinner and then bring you a glass of that whiskey you like while you relax in the den." I pout, playing up the doe-eyed subservient future wife everyone expects me to be.

The coiled tension seeps from his frame under my feigned soft affection and he nods, kissing my cheek. "You're right. After all, I was home early and interrupted your routine. Call me when dinner's done, yeah?" He turns to head out of the room but stops just inside the doorway, turning back to me with a critical gaze. "Oh, and Lyla?"

Anxiety rockets through my system, turning my stomach dangerously. "Yes, honey?"

His expression changes on a dime as a cruel smirk tilts the corners of his lips. "Why don't you take a few minutes to clean yourself up first? You're looking a little... worse for wear."

The remark lands exactly where he aimed it, sending my insecurities spinning with just a few murmured words. Smoothing my long, vibrant auburn hair back into its haphazard bun, I watch as my future husband leaves the room, satisfied for now with only the verbal assault.

I whisper my agreement and keep my spine straight until I hear the TV in the den turn on. The second it does, I slide down the cabinets to the cold tile floor. The volume is nearly deafening as it always is when Bas is watching the stock markets, so I allow myself sixty seconds to break down, setting a timer for my moment.

Exactly one minute later, I wipe the tears from my eyes with a resigned sigh and go about doing what's expected of me as the future Mrs. Sebastian Michael Pennington Junior.

Racing up the stairs, I rush through the fastest shower I possibly can before carefully applying makeup and styling my hair to perfection. Slipping into a tight but modest A-line dress and low heels, I hurry back into the kitchen to put dinner into the now-preheated oven.

Thirty minutes later Sebastian joins me in the formal dining room as soon as I place his full plate down at the head of the elaborately set twelve-person oak table. I track him in my peripheral vision while he inspects the house, ensuring any signs of earlier messes have been taken care of. He must be satisfied with what he finds because all he offers before he sits is a kiss on my sore, rapidly bruising neck, which I dutifully covered with a thick layer of concealer.

I wait until he's seated and eating before following suit, elegantly lowering myself into the chair opposite him and keeping my eyes on my plate. I know better than to interrupt his mealtime with idle chatter. The last time I tried to make conversation earned me a black eye and a steak knife embedded in the wall inches above my shoulder.

The room is blessedly quiet since my fiancé seems to be occupied with his phone during his meal, and a small ember of hope starts to flicker in my chest that tonight might be a good night after all. Forks scraping against fine china plates become a soothing rhythm, settling some of the anxiety that's become a constant thrum through my body and mind.

I should've known better than to trust the silence.

As soon as the last bit of food is cleared from his plate, Sebastian slams his palms down on the table, rattling the glassware and startling me enough that I drop my fork to the floor.

"What did you really do today, bunny?" He spits the word, making it sound less like a term of endearment and more like a taunt.

My jaw drops. "What do you mean?" I choke. "I watched Amelia's kids and then did homework before starting on the dishes. You saw me washing them when you got home."

I don't understand why he's confused that I was still cleaning when he arrived. Sebastian's opulent, 5,000 square foot mansion was a college graduation gift from his father, along with the full maid service he had before I moved in.

Sebastian let them go after we got engaged, citing cleaning as one of my "wifely duties." Between school and watching his sister's three children four days a week, cleaning was taking up every spare minute I had.

I'd asked if he would allow me to hire the service back using my own money so I didn't have to spend hours every day keeping the house up to his standards of cleanliness when I could be using that time to study, and it only took a few seconds to realize my error.

He flew off the handle and told me if I couldn't handle caring for our home, I certainly couldn't handle being a Pennington Wife. My second mistake was bringing up that his parents had an entire staff of people to take care of their house.

Needless to say, I never asked for help again.

His plate hits the wall without warning, shattering all over the floor as I jerk back to the present and let out a startled squeak. Shoving away from the beautiful wood table, he stalks toward me and lifts me by the neck, squeezing hard enough that I have no chance of escaping. Desperate wheezes escape my throat as Sebastian's sweaty palm cuts off my airway.

"Amelia picked up her kids at two-thirty today! What the fuck were you doing for two hours before I walked in that goddamned door? Because it sure as hell wasn't cleaning up your fucking mess. I didn't sign up to live with a slob, Lyla!"

We've been fighting like this more than ever lately, and I'm so tired. Bas wasn't always like this. For the first year we were together, up until we got engaged, he was so sweet. Nice dates, flowers every week for no reason at all, constant love notes, and sweet words. Sure, he could get a little too flirty with other women whenever we'd go out, but I told myself at the end of the day, it was me he was going home with, not those other girls.

But from almost the exact moment he slipped his ring on my finger, it all changed. Instead of treating me like a prize to be won, I became his possession. Our parents treated it like the second coming of Jesus when we got engaged, our fathers more excited than anyone else. That's actually how we met.

Bas's father, Sebastian Michael Pennington Senior, better known as Mike, is the CEO of a massive media conglomerate here in Maryland, while my dad, Colin Kingsley, is one of the most prominent actors of his generation.

Due to my father's wide range of smart investments, he's richer than God and still has a ridiculous amount of pull in the entertainment industry. So despite being mostly retired, he and Mike still work closely together.

My dad dragged me along to an industry party with him one night just before my sophomore year of college, and I refused on principle, not having the energy to deal with more snobby rich girls trying to use me to get to my dad. But he insisted he had someone I should meet.

When we arrived, Sebastian was already there. In a stunning navy bespoke suit, Bas stood out, even in the upper-echelon of the entertainment industry.

Despite being desensitized from growing up around actors and other celebrities, there was this magnetism about him that had me hypnotized from that very first night.

With a full head of dark blond hair, even darker blue eyes, and a sweet, round face, he was the epitome of boy-next-door good looks. That and his charm drew me in like a moth to flame. After being sheltered from dating and boys for most of my life, I didn't hesitate to jump at the chance to be with someone my dad approved of.

I wasn't a virgin by any stretch when I met Sebastian, a fact that irritated him to no end, but I was completely naive when it came to love and what a healthy relationship was supposed to look like.

Which is likely how I ended up in this situation.

A punch to my face knocks me out of my oxygen-deprived stupor, forcing my head to the side in a violent snap as something warm drips down my nose and cheek. Blinking to clear my blurry vision brings me back to a set of blue eyes so dark with anger they're nearly black.

If I was getting more oxygen to my brain, I might be terrified at the dead look in the abyss of Sebastian's glare because even standing at 5'10, my fiancé is still more than half a foot taller than my barely 5'3 frame, which he uses to his advantage often.

"When I ask you a question, I expect a fucking answer. Do you really think I'm going to let my wife act like this?

What if I had brought a colleague home with me?" Sebastian screams in my face. His hand is still wrapped tightly around my throat, but he's moved us closer to the doorway.

He grips my wrist so tight something snaps, forcing me to bite my cheek to hold in the scream. Blood fills my mouth from the fresh cut, making me want to gag, but I don't dare make a sound when he's like this. The smirk tugging up the side of his mouth turns cruel as he yanks me into the hallway, muttering under his breath about teaching me a lesson.

Panic makes me hyper-aware of my surroundings, which is the only reason I spot the baseball bat I left out after playing with Amelia's ten-year-old son earlier.

A plan quickly forms in my mind, and without a sound, I drop to my knees in front of Sebastian, catching him off guard enough that he loses his grip on my neck.

I snatch the bat and tighten my hands around it so hard my fingers turn white with the pressure. "Don't come any closer!" I hiss as harshly as I can. I would have screamed it, but I worried my voice would shake with anything louder than a whisper, and I know that I can't let my fear show right now.

A deranged chuckle leaves his thin lips, sending a bolt of fear skittering down my spine. "Are you going to hit me, Lyla? We both know you're too much of a meek little bunny to follow through with it."

That awful nickname fuels the anger that's been at a low boil in my chest, and I swing with all my might... only to miss him entirely, getting the bat stuck in the drywall. I only have a second to process my own horror until his heavily modified jaw drops in shock, and his dark eyes burn with unrestrained fury.

The fear skittering down my spine causes my hands to

shake as I pull as hard as I can on the handle in a desperate bid to get it free before he retaliates.

"You. Fucking. BITCH!" He leaps forward to attack me just as I manage to yank the bat out of the wall; only it comes out so fast I lose my footing and clip Sebastian's head on the backswing. I watch in stunned silence as he drops like a stone to the ground.

Steeling myself against the panic wreaking havoc on my nervous system, I slowly lean down and press my shaky fingers against his mouth to see if he's breathing.

I realize with a small amount of relief I only knocked him out and sprint up the stairs to the opulently decorated master bedroom, shoving as many clothes as I can into a large duffle bag before making my way to the en-suite bathroom.

Knowing I need to assess the damage, I hesitantly lift my gaze to the ornate circular mirror over the sink. I barely recognize the woman staring back at me.

Blood pours from a thick cut on the bridge of my nose, likely from Sebastian's class ring. Bruises are already forming on my pale skin, made even more pale from the fear coursing through my veins.

There isn't much I can do with the limited time I have left to get out of here, so I quickly open a couple of butterfly bandages to hold the cut closed. Cleaning up as much of the blood as I can, I place a larger bandage over the butterflies on the bridge of my nose to keep it protected. The pain is bad, but not the worst thing I've ever felt, so low-strength over-the-counter medicine will have to do.

After swallowing the pills with water from the tap and gathering the few sentimental things I refuse to leave behind, I hurriedly dump the contents of the cabinet under the bathroom sink, pulling out the small tampon box hidden under a small stack of towels.

I've been hiding away small amounts of money every month for this exact reason.

Sebastian made me quit my job, so I did little things like clipping coupons so I could keep the change from my grocery allowance without him knowing, doing occasional side jobs like housesitting and childcare when he was at work, even selling off designer clothing pieces I had as a teenager that didn't fit anymore.

I squirreled the money away, not knowing if I would ever have the courage to leave my fiancé. I guess some small part of me held out hope he would turn back into that doting man he was when we first got together, but it's clear now that's never going to happen.

After triple-checking how much cash is crammed inside the box, I bury it deep in the duffel bag and make my way back into the bedroom, stopping to take in the grand four-poster bed and antique furnishings worth more than most new cars.

As long as I've lived here, I never felt like this house was a home. It's so much like a museum that relaxing has been nearly impossible, especially since the slightest mess would set off my now ex-fiancé.

If all goes well and I find somewhere safe to land, I'll never set foot inside this lavish prison again. The thought isn't as scary as I expected it to be.

Pausing next to the bed, it takes several tries to slip the tight silver band off my fourth finger, but eventually, I manage. The engagement ring has felt like a shackle for so long that a sigh of relief leaves my lips when I set the diamond on Sebastian's bedside table.

I spare a single backward glance at my ex before

leaving my phone, smartwatch, and anything else that can be tracked nestled inside the lining of the underside of the couch where he hopefully won't think to look. After one last check for anything I may have missed, I walk out the front door, terror and excitement in equal measure fueling my steps.

It's time to start over.

Aidan

"Oh, you've gotta be f— kiddin' me!" My voice is a quiet hiss as I glance towards my playing son, barely catching myself before saying 'fucking'.

"I know, Mr. Black, and I'm so sorry. We simply do not have anyone available on such short notice to travel with you," the accented voice on the other end of the phone says. "I wish you the best of luck in finding a suitable option, and should you need somebody in the off-season, please don't hesitate to call." The click tells me she hung up without waiting for a response, not that I can blame her.

The last in a long line of my son's nannies was unceremoniously fired after I came home from a late practice to find her perched on my bed in nothing but skimpy lingerie while Crew slept down the hall. Needless to say, she won't be getting a reference from me.

"You okay, Daddy?" My son's sweet voice has me taking a deep breath in an attempt to quell my frustration. I do my best not to hide my emotions from Crew, but I also refuse to direct my anger at him in any way.

I've seen enough angry outbursts for both of our lifetimes.

"I'm okay, bud." Reassuring my son is as easy as breathing, even as my mind spins with panic when I realize how royally fucked I really am.

We're still in the thick of Spring Training, with our season starting up again in just over a month, and now I don't have anyone to watch Crew here or for away games. My mama has a bad hip and can't handle a wild, almost 6-year-old for more than a few hours at a time, let alone a week or more.

"Hey, why don't you get dressed, and we'll go see Auntie Wren?"

His eyes light up hearing my question, and even though I see the expression on him almost every single day, it still melts my heart into a puddle in his little hands. I would do anything for my boy, the least of which being both his dad *and mom* on a daily basis.

Listening to his screams of joy over seeing Wren brings a smile to my face in spite of the chaos rioting through my mind over this nanny situation. We've only known my best friend Rhodes's fiancée for a little over a year, but she's become an irreplaceable part of our ragtag family, and Crew and I love her just as much as we love Rhodes.

It really chaps my best friend's backside sometimes that my little hellion prefers the pretty lady over his uncle Rho, given Rhodes has known Crew since he was barely knee-high to a grasshopper.

"Daddy!" My favorite boy shouts at me from upstairs, and I take the steps two at a time to get to him, cursing myself for being so lost in my own head. The same tendril of fear that wraps around my throat every time I hear him scream for me nearly chokes me until I make it to his room.

When it becomes clear he's fine, I heave a relieved sigh and drop down next to him, planting a kiss on the top of his soft blond head. The kid looks just like me with his light blond hair and ice-blue eyes, and I can't help but be selfishly grateful he favors my genes.

Crew is sitting at the end of his brand new "big boy bed" trying to tie his shoes without much luck, and I stifle a chuckle when I see his chubby fingers twisting the laces aimlessly.

Kneeling down, I tie the laces for him, making sure to go slow so he can see how I do it. I untie them again to his frustration, but give him a patient smile. "Try it again little raptor, I know you can do it."

He groans but does as I ask, this time tying the laces like an old pro. His toothy grin lights up the room. "I did it, Daddy!"

I chuckle, ruffling his hair. "I knew you could! So, how are you likin' your bed?" I ask, hiding a small smirk behind my hand. He begged me for *months* for this bed Rhodes showed him on a whim one night after binge-watching all five *Jurassic Park* movies.

So instead of the regular bed I had planned on getting him, there's now a life-size replica of the freaking *Jurassic Park* Jeep in my son's bedroom, surrounded by way too many dinosaur toys.

He stands up and wiggles his little behind in excitement, grabbing my hand to pull me out of the room. "I love it!" he yells excitedly. His inside voice is essentially nonexistent, but I'm working on it with him. "But *hurry*! I wanna go see Auntie and Finny!"

I snicker, knowing how much we all love that damned

dog. Finnegan is a massive grey Newfoundland and the sweetest thing ever, but the big oaf doesn't know his own size when it comes time to show affection. I swear I nearly leave with a pancake for a son every time we make a trip over to the Gray house.

The reminder of Finn makes me realize I need to text Wren before we head over, so I pull out my phone after getting Crew buckled into his car seat.

ME
Y'all busy or can Crew and I come by?

FUTURE MRS. GRAY
Never too busy for you! Rho is at a brand meeting, so it's just me and Finny. Everything okay?

ME
Nanny crisis. Sending up the bat signal.

FUTURE MRS. GRAY
I have beer and takeout menus

ME
You're a saint. You sure you still wanna marry Rhodes?

FUTURE MRS. GRAY
I mean... pretty sure.

Her response earns a chuckle from me. I only ever flirt with her to ruffle my Rhodes's feathers, but she really is a saint of a woman. I can't even count the number of times Wren has rescued me from a babysitting bind, even going so far as getting her dad, Archie, to watch him if I was really stuck.

I never planned on raising Crew by myself, but every second has been worth it. The kid is my clone in every way. Not a drop of his egg donor's looks or personality has shown itself in him yet.

Thank the good Lord for that.

Crew's biological mother, Mia, was a one-night stand gone wrong in every possible way. Just before the start of my rookie year six years ago, I was drunk off my ass and drowning in emotions after losing my father, so I numbed the feelings in any way I could. Mia just happened to fit the bill for a mindless bar hookup.

Seven months later, she showed up on my apartment stoop visibly pregnant after coming clean about the baby and being kicked out by her parents.

Mama nearly tanned my hide when I called her in a panic because I had a pregnant girl sobbing on my couch, but she got on board real quick when she realized how bad off Mia was. Crew was born only a week later, *two months early*.

Thankfully, other than being underweight and in withdrawal, he miraculously didn't have any lasting issues from his mother's drug and alcohol use during her pregnancy.

I didn't know about any of that until his NICU blood tests came back positive for opioids, and Mia disappeared from the hospital without a trace. I always worried she might come back and try to take him, but shortly after his second birthday, her parents notified us she had died in a drunk driving accident.

Her death reminded me so much of my father's that I would have spiraled had I not had my son to take care of. It's been just me and Crew his entire life and although I wouldn't change it for anything, I'm so goddamn lonely.

"Daddy, are you gonna drive, or are you havin' a moment?" Crew's sweet little twang hits my ears and I smile fondly. Raising a kid on your own is hard, but adding in the stress of a professional sports schedule and inconsistent childcare, I've been in over my head for a long time.

When he got older and started noticing my emotions, I tried to explain the concept of being overwhelmed. What came out of my mouth was that sometimes people need "moments" just to be quiet and sit still when their feelings get too big.

At the time, I felt like I was fucking up the explanation of something I so desperately needed, but my sweet toddler took the idea and ran with it. He now freely offers moments to anybody and everybody he thinks is struggling, and pride threatens to bust my chest open every single time.

Gathering my wits, I glance at his concerned expression in the rearview mirror. "I was having a moment, my little raptor, but I'm ready to go if you are!"

I'm ashamed to admit I was an emotionally stunted asshole for much longer than I'm proud of, even after Crew was born. That changed fast when my best friend and teammate Copeland all but kicked my ass into therapy, saying he heard somewhere it would help me be a better father and friend.

The pot calling the kettle black if you ask me.

The drive to our friend's house is only a few minutes, so before I know it we're parked in their spacious driveway with a furry behemoth fogging up my little raptor's window with his slobbery breath. Wren comes running out of the house after her bear of a dog, face bright with laughter as she whips open the back door of my truck.

"Pumpkin butter!" she squeals, quickly extricating my

squirming son from his booster seat with a grunt of effort. I nearly bark out a laugh but manage to choke it down at the last second.

Crew is incredibly tall for his age and built like a dang linebacker, every inch of his small body sturdy as hell. So even though Wren is 5'8 and athletic, she still struggles to cart him around.

He giggles loudly and squishes Wren's cheeks between his small hands. "Auntie! Can we go see the pumpkins?" he asks excitedly.

She smiles softly at him before nuzzling his cheek, ending the affection with a loud raspberry and making him screech with laughter. "Sorry, butter. Mr. Hendrick isn't feeling very good today, so we're going to let him rest up," she says quietly, an edge of concern sneaking into her tone. "Plus, pumpkins are out of season, silly! Now he's got strawberries growing!"

Crew continues to chatter animatedly about all the things he wants to do out at Walter's farm, but a niggle of worry has wormed its way into my chest, hearing the unease lacing my friend's words.

I've gotten to know the old man well the last year or so since Wren moved back because he's a close friend of their family, and in some ways, he's like the father I always wished for growing up.

To hear that he's sick has apprehension bubbling in my gut, and I make a note to call him sooner rather than later.

I watch my son run inside with Finn hot on his heels, but I gently snag Wren by the wrist and hold her back just outside the door. "Is Walt okay?" I try to keep my words to a hushed whisper but can't help the frantic way they come out.

Her pretty blue eyes widen on mine, and I watch them soften with understanding when she gets a good look at my expression. "He's okay, Aid. We're pretty sure it's just the flu, but I'm taking him to the doctor tomorrow just in case."

My breath whooshes out in relief and I pull my friend into a grateful hug. Her soft voice meets my ear a second later. "He would tell you if it was something serious, Aidan. Walter would never keep something like that from you, knowing everything you've been through."

Shooting her a strained smile, I take several deep breaths and force my suddenly tense shoulders to relax. I know she's just trying to help but any mention of my father, brings up things I'd rather not deal with, no matter how abstract. With a silent nod of acknowledgment, I follow her through the foyer and straight into their spacious kitchen.

Where my kitchen is all white marble and sage green cabinets, Wren and Rhodes's kitchen has dark espresso cabinets and pastel yellow walls, making you feel like you're outside on a bright South Carolina afternoon.

A smile splits my cheeks when I walk further into the space and lay eyes on my little hooligan. Crew has managed to open the cabinet nearest the pantry door and is feeding the giant gray Newfie a bully stick, his delighted giggles echoing around the room.

Wren sighs in exasperation but still follows them to the floor, doting on the dog and my son as usual.

"So," she singsongs. "Lost another nanny, did you?"

Her little smirk has me rolling my eyes and leveling her with an unamused look. "This one decided that after puttin' the raptor in his bed, she'd play dress up and wait in *my* bed for me to get home from the second half of a grueling two-a-day."

At least she has the decency to look chagrined while trying to stifle a snort, but she does a piss-poor job of it.

"Sorry, Aid. But wait, won't they just send somebody from the travel agency over for the season? You made it sound like you were up sh—" She glances at Crew with a grimace. "—*sugar* creek without a paddle."

Heaving a long sigh, I sit at the island and drop my head into my hands, using my fingers to massage the renewed throbbing in my temples.

"That's the thing; they don't have a single person available on short notice. Not to mention, Crew is almost six. So unless I wanna hire three different people, I need somebody who can double as a nanny, a teacher, *and* who can move in and travel with us on a moment's notice."

Wren is quiet for several long moments, and when I think she isn't going to respond, her eyes light with excitement. "Okay, before you say no, hear me out! I might just have the perfect idea."

Well, that rarely ends well.

2

"What do you mean, you're letting me go?" I'm grateful my obvious shock seems to mostly cover the panic that colors my tone at my boss's words.

I've been working at *Color Me Crazy* for over a year now, and I love my job. Sure, it isn't my dream career or anything, but it's been instrumental in covering the costs of my living and tuition while I finish university.

Beth's eyes are watery as she delivers the news, her tone solemn as she grips one of my hands tightly. I barely manage to hold back the flinch, hating that even after almost a year in therapy I still occasionally react this way to sudden touch.

Damn Sebastian for making me fear affection.

"I'm so sorry, honey. I wish I didn't have to. I'm closing up shop for a while to go be with my pregnant daughter in Georgia."

Releasing a quiet sigh, I do my best to quell the worry clogging my throat. "I understand. Thank you for taking a chance on me when I needed it, Beth. I'm not sure I'll ever be able to repay you, but if you need anything at all, you've got my number."

She pats my hand with a sad smile before thrusting an envelope into it, making sure I have it in my grip before she lets go. "If *you* need anything, you give *me* a call, ya hear? None of that brave face, lone wolf nonsense."

That pulls a tiny laugh out of me as she leads me out of the shop. I notice the envelope is thicker than usual and when I check the contents, I see more than twice my normal pay lining the inside.

"Beth, wait—"

Rather than hear me out, she shoves me out the back door, slamming it closed and flipping the lock with a finger wave and a wink before she pulls the shade down over the long window, effectively dismissing me.

Stifling a snort at the old woman's tactics, I begin the ten-minute walk home. Beth has always tried to slip me more than I earned when she realized I wasn't being fully honest about my life, but it's never been this much before.

Between this, my savings, and the emergency money I brought with me from Maryland, I have maybe six months before I absolutely *have* to find a new job. Not to mention the fact that I won't have health insurance now.

You wouldn't have to work at all if you'd take the risk and access your trust fund.

But if I did that, Sebastian would have a way to find me. I know my dad was the one who pushed me to meet Bas, but I have no idea if he knew the things my ex-fiancé was doing or what kind of man he set me up with.

Colin Kingsley is many things, but observant is not one of them. My father isn't a bad man, just absent. If it wasn't a movie script or his latest flavor of the month, it didn't get his attention.

I have no idea where my mom is or *who* she is. Unfortunately that means I was raised by a rotating gaggle of nannies, very few of which ever stuck around long enough to make me feel like I was more than just a job. It may have given me some *slight* abandonment issues.

Shaking off depressing childhood memories, I startle when my phone rings. My best friend's name pops up on the screen, and I smile widely. It's been a couple weeks since I last saw Wren, but we text constantly and talk on the phone almost as often.

I met Wren when she came into my job last year looking for a new hobby, and one of the first things she said to me was a warning that there's constantly family and friends around her. The last year of friendship has proven that to be true, but her fiancé Rhodes is the most constant person around when we're hanging out.

No matter how hard I try, I can't help the envy that grows every time the three of us hang out together. As much as I don't feel ready to date again, I can't help wanting somebody to look at me with the depth of affection Rhodes and Wren have every time they look at each other.

"Hey! You will never believe what happened today."

There's tons of barking and other chaos in the background, which makes me wonder where she is. "Uh oh," she responds as I hear a door click shut and the noise dies down. "Good news or bad?"

I groan miserably into the receiver, and she hums. "That bad, huh?"

"Beth is closing the shop," I blurt out, cringing at my delivery. Wren has been painting there no less than once a week since that first day we met, often waiting until I clock out so we can paint together.

Her gasp is loud enough to be heard over the sound of midday traffic where I live in downtown Mount Pleasant. "*Closing?*" she cries. "For how long?" I start to speak, but she keeps talking, her tone growing increasingly distressed. "Oh my god, what does that mean for your job?!"

Sighing, I scrub a paint-covered hand down my face. We had a party of twenty preschool-aged kids this morning and I swear my ovaries nearly exploded at the sheer cuteness, even though every inch of visible skin looks like a haphazardly-painted easter egg.

"She doesn't know how long she'll be closed because she's moving to be with her pregnant daughter, so she had to let me go."

Wren is silent on the other end of the phone before a loud laugh belts out of her, the sound jarring enough that I nearly drop my old flip phone on the sidewalk. "Umm, babe, are you *laughing* at my misery?" I ask incredulously.

Her laughter dies down to quiet giggles, and she explains between gasps for air. "Sorry, I promise I'm not. But I was calling to see how you felt about taking a teaching-slash-nannying gig for the duration of baseball season."

I gape at nothing, questions racing through my brain faster than I can form words. Wren runs public relations for the Raptors, Charleston's major league baseball team, and her fiancé plays first base on the team. "What—I—*huh?*"

"One of our best friends plays on the Raptors with Rho, and he's got this adorable almost six-year-old little boy. Well, they just lost another nanny, and Aidan is looking for a qualified nanny who can *also* teach his son, Crew, and travel with them. You'd essentially be doing three jobs, but I've seen how much he's offering and can confirm the pay is *way* above market rate. The thing is, you'd need to move in to their house down the road from us."

I can hear the smile and barely concealed excitement in my best friend's voice even as my mind spins and everything else becomes background noise.

Living with another man barely a year after getting away from Sebastian? I'm still frequently looking over my shoulder, wondering when the police will come after me for attacking him. It's not as often as when I first moved here, thanks to my therapist, but the possibility is still always there, lingering in the back of my mind.

Clearing my throat, I take a deep breath. "I would need to meet both of them first before even considering a live-in position. How well do you know Aidan?" My voice drops to an anxious murmur.

Wren must pick up on the apprehension in my voice because she's quick to soothe the newly exposed nerves. "Aidan Black is one of the best men I know, Ly. He's a wonderful father and incredibly kind, honest, and respectful. I wouldn't have suggested it if I suspected otherwise."

Some of my worry settles with her words. I know better than anyone how good people can be at hiding their true selves, but I've found that kids are the best judges of character. It should be obvious when I meet them if the son holds any fear or shyness around his father.

Just as I start to agree, part of what she said earlier comes back and makes me pause. "You said he lost *another* nanny? What did you mean by that?"

"Oh, that?" she asks innocently. "Finding qualified nannies for professional athletes is hard enough as is, but some of those women see them as mountains and do whatever they have to do to climb them, if you catch my drift. Aidan is extremely protective of his son and his space so when he came home to yet another nanny almost naked in his bed while Crew slept down the hall? He's real hesitant to try again with that agency."

My apprehension about meeting with Aidan and his son melts away like a popsicle left in the sun. I know exactly how it feels to have your space invaded against your will, and if there's a possibility to take care of a sweet kid, use my degrees, and also make sure someone else feels safe in their own home? I'm going to do it.

"When can I meet them?"

Aidan

My no-nonsense glare unsurprisingly doesn't phase my friend through the small screen on my phone, but her too-innocent smile sure as hell grates my nerves. "So you're telling me you invited a near stranger *to my house* to interview to be my son's nanny? Did the cheese slide off your cracker since I last saw you?"

When Wren told me she had a crazy idea but didn't clarify beyond "I might have a solution to your problem," I idiotically assumed she meant keeping Crew with her in the offices or something during practices and games, not letting someone she's known barely *one year* into my life and home.

Rolling her eyes, the meddling blonde pushes up her dark sunglasses and levels me with her own version of a glare. "*Near stranger* is a stretch, Aidan. I've known her for a year and I am fully confident Lyla is the best person for the job, and from where I'm standing, you're fresh out of options. Just meet with her and let Crew spend some time with her. I promise I wouldn't have suggested it if I didn't think it was the best thing for both of y'all."

A deep chuckle comes from off-screen before Rhodes's face enters the picture next to his fiancé's. "I've met the girl dozens of times, dude. I really think you and the tiny terror are going to love her. Plus, she just graduated college and needs a job."

I lift my middle finger with a sneer I don't really mean. "Y'all owe me big if this blows up in my face."

They share a look and Wren gets a calculated gleam in her eye. "You owe us big if it doesn't."

After saying our goodbyes and hanging up, I place my phone face down on the island with a thump and haul myself off the tall barstool, running my hand over the smooth white surface before making my way up the staircase.

My routine is the same every morning. I rise with the sun, make my coffee, and sit in the kitchen or on the porch so I can admire our home before I have to go wake Crew; a.k.a the sole reason I'm up at ungodly hours just so I can drink my coffee in peace. My whole body relaxes like it does every time I have my son in my sight and can see with my own eyes that he's safe.

Mia has been gone for almost four years now, but that hasn't stopped the constant worry about something happening to Crew, or of someone taking him from me.

I went back to therapy for about six months after she died, but it just felt redundant so I stopped, choosing instead to put all my time and energy into raising my boy.

I crouch down next to the bed, shoving a herd of small plastic dinosaurs aside so my knees don't get shredded by horns. These things are all over the house, and I'm constantly stepping on them.

They might be tiny, but those little fuckers hurt worse than stepping on legos.

Brushing a few stray locks of soft blond hair out of my boy's face, I kiss his nose, earning a grunt of annoyance. "Good morning, my little raptor."

The nickname pulls a smile out of him as his eyes flutter open, revealing an icy blue the exact same shade as mine. "I'm a hungry dinosaur, Daddy."

Chuckling, I widen my eyes at him in mock fear. "Oh no, we don't want a hungry dinosaur on our hands! What does my ravenous raptor want for breakfast?"

He sits up and stretches with a huge yawn, showcasing his first loose tooth. My heart thumps painfully when I see it because it's just another sign of how fast he's growing up. I try not to focus on that too much because it makes me sad, but the little things like this remind me how alone I would be without Crew.

Sure, my Ma is still in town, but she's getting older and spends most of her time catering to her favorite son. I mean, I live five miles away from her and only see her once or twice a month if I need an emergency sitter.

She travels a lot to be with my younger brother Wesley in Seattle and I try not to let it bother me, but after a lifetime of being the one who always had to be okay, it would be great to have someone who cares about how I'm doing.

Not someone who cares about me as Crew's dad, not as catcher for the Charleston Raptors, not as the jokester friend who's always happy to lighten the mood. Just Aidan Black, exhausted man and single father who wants nothing more than a safe space to not be okay sometimes.

A small finger pokes my cheek, and I blink out of my little reverie to see Crew's concerned face. "Do you have the sads?"

His whispered question brings a smile to my face

while I help him out of bed. "I'm only sad because you're getting so big! Pretty soon, you'll be as big as me."

He giggles, wiggling out of my arms and skipping to the stairs. "And then I can play football! Right, Daddy?"

I hide a snicker behind my palm. He has been on this football kick since his third birthday, and Rhodes and Copeland see it as damn near a cardinal sin. "That's right, little linebacker. You can play football. In fact, you can start this year if you want! A few months after you turn six."

Childish squeals of joy bounce around the open concept of our kitchen and living room, echoing against the beams that stretch across the high ceilings. I'd been keeping that little fact a secret from him because I knew he would never stop talking about it once he found out, but his excitement bolsters mine.

Crew turns six in three weeks, just before baseball season starts, and Peewee football runs from mid-September to the end of January, so I should be able to make it to every practice and game, barring any mandatory off-season workouts. But Coach has always been really good about letting me do make-up workouts when I've needed to be with Crew.

I get to work making breakfast for the both of us while my energetic little boy hops around the kitchen pretending he's an actual dinosaur, if the screeches and arm flaps are anything to go by. "Alright, wild one. Go sit down at the table, please. Food's on."

One thing I'm grateful for is that, overall, he's a fantastic kid. I won't say easy because I don't think kids are ever truly easy, but for the most part, he's great at listening and doesn't pitch a fit over too many things.

Just as I move to sit at the table the doorbell rings,

which has me on edge. It's eight a.m. on a Saturday, and everybody close enough to know our address would text first. Checking the doorbell camera, all I see is a head of ridiculously long brown hair tucked into a pink baseball cap.

Suspicion worms its way through me, tensing my shoulders as I pull open the tall front door to what looks to be a young girl standing with her back to the door. I clear my throat loudly, and she whips around with a hand on her chest, a startled expression on her face.

Holy shit.

"Oh! I'm so sorry. I hope I didn't wake you. Wren said it would be alright to come over early and meet y'all, but she also said she cleared it with you... Maybe I misunderstood? I can come back another time! I don't want to impose." Her soft voice is in direct opposition to the frantic movements of her hands, and I want to reassure her, but I'm too stunned to speak.

The woman standing in front of me is shockingly pretty, with long, dark brown hair hanging thick and straight down past her waist and wide, mossy green eyes. Taking a closer look at her face, I see a prominent pink scar across the bridge of her nose, making me wonder how it got there.

She clears her throat quietly, spooking me and making me realize I've been ogling her like a creep while she stands on my front porch. "Sorry." My words are a gruff rumble. "Who are you?"

Her cheeks flush a pretty pink color that almost matches her hat, and I force myself to hold back a chuckle. Sure, she's all kinds of adorable, but she's still a strange woman on my porch. "Oh, um... I'm Lyla Taylor? Wren said you were expecting me?" Her name isn't ringing a bell, so I keep my face blank and lift my eyebrows for her to explain.

Lyla's eyebrows furrow in response, and a flash of irritation crosses her face before her eyes widen minutely, and she settles her expression into something... passive. I don't know why, but the quick change has me more on edge than I already was.

"Wren said you needed a live-in nanny for your son and that she mentioned setting up a time for us to meet..."

All at once a lightbulb goes off in my mind, and I feel like an ass. "Dagummit, I'm sorry. I completely forgot she had set this up for today." Offering her a chagrined smile, I turn to the open door and hold out a hand to welcome her in.

"My mama would tan my hide if she knew I answered the door like that. Crew and I are just eating breakfast if you want to join us. I made chocolate chip pancakes." I shake my head in embarrassment. "Sorry *again*. Crew is my son."

If she thinks I'm an idiot with all the rambling I'm doing, she doesn't show it. Instead, the woman, *Lyla*, I remind myself, offers me a stunning smile and cautiously skirts past me, avoiding all physical contact as she does. "Chocolate chip pancakes are actually my favorite food, so I'd love to join you and meet Crew if it's not too much trouble."

I shake my head at her and lead her to the kitchen after locking up. "It's no trouble at all. I always make too much because I never know how hungry he'll be on any given day. He'll be six in just a few weeks and is growin' like a weed."

Her laugh is light and melodious, reminding me of a Disney movie Crew made me watch with him last week where the fairy voices sounded like bells or something. Honestly between the pink hat, the hair, and the fact that she's at least a foot shorter than me, she kind of reminds me of a Disney character.

Focusing on her laugh distracts me from the way my palms slick with sweat and my heart races. I know we've gone through plenty of nannies, but never one that came recommended from one of my best friends or one whose looks made my breath catch the way hers do. My mind knows she's off limits in so many ways, but my body doesn't seem to be getting the memo.

Not to mention, if she doesn't work out as Crew's nanny, I'm completely screwed this season. I can't find another travel nanny on such short notice, which means I would have to trust someone I barely know to watch Crew for days on end while I'm out of the state and can't get to him in minutes if I need to. And I can't keep burdening my friend's parents just because I'm not able to get my shit together enough to find regular childcare.

"Daddy, can I eat now?" Crew shouts, making me chuckle.

"Yeah, kiddo. We're gonna have a new friend eat with us, too, okay?"

His squeals turn my chuckle into a full-blown laugh, but a glance to my right shows me my latest potential employee isn't laughing. Her shoulders are hunched up by her ears, and her eyes are wide and unblinking, pupils dilating further by the second.

My heartbeat skips for a whole new reason, and I take the smallest step closer to check on her, but she flinches back. That minuscule movement seems to bring her back to the present, even as it sends my thoughts spiraling back to a time when I flinched like that at sudden contact.

Lyla offers me a brittle smile that doesn't reach her eyes as she tucks a lock of hair behind her ear. "Sorry about that. I guess I'm just a little nervous."

I don't believe her, but I figure if she's going to be Crew's new nanny, we'll be spending a lot of time together soon, so I'll have plenty of time to figure out why this little lady seems so skittish.

Lyla

4

Nearly having a panic attack in front of your scary, really good-looking potential employer because their kid yelled and startled you. Great first impression, Ly.

Laughing nervously, I quickly move through the stunning foyer into what looks to be an adorable sun-soaked breakfast nook just off the massive kitchen. A round, stained-white table sits in front of a corner bench the same sage color as the island.

Beautiful cream-colored cushions have been placed on all the seats, and large arched windows take up the entire wall above the bench, letting in the early morning sunshine. Bouncing in one of the seats is a darling little boy with a full head of wavy, white-blond hair that matches his father's.

Crew's grin is toothy, and his face is covered in chocolate, pulling a surprised giggle out of me. I cover my mouth and glance behind me to Aidan, worried about how he'll react to the noise, but he just has that same pensive look on his face as when he opened the door. Deciding to channel my focus on the reason I'm here, I walk straight up to the boy and crouch just a bit so I'm at his eye level.

"Hi!" I say brightly. "I'm Lyla. Your name is Crew, right? It's nice to meet you!"

He looks more than a little wary, which sends a ping of sadness through me, but I keep my smile firmly in place while he shifts his attention to the man behind me. I'm guessing he's looking to his dad for direction, so I wait patiently. Bringing his piercing blue gaze back to me, he grins shyly and holds a sticky hand out to shake.

"How do you know my name?"

I shake his small hand and marvel at how tall he seems to be at not even six years old, though Aidan is probably an entire foot taller than me, so maybe I shouldn't be all that surprised that his son clearly seems to favor his genetics.

"Well, your dad just told me, but I'm also friends with your Auntie Wren! She told me all about you."

Crew gasps, bouncing in his seat. "Auntie Wren is my bestest friend! I just see'd her yesterday!"

Fighting back a laugh, I grin at his excitement. "You *saw* her yesterday. And guess what? I did, too! Wren is my best friend and I see her all the time!"

I listen to him chatter excitedly about all the things he does with Wren with rapt attention while also cataloguing the striking resemblance he bears to his father. They both share golden locks with platinum highlights that are likely from frequently being in the sun, and the same light blue eyes.

The exact opposite of Sebastian's.

"So," I ask, getting Crew's attention as Aidan quietly slides into the booth on the other side of his son. It puts him directly across from me, and I studiously avoid his intense gaze. "Do you like your breakfast?"

A fast nod is the only answer I get for a minute as he shoves a massive bite of pancakes in his mouth. My caregiver instincts go on high alert, and I slide his water cup within reach and watch him like a hawk until he chews and swallows.

I notice Aidan tracking my movements with his eyes, but he also slides a few inches closer with a hand out toward his son, ready to intervene if needed.

I let out a sigh of relief when he successfully swallows the bite and chases it with several gulps of water. "Chocolate chip hotcakes are my favorite!"

Aidan snickers quietly as he starts to wipe his son's hands and face, causing me to raise a brow in question. "Wren's dad calls 'em hotcakes, and Crew has spent a lot of time over there the last few months, so he's adopted the word and corrects anybody that says pancakes within his earshot."

Crew rolls his eyes at his dad, sighing in exasperation. "They're called hotcakes, Daddy. I'm just tellin' 'em so they know the right word."

I laugh, but lean in conspiratorially. "You're right, Crew. They're definitely called hotcakes."

He grins in triumph, sticking his tongue out at his father, and the amount of attitude packed into such a little human is hilarious. "I like you, Miss Lyla. Will you stay after breakfast and play?"

The quiet words have me straightening my shoulders with pride. I went to school for years to learn how best to interact with children of all ages, and the fact that Crew is accepting me so easily makes my heart swell. Aidan clears his throat gently before I can get too excited and say yes.

"Raptor, Miss Lyla and I need to talk for a bit first, okay? Do you wanna watch the fairy movie again while we do?"

He's up and out of the kitchen in a flash, sprinting to the sunken living room that's semi-visible from our position in the breakfast nook. I turn back to Aidan with wide eyes, and he belly-laughs, sending shivers down my spine.

His voice and laugh are deep and smooth, and the theater kid in me wonders briefly if he can sing. "You promise my kid Disney movies, and he'll do just about anything you ask."

Understanding dawns on me, and I grin. "Good thing I love Disney movies, then, huh?" He just chuckles quietly and finally serves himself from the platters of food on the table.

Now that I'm not so nervous, I notice more pancakes, bacon, eggs, and fruit than two people could reasonably eat, not to mention the large pitcher of orange juice. "You really weren't kidding when you said you make too much!"

Aidan snorts. "I wish I was kidding. I've been cooking for two since Crew was a year old. You would think I could figure out how to make smaller portions. Please help yourself if you're hungry. I figured we could talk about the job now, and then you're more than welcome to hang out and get to know us if you want."

Confusing butterflies take flight in my belly at the mere mention of casual hangouts with my handsome boss if I get the job, but I know it likely won't be something I have to get used to since it sounds like he's gone a lot during the season. Perusing the spread before me, I grab two pancakes, some fruit, and a few pieces of bacon, nearly moaning at the competing aromas of chocolate and bacon.

The man across from me keeps his gaze laser-focused on my face until I take my first bite, and only then does he dig into his own meal. We eat in comfortable silence for several minutes with only the sounds of Crew's movie and commentary as background noise.

"So, I guess Wren already told you this would be a live-in position?" he asks, his voice guarded.

"She did, and she also said it would be a travel position as well?"

Aidan nods, his firm expression easing the slightest bit at my acknowledgment of the travel. Wren said that's been the hardest part of finding a nanny for them.

"Obviously I travel for work quite a bit, and I don't like being away from my son for days, sometimes weeks on end. It makes me feel a lot better when I can have him on the road with me for the longer stretches without the added stress of rotating babysitters."

Nodding, I smile gently at him. "I completely understand. I can't imagine how stressful your job is already as a professional athlete, but adding on to that being a single parent with unreliable childcare? The kind of pressure you're under must feel crushing."

I watch as his glittering eyes widen a fraction before he quickly schools his expression. "Exactly," he says quietly. "That's why I need somebody I can trust with Crew. Somebody reliable and good with kids and who won't need to call me during a game for every sliver or scrape. He's my top priority, so while I would hate to break my contract and quit the team if I can't find somebody, I'd give it all up without question to keep him safe and happy."

Can ovaries actually explode?

Rather than voice the incredibly inappropriate

thought, I thread my hands together and rest them on the table. "You don't know me and have no reason to trust me. What I can tell you is that even though I'm only twenty-two, I just graduated with a double Bachelor's degree in Childhood Education and Psychology. I have some great references from my professors and the teachers I worked with during my five years in school that I can provide as well. I also have up-to-date certifications in CPR and water safety."

"You said Crew is your top priority? If you give me a chance, he will be my *only* priority. His safety, his education, his comfort, and happiness. I'll treat your son exactly like I would treat my own child because I know all too well what it's like to be just another job to a rotating roster of nannies and sitters."

I don't even realize I'm breathing heavily until I finish my unplanned speech and see Aidan's wide eyes locked on mine. My cheeks heat with embarrassment. Slumping down in my seat, I struggle to meet his eyes. "Sorry."

He shakes his head, a lock of wavy blond hair falling across his forehead. Brushing it back, he graces me with a small but genuine smile. "You're easily the most passionate person I've ever hired."

The quiet words make me choke on my juice. Coughing, I stare at him with eyes wide as saucers. "*Hired?* You mean you're giving me the job?"

"I honestly can't think of a single person, let alone a *nanny* that's ever offered to treat my son like their own. If I'm being completely transparent, you're way overqualified, but if you want the job, there's no way in hell I'm going to say no," he says with a laugh. "When can you move in?"

My mind is already racing with ideas for a curriculum

and activities I can plan to keep Crew entertained on the road, so I know I'm beaming when I respond.

"Does today work for you?"

———

"Good morning, sleepyhead!" I sing as I walk into Crew's dimly-lit bedroom. The smallest sliver of light gives me just enough visibility to see that his floor is still clean after we picked up yesterday afternoon, making me smile.

Aidan only hired me a few days ago, and already, I don't think I've ever loved a job more than this one. Crew is the sweetest kid ever, and his dad has gone out of his way to make me comfortable in their house.

Muffled grumbles are my only response, so I give him another minute of quiet, open the curtains, and then the window, letting in the warm salty breeze.

Crew's bedroom is on the left at of the stairs, so it faces the back of the house, meaning there's an amazing view of the water from the large window above an adorable window seat.

"Miss Lyla?"

I turn to the sleepy boy behind me with a soft smile and move to crouch next to his oversized bed. His platinum blond hair is all I can see over the comforter, and it's sticking up at all angles. The sight has me rolling my lips together to stifle a laugh. "Yes, Crew-bug?"

"Did Daddy go to work already?" he asks, sniffling.

My stomach drops. Crew has one of the most severe cases of separation anxiety I've personally seen, which means the last few mornings have been especially hard since Aidan has to leave before the sun comes up. He let me know right away his days are pretty much all the same during training camp: lots of workouts, practice, and games, so he would likely get home around the same time most days.

Thankfully, getting Crew into a routine has been easy so far, but the devastation on his sweet face every time he wakes up and finds his dad gone is heartbreaking. Every day gets a little bit easier, but I know all too well how hard it is to wake up to a nanny when all you want is your dad.

I clear my throat and place a gentle hand on his back. "Yeah, he did. But today is the last day before he has the weekend off! So you'll get two whole days to hang out with him." An idea dawns on me when I remember the note Aidan left on the kitchen island this morning.

Lyla,

I know Crew's been having a hard time with me being gone this week, so I was thinking maybe some time at the stadium would cheer him up. If you don't have any other plans, I would love for y'all to come hang out for a bit. I won't have my phone on me, so if you do decide to come just show this badge and your ID to security, and they'll bring you out to the field.

Thank you for making this transition so easy, Lyla. You have no idea how grateful I am.

Aidan

My heart speeds up thinking about my gorgeous boss, but I lock those feelings down *fast*. The last thing I need is to lose a perfect job because of my inconvenient attraction to an incredibly off-limits man.

Plus, it's one thing to be attracted to someone after healing from an abusive relationship, but actually making that leap is a whole other qualifier I'm not sure I'm ready to tackle yet.

"Hey, what do you say we take a little field trip today?"

Crew's screech of excitement nearly pierces my eardrums, but the tears have thankfully abated with the distraction of getting out of the house. "Can we go now, Miss Lyla? I wanna go now! Where are we going? Will there be food? Can I wear my dinosaur costume?"

Laughing, I watch as he fights the sheets and tumbles out of bed. "No costume, but let's get you dressed in something you can get dirty. Maybe some shorts and a T-shirt and your sneakers?"

He nods frantically, skipping to his dresser in search of an acceptable outfit. It seems like he forgot about the rest of the questions, so rather than remind him, I make sure to grab everything I think we might need at the field today. A change of clothes, sunscreen, and baby wipes all go in a small backpack I'll load with snacks and water when we make it downstairs.

"Crew, come in here and brush your teeth, please!"

"Yes, Miss Lyla!"

Heavy footsteps reach my ears, and I'm surprised to find that he already has his shoes on. "Do you know how to tie your shoes, Crew-bug?"

He offers me a proud grin and nods. "My daddy just teached me how!"

I smile at him, matching his excitement with my own. "Your daddy *taught* you how, and that is so cool, dude! I don't know very many five-year-olds who can tie their own shoes, so you must be *really* smart."

Crew beams at me, and within ten minutes, we're in the SUV and headed to the stadium. I listen to his animated stories the whole way there and fiercely try to ignore the butterflies that erupt the closer we get to seeing my boss.

Aidan

5

"Hey Preach, I heard you got another new nanny. This one crawl into your bed yet?" Davis's mocking words threaten to upset the delicate balance of my mood today, but luckily a mild glare aimed his way has him raising his hands in surrender as he backs away slowly.

Ethan Davis is a rookie and a pain in our asses on his best behavior, so I'm normally immune to his needling. However, the last few days have me on edge.

Lyla has most definitely *not* crawled into my bed, and I can't tell if I'm more happy or disappointed by that. I should be happy, right? I've fired no less than a dozen nannies for invading my space and hitting on me when they should have been doing their jobs.

So why does the thought of coming home to Lyla in my bed appeal to me so much?

I sneer at Davis with a flick of my middle finger before gulping more water. It's hot as hades today for it only being March, and I'm sweating buckets. "Fuck off, Rook. Not all of us are only capable of thinking with the heads located below our belts."

The few guys in the dugout with us let out a collective "oooh" that has me laughing until a flash of color catches my attention from the tunnel leading out of the stadium. A smile grows unbidden on my face when I see a mop of wavy blond hair above the neon blue shirt that caught my eye.

"Holy shit," Daniels chokes. "If you're not into the nanny, then I definitely am."

His comment pisses me off because it's not like I'm blind. Lyla Taylor is drop-dead gorgeous. The kind of stunning that steals your focus and makes your mouth go dry at the thought of approaching her. The kind of unattainable beauty you see in movies and in your wildest fantasies. But she's amazing with Crew, so no matter how attractive she is, it's more important that she sticks around.

It doesn't matter that I want to wrap her long, dark hair around my fist as I slide my tongue in her mouth. Or that her green eyes look like the Spanish moss that hangs from the trees in our backyard after a tropical storm. Or that she always smells like sweet cherries steeped in vanilla, all soft and sexy and tempting.

It doesn't matter that I want her more than I've wanted anyone in years because Lyla is off-limits.

I barely manage to shake out of my haze in time to catch the fifty-five-pound bundle of excited energy flying at me before his knees connect with a part of my anatomy I am *not* ready to lose function in yet. "Woah there, little raptor!"

His giggles are music to my ears after such a stressful week, and I'm even more thankful Lyla accepted my invitation to the field today. Leaving Crew every day is hard, but leaving him alone with someone I don't know very well has felt like a puncture wound to a balloon, slowly deflating my energy and mood.

"Daddy! Miss Lyla didn't tell me we were coming here and I'm so excited, but I didn't bring my bat! I wanna go play with Uncle Rho."

Shaking my head, I look up to find Lyla smiling softly in our direction. At least she *was* smiling, until Rhodes tossed his beefy arm over her shoulder with a smirk and made her jump about a foot in the air. I see him grimace at her and say something but it's too loud for me to catch exactly what he says.

My curiosity peaks when he turns the arm on her shoulder into a full-blown hug. Rhodes has always been a hugger, but Lyla seems pretty averse to touch, so seeing him with her like that makes me a little uneasy.

It's absolutely not because I'm jealous he can touch her, and I can't. Not even a little bit.

Turning back to my son, I ruffle his soft hair. "I guess it's a good thing we keep your backup bat in the equipment room then, huh? Why don't you go with Uncle Rho to find it," I say with a brow raised towards my best friend. Thankfully, he knows me better than almost anyone else, and takes my son with him no questions asked.

I feel this ridiculous urge to check on my son's nanny, even though she's standing right in front of me, and Rhodes would never do something to intentionally hurt her. The second Crew is out of sight, I make my way over to Lyla with slow, measured movements.

"Hey, you okay? It looked like Rhodes took you by surprise for a second there."

The smile she gives me is brittle at best, but I don't call her out on it. Maybe she's just nervous.

"I'm okay. Like you said, it was just a surprise. And, um..."

Keeping my hand in her line of sight so I don't freak her out, I place my hand on her shoulder and duck, so we're eye-to-eye. "And what, Lyla?"

She sighs, glancing around us warily before leaning in and dropping her voice to a whisper. "I don't know any of these guys, and they're all staring at me. It's just making me a little anxious."

My back immediately snaps ramrod straight, and I turn to glower at my teammates. "Hey! Don't you assholes have drills to run or somethin'? *Back. Off.*" My voice is a harsh bark, and I catch more than a few of the guy's mouths opening in shock.

I can count on one hand the number of times I've gotten onto my teammates like that, but even then, I've never felt the kind of irritation I do right now, knowing they've made her uncomfortable.

If this is how I feel after less than a week with the girl? I'm so monumentally screwed.

"So." Rhodes's elbow nudges my ribs a few hours later, effectively knocking me out of my transfixed stare. "Those two seem to get along well, huh? How's it been at home?"

I turn to my friend with a frustrated huff and drop the mitt I've been ignoring for the last half hour. "Things have never been better at our house, honestly. Lyla does so much more than I ever expected from a nanny, and she and Crew get on like fleas and a bluetick hound."

Every word is the truth. Lyla has been going above

and beyond every day she's been with us, going as far as cooking meals even on her day off and starting a load of laundry if I go more than a day or two without doing it. I've already mentally bumped up her salary to compensate for all the extra things she's been doing.

Rhodes crosses his arms in smug satisfaction, no doubt hearing the awe in my voice. I collapse to the ground with a sigh, uncaring that my back is likely covered in dirt and chalk right now. "She's incredible, Rho. She's endlessly patient with Crew and constantly doing little things to make our lives easier. It's been a blessing having her around so far."

He nods like this is what he expected me to say. "That all sounds great, Aid. So why do you sound so miserable?"

I try to come up with something that won't make me sound like a creep, but the truth comes tumbling out of my mouth anyway. "I'm miserable because Lyla is so goddamn gorgeous it physically hurts to look at her. She's so sweet and smart, and I can smell her perfume in every room of the house, and it's driving me fucking crazy. I haven't been this attracted to someone in years, *if ever*, and of course, this perfect angel comes along, and she's totally off-limits."

It looks like he's trying to keep a straight face, so I lift my hand off the ground and halfheartedly punch him in the arm. The pathetic attempt to cause him pain cracks his composure, and he bellows out a laugh, catching the attention of Lyla and Crew where they're eating lunch on a picnic blanket she must have packed.

"Sorry, I don't mean to laugh at you, but Wren totally called it. She said you'd be half in love by the end of the first week, and here we are."

I scoff, sitting up with a groan. My lower back always kills after hours of catching, and it's even worse than usual today. Copeland isn't here this week, so I've been practicing with our backup pitcher, who's off his game. That means I'm constantly rotating in place to catch his pitches, and I'll need to spend some quality time with one of the therapists and maybe even a heating pad when I get home.

"I am not *half in love*, you jackass. I just think she's pretty and smells good. That's all. Sue me."

Rhodes snickers quietly, laying a heavy hand on my shoulder. "You know it's not a crime to be attracted to the pretty girl, right? Just because you're attracted to her doesn't mean you have to act on it. You've been alone for a long time, Aid. Maybe this is your sign to jump back into the dating pool."

The words aren't even all the way out of his mouth before I'm shaking my head vehemently. "No fuckin' way. You know me better than that. Casually dating is hard enough when you're a professional athlete, but add in that I've got Crew to think about? It's just not worth it."

He shakes his head with a frustrated huff. I know he and Copeland are both tired of my resistance to dating, but I haven't found someone worth putting myself at risk for. Even though Mia and I weren't romantically attached, her leaving still fucked with my head. It was too soon after my father's death, and I was feeling too guilty to handle it well.

"Aidan..."

"Stop, Rho. I know, okay? But I'm not willing to risk Crew's happiness if things go south. He has to be my priority always, and he's just starting to get comfortable with having Lyla around all the time. I'm not ready to upend his life again when we're just settling into a brand-new routine. I have my boy, and that's enough. Maybe one day I'll meet someone who changes that, but for now, I'm fine with how things are."

I can tell he wants to continue the conversation, but Coach saves me when he pulls Rho away for batting practice. Taking a few deep breaths to collect myself, I amble over to see what Crew and Lyla are up to, only to be stopped when her bright laughter rings out around us.

This is the first time I've heard her truly uninhibited with her laughter, and the only way I can describe it is *arresting*. The sound stops you in your tracks and makes you smile, even if you were frowning seconds before. I make a silent vow then and there to hear it as often as I possibly can.

Lyla must feel me staring because she glances up with a bright grin and waves me over. "You have a brilliant boy on your hands here, Aidan. Crew was just showing me how you taught him to tie his shoes."

Between her complimentary words and my son's toothy grin, I can't stop the smile that spreads across my face as I join them on the outdoor blanket they have laid out on the grass.

"He shows that skill off to everyone who'll let him, huh, raptor?"

Crew nods with a giggle, and Lyla smiles fondly at him. "I can see why! It's a great skill to have." Turning to me, her smile gets a bit shyer but no less bright. "I packed extra if you're hungry. You do high protein-low sugar, right? I made a modified version of our lunch so it would align more with your meal plan."

I shouldn't be surprised she knows I'm on a specific

diet, but I am. I'm honestly stunned. "Lyla," I choke out. "You didn't have to bring me anything, let alone make a special meal just for me. I have a meal prep waiting in the training room."

She shrugs. "I know, but I thought you might like something fresh, too. I know you have to microwave those trays to reheat them."

Lyla says the word 'microwave' with so much disdain I glance at her in surprise. "I wasn't aware you had such strong convictions about microwaved food, Miss Taylor."

Her cheeks flush bright red at my words, and she ducks her head, letting her long hair cover her face. "I know it seems silly, but we had this French chef growing up who vehemently opposed them. So much so that we didn't even have one in the house until I was well into my teen years. And that was only because I love microwave popcorn so much he finally caved and had my father buy one. I can still hear him cursing at me in French his first day when he caught little six-year-old me microwaving pizza rolls."

I watch her expression closely because whether she realizes it or not, this is the first thing she's ever willingly volunteered about her childhood. It's clear she grew up with money, the complete opposite of how my brother and I grew up. If you didn't know her though, you'd never be able to tell.

Wren told me that she'd been working for the painting place for a year, and they paid her under the table in cash. She was living in one of the run-down month-to-month apartments in Mount Pleasant.

She doesn't dress in expensive clothing or have a car, let alone one that would suggest she's rolling in dough. Sometimes, you can just tell when someone has money, and the only thing that gives any indication she did is the refined edge to her mannerisms and language. She's incredibly eloquent for someone who's only twenty-two.

There's just something about her that fascinates me and makes me want to dig deeper, so I make a note to push her background check through as soon as possible. Maybe I can get some answers that way.

Part of me feels like I'm invading her privacy, but the rest of me knows that doing a background check is a smart move, both as her employer and because she's caring for my son and has unfettered access to him twenty-four-seven.

Realizing I've been silent for too long, I chuckle. "He sounds like a character. My brother and I pretty much survived on the microwave growing up. Mama tried to cook when she was home, but more often than not, she was picking up extra shifts at one of her jobs."

Lyla looks sad for a moment but shakes it off quickly. "What about your dad? Did he ever cook for you?"

Any levity I had been feeling dissipates with the mention of my father. I don't want to be rude, so I quietly clear my throat and shrug as if the mere mention of him doesn't threaten to send my stomach straight out through my throat. "No, my dad didn't cook for us. Unless it came out of a bottle, he wasn't interested."

The last thing I need is to see the pitying look she's likely aimed my way, so I grab the meal she made me and give her a fake smile. She makes it too easy to say more than I should when she gives me those doe eyes and acts like she cares.

"Thanks for this! I'm going to eat real quick and then head inside for our last workout of the day. Feel free to head home if you want. I should be done here in an hour or so."

Without waiting for a response, I grab the warm container and kiss Crew's head before stalking off, desperate to unleash some of this tension on the heavy bag in the gym before I do something stupid.

Like turn around and kiss my son's nanny.

6

Aidan

Tires screeching, the sickening crunch of metal folding in on itself. Why is it so hot in here? The sound of my father cursing and screaming for help assaults my ears on a never-ending loop as lines of something thick and hot pour down my face. I should never have let him drive tonight.

I wake with a jolt, my entire body drenched in sweat and shaking with adrenaline. Nightmares about the night my father died have gotten less frequent over the years, but I've had one nearly every night since Lyla asked me about him at the field last week.

Having her here has been a godsend for Crew, but she's still nervous, reactive, and quiet, which reminds me way too much of how my mom was while I was growing up.

She dropped a mug in the kitchen early the other morning after I startled her coming down for my usual coffee and immediately dropped into a panic attack. I watched her cower by the fridge, apologizing frantically, while my heart twisted uncomfortably in my chest. I could barely keep my own panic at bay long enough to clean up the spilled coffee and talk her down.

It took almost ten minutes for her to come out of it, and when she did, she immediately excused herself and sprinted up the stairs on unsteady legs. We didn't see her the rest of the day since it was her day off.

I tried to keep my focus on Crew and all the things I needed to do to prep for this season, but I kept finding my gaze drifting to the stairs during every quiet moment, wondering if she was okay up there by herself and fighting the urge to check on her.

But as anxious as she's been around me, she's the exact opposite with Crew. When her sole focus is on him, her entire face lights up with no traces of hesitation or anxiety. Just in the last two weeks, she's gotten him started with a whole kindergarten program, and seeing his excitement to recount every moment of his days to me makes me feel like my throat is in a vice.

Part of me is grateful he isn't in school yet because he doesn't seem to know what he's missing by not having a mom in his life. Wren is amazing with him, and I'm so grateful Crew gets the fringe benefits of having a positive female influence. However, it's not like she can act as a mother figure for my son.

With a sigh, I climb out of bed and strip the sheets for the fifth time this week, making a note to grab some more sleep tea at the store later to try and combat these nightmares. My entire body is coated in a film of dried sweat, so I take my time in the shower, letting the scalding water beat down on my tense muscles.

Even after waking up the way I did, my cock is standing at attention against my lower abs, a combination of morning wood and the warmth from the water making me ache. How long has it been since I took the edge off? I haven't had sex in years, but even touching myself has felt more like a chore than anything lately.

It's still really early, so I decide to take advantage of the quiet for a little self-care, wrapping my fist around my straining erection. A guttural groan works its way out of my throat as I tease my hand up and down my length slowly, a faceless woman starring in my fantasy.

A dark-haired woman sinks down to her knees in front of me just before her tiny pink tongue darts out to lap at the precum gathering on my slit. I choke out a surprised whimper and tangle my hand in her thick, glossy hair.

"Fuck, sweetheart. Take me in your mouth, just like that."

She moans around my cock, the sound vibrating down through my balls.

The sounds coming out of my fantasy woman have me close already, so I tighten my fist and squeeze over the head on every upward stroke, my hips stuttering when I start to fuck into my hand.

"Is this okay?" she gasps, a string of spit connecting her mouth to my cock.

"Fuuuck," I growl. "Do you have any idea how fucking sexy you look down there on your knees for me, darlin'? You're takin' my cock so well." She preens at my praise, so I smirk down at her and tighten my hand in her hair just enough to ride the edge of pain. "Now, how 'bout you put your mouth back on me so I can come down that perfect little throat?"

Her pupils dilate, and like the good little girl she is, she dives back in even more enthusiastically than before. She takes me to the back of her throat and pauses to look up at me. Only this time, her face transforms. Mossy green eyes stare up at me, wide with lust.

It's that final image that sends me over the edge, and I bite my lip so hard I draw blood to keep myself from saying my nanny's name as ropes of cum paint the tile before sliding down the drain.

Jesus Christ, Aidan. What the fuck was that?

My mind races the entire time I'm getting dressed until I make my way downstairs. The sight of our perfect living room forces me to stop and marvel at the sunrise coming in through the wall of windows that face our backyard and the water beyond.

I bought this house nearly three years ago now, but the view never fails to amaze me. The giant wall of windows open up to the heated pool directly outside, the back porch, and our private dock that juts out into the river.

Crew and I always fish out there, and it's my favorite way to spend time with him. He gets so excited every time he catches a fish, and it makes me feel like I'm giving him the childhood I always wanted.

We didn't have much money growing up, so it's still a shock sometimes when I can just go to the grocery store and not have to count every single cent, but living in a place like this? It's beyond my wildest dreams. Every day feels like a delicate balance with Crew, wanting to give him everything I never had while still making sure he grows up appreciating what he has and paying it forward whenever possible.

"Oh! Good morning." I stumble to a stop on the last step and desperately fight back a blush as Lyla's quiet voice punctuates the early-morning silence.

She's curled into the corner of the couch, her small

form engulfed by the thick fuzzy blanket we keep draped over the back. I would never say it out loud, especially after what I just did, but she looks downright adorable right now.

Her long brown hair is tied up in a messy bun on the top of her head and flopped over to the side making me wonder if she slept in it and just left it like that when she woke up.

The way the sun hits her hair gives it almost a reddish tint that brings out the delicate freckles on her cheeks and nose. Sleepy eyes stare at me over the rim of my favorite coffee mug and make my mouth go dry.

Clearing my throat, I try to smile genuinely at her and hide how fast my heart is beating all of a sudden.

Off. Limits.

"Hey, you're up early. Did you sleep okay?"

She beams, a gentle flush lighting the apples of her cheeks. "I did, thank you. Being up with the sun is just a habit I can't break, I guess."

"I get that," I laugh. "I started getting up around this time when Crew was little just so I could have an hour or two to myself to wake up and mentally prepare for the day."

Her face falls, but as quickly as it does, she fixes it back to some semblance of a smile. "Oh, of course! I totally understand. I'll get out of your hair and—"

"No!" The word comes out way louder than I meant for it to, making me glance between the bundled beauty and the second-floor balcony with a grimace. "Sorry, I just mean I'd actually like the company if you don't mind hanging out with your boss."

I meant for the words to come out teasing, but it sounded more like a pointed reminder. One I clearly need if my shower thoughts are any indication. She probably thinks I'm insane now, Jesus. It's like I forget how to act like a normal human being when Lyla is anywhere in my general vicinity.

Don't catch feelings, Aidan. She's here for your son, not so you can make her uncomfortable by staring at her with lusty eyes and letting her face fuel your fantasies.

Her jumpy behavior isn't the only reason I've been spending more time in my room than normal. While she doesn't go out of her way to show it off, Lyla is *sexy as hell*. She's petite but has the most incredible hips that I can't help but think would make perfect hand holds for...

"Are you okay?" Her gentle question shocks me out of my wildly inappropriate thoughts and guilt turns my stomach when I see the genuine concern on her face.

Fucking hell, what is wrong *with me today?*

"I'm okay." I try to laugh it off but some of that concern lingers in her eyes. The start of my second erection of the day thoroughly deflates under her assessing gaze. If I didn't know any better, I would think she could read my mind. I doubt it, though. If she could, she'd probably run screaming to the nearest lawyer to file a sexual harassment lawsuit.

"Are you sure?" she asks quietly. "I know it's not my business, so don't feel like you have to answer, but having someone new around can be a big change for everyone in the house, not just the child. And that doesn't even include all the issues you had with nannies before I came around."

Snapping my head to the side, my lips part as I stare at her with wide eyes. "Who told you about that?" I already know the answer before the guilty look crosses her face. "Wren," I sigh. I love the girl, but she has a big mouth when she's meddling.

"I know what it's like to have your personal space violated," she whispers. "And nobody should ever have to deal with that. Especially not in their own home." Shadows darken her green eyes to a deep sage that reminds me of our kitchen cabinets, and also happens to be my favorite color.

Curiosity flames in my chest right below the rage that bubbles just under the surface of my skin. Whatever, *whoever* made her feel like this deserves a special place in hell.

Taking a risk, I sit down next to her on the couch and take her soft hand in mine. "Lyla, if you ever want to talk about anything, I'm here." I keep my expression as open and honest as possible so she knows how serious I am. I don't know how or when it happened, but sometime over the last two weeks, I've come to care about this sweet little thing and would give anything for her to open up to me.

She clears her throat and changes the subject. "Do you want coffee? I made extra. It should still be hot since I haven't been up for long. I was going to relocate to the swing if that's okay. I'm still in awe of the beautiful weather here, and I make it a point to get outside and soak it up every chance I get."

"You don't have to ask to go anywhere in the house, Ly. As far as I'm concerned, you can treat our house as your own for as long as you're here."

The flush staining her cheeks deepens to a dark pink, and I'm struck again by just how delicate her features are. "I appreciate that, *Aid*," she murmurs with a shy smile, clearly following my lead on the nickname front. "I appreciate everything you've done."

Something dangerous tightens in my gut when I hear those words come from her pretty pink lips. Seeing the way she stares up at me without the hesitation that's been present for the last two weeks has my heart nearly skipping a beat.

I'm in so much fucking trouble.

"Miss Lyla, can we have ice cream and popcorn when Daddy goes to his game?"

She places a hand on her chin and pretends to consider his request. "Hmm... why don't we do one better and have a *movie night*? You can pick what we have for dinner, we can do ice cream sundaes, *and* we can build a fort!"

A wide grin splits my face at the girlish laughter that's nearly drowned out by the ear-piercing squeal Crew lets out at his nanny's words.

Making sure they're distracted, I discreetly flip off the man who glares our way, watching as he huffs before stomping past us. His little tantrum has me snickering until I notice how Lyla reels back with a flinch as he passes a little too close with a sneer.

I'd been walking a few feet behind, content to just watch Lyla and Crew interact, but the look on her face as she watches the man with wide eyes has tension tightening my body in alarm.

When I place a gentle hand on the back of her shoulder, she snaps her head in my direction so fast her long, heavy hair whips me in the face, making me sneeze as I bat the strands away from my face.

"Sorry," she gasps. Her plush lips pull down in a

grimace even as her breathing speeds back up after the momentary distraction. Crew is still playing happily in the buggy, so I try to think of anything I can do that might bring her out of this panic attack before it gets worse.

I don't give myself a chance to think as I cup her face in my hands and coax her eyes up to meet mine, so I'm incredibly relieved when she doesn't jerk away from my soft grip. "Trust me for a minute?" I whisper.

With her barely perceptible nod as confirmation, I wrap my arms around her slight frame and squeeze with a bit more pressure than I would usually use for a hug. "Now focus on my heartbeat and my breathing. Try to match your breaths to mine." I take a deep inhale, getting a wave of her perfume in my nose.

The smell nearly has me groaning in the middle of the damned market. She smells like cherries and something else creamy and sweet. Sometimes, I think it's vanilla, but other times, it's a little bit darker, almost seductive.

"That's it," I praise when I feel her chest rise in time with my own. "You're doing so good, angel." Her grip tightens around my waist, and I hope I didn't make her uncomfortable with the nickname. It just slipped out, but I don't regret it. She really is an angel.

"Daddy?" Crew's concerned voice pulls my attention to where he sits in the buggy, watching us with rapt attention. "Does Miss Lyla need a moment?"

His whispered question has me huffing a laugh even as I quietly count the number of times her back moves with each exhale, squeezing tighter when I notice her breathing speed up again. "Yeah, buddy. She needs a moment."

He nods solemnly before going back to his game of pirate ship, and Lyla even laughs this time, sending a wave of relief over me. "How are you feeling now, darlin'?"

She relaxes fully against my chest with a deep sigh. "I'm better now, thank you. Why did that help so much?"

I shrug, but a shy grin tips up the corners of my lips. "It's called co-regulation. I used to do it when Crew was a baby, and he had issues regulating his heartbeat and breathing. The nurses at the hospital taught me that trick during some of his worst nights in the NICU."

Her breath hitches. "The NICU?"

The thought of getting into the whole Mia thing right now and knowing what else that could lead to makes me feel sick so I quickly change the subject, hoping she lets it drop. "Yeah, but he's perfectly healthy now. So, Crew," I turn to the tiny Raptor in our buggy. "What do you want for your special dinner with our Miss Lyla?"

I normally hate going to the market because buying food for two people only reminds me of how depressingly single I am. The team's nutritionist usually sends me meals during the season anyway because I have a hard time getting in enough protein with how busy I always am. So grocery shopping during the season consists of my six-year-old's favorite foods and the few healthy things I can successfully get him to eat.

"Why are you getting cauliflower?" Crew nearly gags in disgust as his nanny places the offensive vegetable down next to him. He scoots as far away as possible in the limited space like it'll reach out and bite him if he gets too close.

She snickers and leans over the side of the buggy. She's so small she can rest her arms on the edge of the basket and barely have to bend over. "Wanna know a secret?" she whispers, eyes shining with mischief. "I have a super special recipe that makes cauliflower taste *delicious.*"

The skepticism is clear on his expressive face, and I cover my mouth with a hand in an effort to hold back my laughter. If there's one thing I know about my son, it's that he's as stubborn as they come when it comes to trying new foods and isn't afraid to show it.

Lyla grins. "How about I make my special recipe, and you try it, and then if you don't like it, I won't make you eat cauliflower again for, hmm..." She taps a finger against her chin. "A whole year."

His eyes light up. "A whole *year*? I'll be almost seven by then!"

She raises a questioning brow at me, and I nod, thoroughly enjoying their exchange. "Okay, so if you don't like it, I won't make you eat it again until after you're seven, deal?"

He beams. "Deal."

7

Lyla

I wonder what kind of comment Sebastian would make if he could see me right now.

I mentally flip him off with both hands, and pride fills my chest as I dig into the pint of chocolate cherry ice cream in front of me to take my first bite. The nostalgic flavors coat my tongue, and I nearly sigh in bliss.

Towards the end of our relationship, Bas was such an asshole about everything I ate and kept meticulous track of my calorie intake. It's taken me nearly nine months to stop feeling like a failure if I wake up hungry in the middle of the night or eat more than a thousand calories a day.

A quiet scuff on the hardwood floor spooks me enough that I jump forward and bump my ribs into the island. "Oh *shit*. Oh my god, you scared me," I breathe with a hand held protectively to my side. I didn't hit them hard, but the phantom pain from past broken ribs has me acting on instinct. "You're a freaking giant. I don't know how you're so dang quiet all the time."

Aidan lets out a husky chuckle and moves to grab a

water bottle from the fridge before placing his palms next to me on the glittering white marble of the kitchen island. His tan, muscular arms flex as he leans forward, bringing my attention to his sculpted chest, bare save for the light smattering of fine blond hair and Crew's birth date tattooed over his left pec.

I feel my eyes widen as desire pools in my lower belly quicker than ever before, and the feeling is nearly enough to send me running back to my room. The only guy I've ever been attracted enough to want to date was Sebastian, and even that was lukewarm compared to the feelings my new boss has been stirring up. I need this job, and I adore Crew, so I need to do what I can to ignore any budding attraction to the single father.

Even if he does look like he was carved by Michelangelo himself. I mean, David who?

"Whatcha got there?"

"Oh... so, I kind of have a terrible sweet tooth, and sometimes, I'll wake up in the middle of the night craving something sugary. Tonight, I just felt like I needed ice cream." A blush heats my cheeks, waiting to see how he responds.

His stunning eyes light up as he clasps his hands together over his heart in a dramatic gesture that makes me smile. "Ah!" he gasps. "A woman after my own heart."

A quiet giggle falls from my lips, and his smile grows.

"Okay, follow-up question. What's your favorite flavor?" Aidan grabs the pint sitting in front of me and examines the label, raising his brows in my direction and intentionally dropping his gaze to my cherry print sleep set with a smirk. "I'm sensing a theme here."

Shrugging, I take advantage of him still holding my ice cream to stick my spoon in the creamy goodness and take another bite. "What can I say?" I ask around a mouthful of heaven. "I have a thing for cherries."

His laugh is full and loud and so happy in that moment that it freezes me to the spot, spoon in mouth and all. The smirk returns to his handsome face and fans the heat still simmering in my veins to boiling levels, and I know I need to get the heck out of here before I say something monumentally inappropriate.

I fake a yawn and stretch, trying to take the ice cream from him to put it back in the freezer. My fingers cover his when I grab the carton, sending chills up my arm. Aidan's eyes fill with heat the longer they stay locked on our overlapped hands.

My words are barely more than a whisper as I stare into his eyes. Their glittering blue reminds me of ice chips, only instead of cooling me off, the look in them has me quickly overheating. "I should probably get back to bed."

He drops my gaze as he clears his throat and releases the melting container back to my waiting hands. "Right, yeah. I should, too."

"Night, Aidan."

I'm already at the stairs before he responds, but I can swear I hear him whisper back, "Goodnight, angel."

———

"Okay so you have the list of emergency numbers? And you know he's allergic to shellfish? Do you have the route to the hospital memorized from here?"

I don't get a chance to answer any of Aidan's panicked questions before he thinks of more. "And you know all the alarm codes and where the car keys are?"

Rolling my lips together to hold back my own nerves, I place a hand on the anxious man's forearm. "Aid, I got this. We've been over everything and I'll treat Crew as if he's my own. He'll call you every night, and I promise I'll text or call you *if* something goes sideways. Which it won't."

"But—"

I shake my head firmly. "No buts. You'll be two hours away for three days. If, for some unknown reason, I can't reach you and it's an emergency, I have Wren, Rhodes, and the coaches numbers on speed dial. I think some time apart will be good for both of you. Remember what I said during my interview? Crew is now my only priority. Trust me."

His worried blue eyes study my green ones for several intense moments before he relents with a small but anxious smile. Turning to where the subject of our discussion sits on the living room floor, happily munching on his lunch of sweet chili cauliflower wings, Aidan gives his son a lingering kiss on the top of his head.

"You're gonna call me every day and be good for Miss Lyla, right, my little raptor?"

His sticky face lights up. "I'll be the goodest! And I'll call every day right before bed so you can read me my story."

Watching Aidan interact with Crew always makes me feel all melty inside, but seeing just how much he loves and cares about him? Cue the pesky butterflies. Those inconvenient little jerks have been around way too often the last few days.

"Lyla, can I talk to you again for a sec before I go?"

The butterflies turn to ash and sit heavy as a stone in

my gut at the question, but I nod anyway and follow him back to the kitchen.

"I just wanted to ask for your bank information so I can send over your pay for the last two weeks," he says with a kind smile.

My heart stops. I feel my eyes grow impossibly wide with panic as I stare at him and scramble for anything that sounds even semi-reasonable. After all, what kind of twenty-two-year-old woman doesn't have a freaking bank account?

Why did I not prepare for this exact question?

"I, um..." Absolutely no good excuses are coming to me, so I reluctantly tell the truth. "I actually don't have one. My last job paid me in cash."

He blinks owlishly at me. "Oh, right. Okay, well, do you need help setting one up? Honestly, I could have my agent do it for you if you don't want to take Crew to the bank. I'd just need your social sec—"

"No!" Shit, shit, shit. How do I get out of this? I probably look insane. "I just mean... I don't really trust banks," I mutter with a grimace.

The curiosity burning in his arctic gaze is impossible to miss, but he takes it in stride rather than calling me out on my obvious lie. "I'll swing by my bank on the way back and grab cash then if you don't mind waiting. No need to open an account if you don't want to."

I can't disguise the gust of air that escapes me as anything other than relief. "That's perfect. Thanks, Aidan."

His returning smile is sad and doesn't reach his eyes when he nods and goes to give his son a final hug goodbye. Aidan Black is a dangerous man, just not in the way I'm used to. He sees everything, and for a girl who's desperate to hide, that's almost scarier than anything I've faced before.

This new life in Charleston was supposed to be a fresh start for me to heal, and until now, it has been, but I'm starting to wonder if this security I feel is too good to be true.

If Aidan goes digging into my past or I get tangled up in his professional or social life, I have no doubt Sebastian *will* find me. I honestly don't know how he hasn't already. I know he's alive from the few times I've seen him on TV with his dad or various actresses.

Staying here might put me in more danger than being alone, but the thought of being just another nanny in a long line to leave Crew makes me feel sick. I can shut down any budding feelings I might have for his dad and focus solely on my job. Keeping my head down until the season is over and they don't need me anymore will be best for all of us.

Why does the thought of them not needing me hurt so much?

"Ly, can we watch *Tinker Bell* now?" Crew is bouncing on his toes in front of the massive fort we built over the couch, his face covered in the crusty remnants of the pasta he ate for dinner.

Giving him a big, goofy grin, I nod and point a finger. "But first, messy little raptor, you need a bath. Do you want to go start the tub and put in your favorite bubbles?"

He shrieks in excitement and sprints to the first-floor full bath to do as I asked, making me laugh. Crew is such a sweet kid, and the more time I spend with him, the more confused I get about why they have such a hard time keeping a nanny.

I know Wren said it had something to do with them hitting on Aidan, but would someone really use an innocent child like that just to get close to the parent?

It's obvious he has some of the same attachment issues I had as a child, but his father, unlike mine, seems to be incredibly present and active in his son's life. I quickly make my way into the bathroom to distract myself from thoughts of my dad, knowing if I continue down this path, it will quickly lead to tears or, worse, a panic attack.

Bath time with Aidan's little clone ends with me and the floor looking like we got baths, too, and Crew's infectious giggles successfully distract me from spiraling. I wrap him up in his dinosaur towel and laugh at the crown of horns across the hood before helping him dress in his, you guessed it, dinosaur pajamas.

"Are dinosaurs your favorite animal?"

He nods frantically, declaring, "Raptors are my most favorite!"

"I bet that's because of your daddy's baseball team, huh?"

"Yes!" he yells. "Daddy is the catcher, so he uses a mitt to catch the balls Uncle Cope throws at him!"

I nod like I understand, praying he doesn't ask me any questions about how baseball works. The truth is, I know next to nothing about the sport despite my near-constant education over the last year.

Wren, my best friend, manages the Raptor's PR department and frequently talks baseball stats, but I swear it's like it's in one ear and out the other; I can't retain the information to save my life. Though maybe that will change working for a player since Crew and I will be attending some of the home games and further away games.

The promise of Disney and ice cream is enough to derail the conversation and remind Crew why he had to take a bath in the first place, so we rush back out to the living room and dive into the fort, creating the perfect little nest bed.

I promised him we could sleep out here tonight since he seemed so panicked about Aidan leaving all day. I don't want to encourage his attachment issues, but with a kid this young, it's important to enforce healthy boundaries and give a little when big changes happen. Hence, the fort sleepover.

I set the alarm and triple-check that all the doors and windows are locked before I truly allow myself to get comfortable, a habit I've developed since leaving Sebastian. The next several hours are spent watching fairies chase a crazy beast while Crew plays with my hair, and despite my best efforts to stay awake, I feel my eyes closing as sleep quickly overtakes me.

"Where's my sweet little future wife, hmm?" Sebastian's deceptively calm voice reaches my ears where I'm hiding in the hall closet. We attended a charity gala tonight that should have been a fun night out as a newly engaged couple.

That "fun" lasted less than an hour until Sebastian saw one of Dad's friend's sons making me laugh with a story of our time together on set as children. Apparently that pissed him off, because he stormed up and gripped me tightly around the bicep before pulling me away mid-sentence.

On the way home, he made his anger known with several cutting remarks, and I knew that if I didn't hide until he lost interest, I would be in considerable pain for the next week, so the minute we arrived at the opulent home we share, I hid as fast as I could in a hall closet.

My heart feels like it's seconds from beating out of my chest as I listen to him pace around the sitting room, no doubt with a glass of expensive bourbon in his well-manicured hand. Keeping my movements as silent as possible, I peek out of the mostly closed door only to come face to face with the man who haunts my nightmares.

A muscle in his cosmetically altered jaw tics as his sinister smile widens, and I know I've just sealed my fate by hiding rather than facing my punishment head-on.

"Lyly?" A tiny cry startles me out of my nightmare, and it takes me several seconds to process where I am. When my vision finally comes into focus, I see Crew standing in front of me with tears streaming down his ruddy cheeks. My stomach drops, worry overtaking any lingering fear from my dream.

"Little raptor," I coo. "What's the matter?"

His tears fall faster, and he throws himself into my arms, knocking me back against the couch in our fort bed. "I had a bad dream," he whimpers between sobs.

My heart breaks for this innocent kid and all he's been through in such a short time. "I'm so sorry, Crew-bug. Do you want to tell me what your bad dream was about?" I keep my voice low so I don't overstimulate him, especially since he's already upset.

He sniffles and twirls a long strand of my hair around his small fingers, tears slowly drying the longer his gaze stays transfixed on the repetitive motions. "A bad man hurt Daddy," he whispers. "And then Daddy had to leave, too. Just like my mommy."

A chasm opens up in the pit of my stomach and I'm

pretty sure my heart falls into it. Most six-year-olds aren't so worried about their parents leaving them that it manifests in nightmares, so to know that this is something that affects Crew *this much* is heart-wrenching.

I don't know anything about the situation with his mother, so I need to tread carefully and remember to ask Aidan about it when he gets back to avoid a situation like this again. I understand he might not want to talk about it, especially after he brushed me off in the grocery store yesterday morning, but I can't properly care for Crew during moments like this unless I have all the facts.

I run one hand over his soft hair in soothing motions while I use the other to hold him to me as tight as I can without hurting him. "Crew, listen to me," I murmur. "Your daddy is one of the strongest guys I've ever met, and I promise that even if a bad guy did try to hurt him, he would still come home to you."

He still looks distressed, so I scan the fort for my phone and find it sitting on the couch cushion where I left it to charge. Picking it up, I see it's already well after one in the morning, and I have a missed call and a text from Aidan, that came in around ten, apologizing for missing their bedtime call. "Would it make you feel better if we called your dad so you could see for yourself that he's okay?"

He hesitates but eventually offers me a tiny nod just as a snot bubble pops on his upper lip. I bite my lip to stifle a laugh and use one of the leftover napkins to wipe his nose before pulling up Aidan's contact. He told me to call him any time, day or night, but I still find myself worrying he'll be angry if we wake him up.

The little FaceTime tone only sounds twice before Rhodes picks up, startling me enough that I almost drop the phone. Why is he answering Aidan's phone? Someone would have notified me if he was hurt, right? With shaking hands, I do my best to steady the screen as Crew starts to panic in my arms.

"Where's Daddy, Uncle Rho?" he whimpers. Rhodes' eyes go wide when he sees my own panicked eyes and Crew's crying form molded to me.

Please tell me I didn't just screw up.

8

Aidan

My fingers twitch to pick up my cell phone, and it takes everything in me to leave it where it lays face-up on the bed. The ringer is turned all the way up, and I have Lyla set as an emergency contact, so her calls and texts will come through even when my phone is set on do not disturb during games and media.

Missing my first nightly call with Crew and breaking my promise made me feel like a shit dad, but our post-game debrief went way later than normal, and I knew he would be asleep by the time I got back to the room, which was confirmed by the fact that my text still sits on delivered two hours later.

"Dude," Rhodes laughs. "It's after midnight. They're going to be fine. Lyla is one of the most responsible people I know, and you've already told me multiple times how good she is with Crew."

Rhodes has been my best friend since he was drafted five years ago, and aside from his fiancée Wren and our other friend Copeland, he's the only person I can be honest with about how I really feel. I glance up and meet his skeptical look with a grimace, shrugging defensively. "What if he needs me? And I still don't know Lyla very well. I mean, she doesn't even have a bank account. Doesn't that seem a little suspicious?"

His eyes widen the tiniest bit, and my stomach sinks. Was I stupid to trust Lyla with Crew after only knowing her for a couple of weeks? Sure, I've been hearing about her in passing for months, and my gut tells me she's the real deal, but Christ's sake, I didn't even know her name until the day she showed up on my doorstep a few weeks ago.

Rho's heavy hand lands on my shoulder, snapping my attention to his. "I can see the wheels turning in your head, man, but I don't think it's as weird as you think it is. When Wren first started going to therapy again last year, Doc told her to find a hobby, and that's when she met Lyla. Wren adopted her right away for obvious reasons, but the non-obvious ones were the tan line on her ring finger and the shadow of bruises under her collar that looked like fingerprints. She tried to hide them, but Wren and I both noticed."

His sigh is loud in the quiet hotel room. The video game we had been playing is paused and temporarily abandoned as I hang on to every word of insight he has about the gorgeous woman currently occupying my mind, living in my house, and caring for my son.

"I just... she's been extremely secretive about her life before moving to Charleston, but from what I can guess, it was a really bad situation. I know she's told Wren as much, but even though they've been inseparable the last year, we still don't know anything about her life before she arrived in South Carolina other than that she came from Maryland. But Aid? We trust her. Whatever is in her past, I don't think it was something *she* did. I'd bet my contract she's running from something. Or some*one*."

My heart falls at the thought of someone hurting that sweet angel of a woman, and my earlier suspicion fades away with the reassurance from someone I trust implicitly. I already submitted a background check, so I guess I'll tone down the panic unless that tells me I have something to worry about.

Scrubbing my hands down my face in exhaustion, I glance at the clock to see it's nearly one in the morning. "I'm gonna take a shower. Keep an eye on my phone for me?"

He smirks, giving me a faint eye roll.

I flip him off before shutting the bathroom door and twisting the lock. "Just humor me, you dick."

My thoughts are all over the place as I step under the steaming spray, but as much as I try to keep them on other things, they keep looping back to my son's nanny. What kind of person has a woman as gorgeous and kind as Lyla and puts their hands on her in any manner less than the reverence she deserves?

Just the thought of the stunning brunette who sleeps down the hall from me has me hardening even as guilt eats away at my conscience for thinking of her in that way again. Flashes of her toned thighs and the crease of her ass from our midnight run-in a few days ago assault my vision and I groan quietly, stroking a hand down my aching length.

There's no harm in another silly little fantasy as long as it stays a fantasy... right?

Fuck, I'm definitely going to hell.

My imagination takes control as I let myself think

about what might have happened in the darkness of my kitchen that night if we were different people.

I think about the way she stood bent over the counter, her pert ass hanging out of those adorable little cherry print shorts she loves so much. I think about the look on her face as she enjoyed her ice cream, and the sass on her pouty mouth when she told me she had a thing for cherries.

It was late, just like it is right now, but I woke up from a nightmare, thirsty as hell. Only when I walked into the kitchen to grab a water, Lyla was already there eating ice cream straight from the container. Watching the way she wraps those plush lips around the spoon nearly brings me to my knees and forces me to bite back a groan.

She's in one of her tiny, cherry-printed sleep sets, and it exposes the clear pale skin of her shoulders and tight buds of her nipples. My mouth waters as I take in the stunning woman camped out at my kitchen island.

The fantasy starts to take shape as I slowly stroke myself, the guilt fading quickly into pleasure.

Hearing her admission about liking cherries makes me chuckle as I place my palms on the solid marble and subtly flex my arms. I watch her mossy green eyes deepen to emerald, desire flooding her heated gaze as she locks on to the subtle movement.

Leaning forward, I take the spoon out of her tiny hand and scoop up a bit of the chocolate cherry ice cream, flipping the spoon over to take an exaggerated lick.

I stay silent and wait, nearly smirking at the quiet gasp she lets out. "You have your tongue pierced?"

Nodding, I stick my tongue out so she can see the little silver ball in the center of my tongue. It's not really visible unless you know to look for it or I make a point to show it off, which I was absolutely doing just now.

Copeland was spiraling last year after receiving yet another text from his cheating ex, and I made the mistake of getting black-out drunk with him in solidarity. The next thing I know, I'm waking up in bed with the idiot, both of us suffering from massive hangovers and throbbing tongues.

Lyla reaches up like she's going to touch it, and even though I know she's my son's nanny and this is definitely a terrible idea, I can't stop myself from gripping her wrist and bringing her finger to my mouth. Checking to make sure she's not freaking out, I wrap my lips around her finger and suck.

I groan out loud as my fantasy Lyla moans at the contact, stroking my cock faster and slapping a hand on the tiled wall to steady myself when my legs start to shake. The pleasure is so overwhelming my vision starts to spot, but it leaves room for the fantasy to become even clearer.

"What do you think?" I ask her after releasing her finger. Her gorgeous eyes are glassy with desire.

She blinks, swaying a little so her wet finger rests against my chest. In a move I'll likely never get to experience in real life, Lyla trails her moistened finger over my chest to circle my nipple, leaving it wet with my own saliva. She grins when I shiver, a layer of goosebumps covering my overheated skin.

"Fuuuck, angel. That feels good," I breathe out loud. The sounds of the shower around me are loud enough to drown out my panted words, but at this point, not a single part of me cares if Rhodes hears me fucking my fist to the thought of my sexy nanny. I stroke my fist up over the head of my cock, spreading the beaded precum down my aching length.

A smug grin crosses her pretty pink lips, and with that single tilt of her lips, my carefully held control snaps. Gripping the backs of her thighs, I lift her up and drop her on the counter. The move places her at my eye level, and I'm taken aback by how sinfully hot she looks in her sleep-mussed state.

With a dirty smirk, I drag my tongue up the delicate column of her throat. "You think it felt good on your finger? Wait until I show you how good it can feel somewhere else. Somewhere more... intimate."

Her breaths are coming in small gasps now, but she nods, lifting her hips for me so I can slide her teeny little shorts down. Taking the spoon out of the now-melted ice cream, I tease it up her inner thigh, leaving a trail of the cold treat as I go. Offering her a heated glance, I lick a path across her velvety skin, groaning at the taste of my angel combined with the sweetest fucking cherries.

Just as her hips buck up into my mouth in the fantasy, I lose it. Cum lands in thick ropes on the floor as I quietly growl out Lyla's name.

I enjoy the post-orgasm haze while I wash up, but the cold air outside of the glass-walled shower brings with it a flood of intense guilt over what I just did.

Banging on the door distracts me from the lingering shame of my new favorite fantasy, and I open it to see a panicked Rhodes holding up my phone. "It rang as soon as I heard the shower turn off, so I rushed over here to get it to you. I know I told you they would be fine, but Crew is crying!"

Normally, I'd laugh at Rhodes' inability to handle tears of any kind, but my focus immediately sticks to the fact that *my son is crying*. Snatching the phone out of my best friend's hand, I bring the screen to my face in a panic until I see both Lyla and my boy giggling in a dark room, their faces lit up by what I'm assuming is the TV.

She snorts, waving a hand. "Sorry, you guys are too much. I was trying to explain to Rhodes that Crew is fine, but he started to panic, and then everything went blurry until he handed you the phone."

I *hear* her words, but I don't think they fully register until I see with my own eyes that my son is okay and sitting on his nanny's lap. There are tear tracks on Crew's cheeks, but his eyes are dry, and he has a happy look on his face. "I'm okay, Daddy. I had a bad dream, but Miss Lyly helped."

My heart swells with renewed attraction when I see the look of adoration Lyla holds for my son, and I know without a doubt that when it comes to her, I'm screwed six ways to Sunday.

My heavy duffel bag drops to the wood floor with a thud, and my shoulders sag in relief. The awe and gratitude I feel coming home to this house hasn't worn off in the three years we've lived here, and I'm not sure it ever will.

If anything, it might be even more since Lyla moved in and made our lives so much brighter. The smell of coffee permeates the early-morning air, making me groan. I'm so damn tired, and I still have a full day of work to do at the stadium.

Following the aroma of the freshly-made Holy water, I stalk into the kitchen and pour myself a massive cup before making my way outside to the back porch.

Lyla sits in her new favorite spot, tucked into the corner of the large porch swing. A surprised smile lights up her sleepy face when I emerge through the sliding-glass doors.

"Aidan! I didn't know you'd be home so early. Come, sit!" She pats the cushion next to her.

I sink down with a moan, dragging a hand down my face. "I'm only here to drop off my bag and get my caffeine fix, unfortunately. Someone thought it would be a great idea to schedule a full day of press today, so I'm due back at the stadium in an hour."

"Oh." Her face falls. "So you won't get to see Crew until tonight?"

My heart drops, and I shake my head. "Don't get me wrong. I love playing ball, and I know I'm so privileged to live the life I do, but sometimes the schedule really grates on me. I miss my boy, and I feel like a half-assed father being away from him so often."

Lyla's soft hand slips into mine and squeezes tightly, surprising me. I don't move an inch, too afraid she'll let go. "Aid," she huffs. "No offense, but that's the dumbest thing I've ever heard."

I turn to her, my brows raised in surprise.

She rolls her eyes, an exasperated smile tipping her lips. "Crew worships you. To him, you're super dad who can do no wrong. Sure, he misses you, but he also thinks you're the coolest person ever because baseball is what you're paid to do *every day*."

Something in my chest settles with her reassurance. I still feel like I need to apologize to Crew, but knowing Lyla doesn't think less of me for being gone so much lifts a burden I've been struggling with for a long time.

Taking a chance, I lace our fingers together and

scrunch down to lean my head on her shoulder. A quiet intake of breath is her only response, but she doesn't stiffen or move away.

"Thanks, Ly."

Her body melts into mine, and for the next half hour we drink our coffee in silence, simply enjoying the feeling of not being alone.

Happy giggles and the smell of sugar and chocolate emanating from the kitchen catch my attention and pull an exhausted smile to my face.

I can tell they were busy while I was gone because the house is spotless, save for the enormous blanket fort currently engulfing my cream-colored couch.

"I was gonna take it down before you got home, I swear! But Crew begged me to keep it up, and he just loves it so much that I figured maybe a few more days living with the mess wouldn't hurt."

I know before I even turn around that Lyla is wringing her hands together in a panic, and I'm not wrong. I turn to face her only to see her eyes wide and glistening with unshed tears. She stands in the entry to the room, her pale arms crossed over her cherry-print apron.

I give her a soft smile to show her I'm not angry, doing what I can to disguise the way my entire body tenses when I see the fear radiating from her in near-tangible waves.

She had been doing so well overcoming her fear around me, but it seems like the idea of leaving the house messy might be a trigger for her. I fucking hate that thought. Kids are messy, and I don't expect her to constantly keep the house spotless.

Glancing over the fort again, I inspect it thoroughly before turning back to her with my hands out in a placating manner. "Lyla, I promise I don't care about the mess. If it makes him happy, leave it up as long as he wants." I look over just in time to see her shoulders drop in relief. "Plus, I'm kind of impressed with the structural integrity you managed to pull off only using sheets and clothes pins."

The panic in her eyes fades, and she shakes her head with a small smile at my attempt at levity.

"Lyly! I got some dough on the fridge!" Crew's voice rings out from the kitchen, making me snort. *Of course he did.*

I follow a now much-calmer Lyla to the kitchen and come face to face with an absolute disaster. My eyes don't know where to look first, but my kid is standing on a stool at the island, and the second I catch sight of him, I break out into raucous laughter.

Crew is covered head to toe in flour, and his lips and the tips of his fingers are stained bright red. I bite my fist to calm the laughter and hear sweet giggling at my side.

When his big blue eyes finally land on me, he gasps and nearly face-plants in his haste to get down, making me lurch forward in a panic. Dropping to my knees, I let him barrel into me and take the opportunity to squeeze him as hard as I safely can. I was only gone for three days, but with every fresh inhale of his watermelon shampoo, the bridge of my nose burns hotter with impending tears.

A quiet sniffle reminds me we have an audience, but the shame that would usually come from openly showing emotion like this in front of anybody but Crew is suspiciously absent in the presence of the angel standing behind us. Placing my hands on the shoulders currently digging into my ribcage, I push him back with a hum of amusement to assess the damage.

"Raptor, did any of the dough actually make it into the oven?"

He giggles, showing me his red fingers. "We made them special for Miss Lyla's birthday next week, Daddy! Cherry cookies with chocolate chips! Did you know me and Lyly have the *same* birthday?!"

Lyla freezes halfway through pulling on the oven mitts, with a look of chagrin aimed our way. "Crew-bug, that was supposed to be our secret," she murmurs, a blush lighting her cheeks. "You're turning *six*! That's a big deal! We don't need to do anything for me."

My eyebrows nearly touch my hairline as this new information registers. "Your birthday is on the 15th, too?" I ask quietly.

She nods slightly before turning back to her task of pulling some delicious-smelling cookies out of the oven. Outwardly, I keep my expression blank, but in my head I'm doing a fist pump. I'm thrilled to get another small piece to the puzzle that is Lyla Taylor.

I don't know if her birthday is another trigger for her like loud noises seem to be, so I decide to tread carefully. Ruffling Crew's flour-dusted locks, I encourage him to go pick out jammies and bubbles so I can get him clean for what I hope will be an early night. I'm beyond exhausted. We won both of our games, but they were hard-fought, and we almost didn't.

Copeland has been having trouble with his throwing arm, and it's driving the rest of the team out of sync. Our guys were making rookie mistakes, missing simple pop-flies in the outfield, and being too slow to tag out a runner before they get on base, even if they already had the ball in their possession. We weren't working as a cohesive unit, and Coach reamed our asses for it, too.

Because of the way we played, the press interviews we had today were actually just thinly-veiled interrogations about our roster and strategy for the season.

Turning to Lyla, I offer a gentle smile. "Would you mind hanging out with him a bit longer so I can run to the market? I was going to stop on my way home but got too excited about seeing my boy."

The bright smile she had on her pretty face earlier slides back into place at my change of subject. "Of course! Why don't I take care of his bath so you can go now and be back for bedtime?"

I thank her and grab my keys to make the quick trip to town. I have another birthday to plan.

9
Aidan

The first thing I do when I get in my truck is open a new text to Wren, hoping she'll let me pick her brain for the answers I know I probably won't be able to get out of my nanny.

> **ME**
> Please tell me you know if Lyla likes her birthday
>
> **FUTURE MRS. GRAY**
> I'm not sure, but thanks for reminding me it's coming up! Why do you wanna know?
>
> **ME**
> ... No reason.
>
> **FUTURE MRS. GRAY**
> Aidan, you need to be careful.

Her comment digs at me for the rest of the drive, so I call her once I navigate the mostly empty parking lot and find an open space.

She answers on the first ring. "Before you get all huffy with me, I didn't mean it like that. Out of all the men I know, you would be so good for her, please don't doubt that. But from everything Ly told me, she left a really awful situation back in Maryland, which wasn't exactly resolved. I don't know exactly what it was, but what if y'all get involved, and her past comes back to bite her? You're a public figure and a father, Aidan."

Shit. I didn't even consider that. I heave a deep sigh into the receiver, and it echoes on the other end of the line. "I think I like her, Wren."

"I figured. Has she given you *any* indication that she feels something for you beyond friendship?" she asks.

Has she? Not really. "Honestly, I don't think so. But I'm not sure I'd know even if she had because I've been so adamant that she's off limits. I don't even know why I feel like this. I just know how I feel when I see the way she looks at Crew."

My words trail off because that's not entirely true. "I also know how it makes me feel every time she talks to me like I matter. Not because I'm her boss or because I'm Crew's dad. She talks to me like she cares about my well-being," I murmur.

Wren lets out a quiet sigh that echoes through my car. I run my hands through my shaggy hair and make a mental note to get it cut before the season officially starts. "You feel all that even though she's only been around for a few weeks?"

A self-deprecating chuckle escapes. "Fucking insane, isn't it? Jesus, listen to me! '*I like her because she acts like she cares.*' I'm her boss. Of course she's nice to me!" Confusion thrums through me as conflicting thoughts run rampant in my brain. Am I so lonely that I see something that isn't there?

"Aidan," Wren scolds. "*Breathe*. If Lyla didn't like you or you were making her uncomfortable, you would know. She has had nothing but glowing things to say about you *and* my little pumpkin butter. I know she loves her job, and I could easily see her loving y'all. I just want you to take it slow and be cautious for all three of your sakes."

Her words soothe some of the overwhelming turmoil coursing through my body, and I take a deep breath. "Level with me here: is it selfish for me to want her? To think about going after her this soon? She's been everything to Crew the last few weeks, and I can't handle watching him lose someone he cares about so much. But she's... god, she's unreal, Wren. She's sweet and smart and brave and she makes me feel seen."

She's quiet for several beats but eventually hums in contemplation. "I don't think your needs can take a backseat for his entire life, Aid. If you're serious about wanting Lyla, even knowing there are things in her past she isn't ready to share, then I say be a little selfish. I said it once, and I'll say it again. She couldn't end up with a better guy than you."

I'm thankful she can't see me when a blush heats my cheeks.

"Hey, why did you ask me about her birthday, anyway? We have the last set of spring training exhibition games next weekend, so you won't be around."

A smirk tugs at my lips, because I already knew that. "I know. Any way you can help me rearrange things and turn Crew's party into a surprise *joint* birthday party for Friday before we leave? And also possibly swing me a ticket on the home side for both games?"

Wren hesitates for a moment before an offended scoff escapes. "Have you met me? Of course I can."

I hesitate on the next part but ask anyway, knowing it's important to the plan. "And how do you think Kaci and Dominic would feel about having a sleepover with Crew for the weekend?"

Rhodes's folks always ask to see Crew, but I feel guilty whenever I ask them to keep him longer than a few hours. All I can hope is that the time alone with Lyla will be worth missing him for a few days.

Her smug look is practically slapping me across the face through the phone, making me groan as she cackles wildly. "Oh man, this is gonna be great. I'll text Kaci now and let her know they'll get to play grandparents for the weekend with Finnegan *and* the birthday boy."

Thankfully, we already have Crew's party planned, so he hasn't been upset knowing I'll be gone on the actual day.

Here's hoping this doesn't all blow up in my face.

The next morning, I hide a nervous grimace behind my overly large coffee cup when I hear Lyla's soft footsteps padding down the staircase.

I couldn't sleep for shit last night with the way my nerves were eating me alive, so I tossed and turned until four before I finally gave up and went down to the basement to work out. I pushed myself harder than I have in months in a futile attempt to burn off some of the anxious energy that's been plaguing me since my conversation with Wren.

The fear of being rejected by the first woman I've

genuinely been interested in since Crew was born has my stomach violently twisting in on itself.

Each soft step I hear threatens to make the coffee I've been sucking back for the last half hour come back up. It's been tortuous waiting to see if she would be up for what's become something of our daily routine.

Every morning since the first time I came down to find her cuddled into the couch with her coffee, we've ended up on the back porch swing together.

Some days, we talk about a little bit of everything, and some days, we don't talk at all, but I cherish our quiet time together so much. She's vulnerable and soft and so damn sweet, it's no wonder I developed feelings for her so fast.

"Good morning!" Lyla chirps with a sleepy smile as she makes her way to the coffee pot. God, she's even more stunning first thing in the morning. As usual, her long brown hair is tied up and messy on top of her head, and she's in yet another cherry-print sleep set.

I almost let a laugh slip free when I see her cute little shirt. Two cherries on the stem are holding hands underneath the words "I'll always pick you."

I wait for her to doctor up her tooth-achingly sweet coffee before asking if she wants to go sit on the porch swing and watch the sun rise. She nods with a smile and follows right behind me, none of the hesitation from her first week with us present in her movements.

"Everything okay?" she asks softly. "You seem more keyed up than usual for six in the morning."

Oh, angel, you have no idea.

Clearing my throat, I stare into the mug in my hands as nerves steal my voice for several long moments. "You know I have another away series this weekend in New York, right?"

"Of course! I have your whole schedule memorized," she titters nervously, her cheeks flushing just a bit as she sips her coffee.

Wringing my hands together nervously, I ignore the way her perceptive eyes track the action. "So, um... I was wondering if you would maybe want to come with and make a weekend out of it. Wren snagged me some tickets, so you can come to the games if you want. We can go sightseeing, find some really good pizza..."

Lyla's face lights up brighter than I've seen it in the month she's been with us. "I would love that!" She bounces around in her seat, making me laugh when the wide swing begins to sway back and forth.

Her grin settles some of my worry, at least until she says her next words, and then my insecurities come roaring back in full force. "Has Crew ever been to New York before? He's going to have a blast. I wonder if—"

Taking a risk, I set my free hand on top of hers on the lounger, startling her into silence.

But again, she doesn't flinch or pull away.

Leaning down the slightest bit to catch her eye, I take a deep breath, my heart pounding so hard that I absently wonder if she can hear it. "I was kind of thinking Crew could spend the weekend with Rhodes' parents."

Her eyes widen in confusion and I almost lose my train of thought when I see the way they sparkle in the golden light of sunrise. The green lightens to that perfect sage color I love so much, and what looks like brown freckles dot her irises.

"But..." she pauses, brows furrowing. "If Crew is staying here, why would you need me to go with you to New York?"

I keep my expression open and don't say anything for

a minute, waiting. I see it the second the wheels start to turn in her head, and she exhales softly.

"Oh."

She doesn't say anything else, and I school my expression, keeping the disappointment off my face at the sharp sting of her rejection. Removing my hand from where it still rests on hers, I try to fix the mess I just made. "I'm so sorry. I didn't set out to make you uncomfortable, and maybe I'm just seeing things that aren't there, but I thought…" I sigh, rubbing my hands down my face, hard-earned calluses catching on the thick layer of blond stubble that currently covers my cheeks and jaw.

Her frown is like a punch in the gut, stealing any semblance of hope and making me nauseous.

God fucking dammit. You're her boss, Aidan. She's been here a month and has given no clear indication she's even slightly romantically interested in you. Just because you're pathetically lonely and desperate for attention doesn't mean your son's nanny is interested in anything more than friendship.

I'm pretty sure I just ruined one of the best things my son and I have ever had.

Lyla

My heart is beating so fast I feel like I might pass out right here on this swinging outdoor bed. Did Aidan just ask me out? My boss, Aidan? Crazy handsome, single dad, Aidan? I don't know if I'm more excited or terrified.

I feel like I need to get some clarity here before I make a fool out of myself. "I'm sorry," I shake my head and tentatively lay my hand over his, still feeling cold from the loss of his comforting touch. "Are you—"

"Askin' you out in the most indirect, and likely inappropriate, way possible?" he interrupts with a nod. "Yeah. In my defense, I haven't done this in six years." A blush lights the tops of his cheekbones, and it's so endearing that a shy grin makes its way onto my face.

That small physical response eases some of my terror. Aidan's eyes flash with excitement when he spots my smile, and he flips his huge hand over to twine our fingers together.

"Listen, Lyla. I want you to know that telling me no will in *no way* impact your place here with Crew if you want to stay on as his nanny. And if I crossed a line and you're uncomfortable and want to quit, I'll help you find a new gig and give you the best-damned recommendation I can possibly write."

He pauses, letting me see the emotions playing across his face. "But you're so wonderful with Crew, and you're kind, compassionate, and a great listener. Becoming friends with you the last few weeks has been the most fun I've had in a long, *long* time, and I really like you. So, if you're open to it, I would like nothing more than to take you on a date. No kid, no responsibilities, no pressure.

Just you and me and one weekend to see if this could be something more than friendship."

Thoughts of Sebastian and the overwhelming charm he showed me at the beginning of our relationship play on a loop in the back of my mind, but am I really going to keep letting his actions control my life?

I'm still in therapy, doing the work to continue to heal from his words and the lasting trauma he so generously gave me. Aidan has proven time and time again that even though they may look similar, he's the exact opposite of my ex in every way that matters.

"Can I take some time to think about it?"

His grin softens. "You considering it at all is probably more than I deserve."

Lyla

10

"Lyly!" Crew's shout has me sitting up so fast I nearly fall out of bed, barely managing to catch myself at the last second. I blink in confusion against the brightness of the beautifully decorated bedroom I've lived in for the last month.

What time is it?

Glancing at the clock on the white nightstand, my eyes fly open in shock when I see it's after nine a.m. already. Pounding knocks on my bedroom door send panic racing through me, and I don't even think, jumping out of bed and ripping open the door to see Crew and Aidan with matching smiles.

"Happy birthday!" they shout in unison.

Aidan holds up a tray of chocolate chip pancakes with what looks like cherry compote on top, a wide grin marring his handsome face and forming little wrinkles in the corners of his light eyes. My mouth waters, but I'm not sure if it's from the food or *him*.

My boss towers over me, clad in light wash jeans, a faded black Raptors muscle tee with obscenely cut armholes that offer flashes of his bulging arms and chest, and bare feet. His messy hair is just on the verge of too long, but it's a good look on him.

Now listen, bare feet usually freak me the hell out. I don't like looking at them, touching them, or even *thinking* about them. But *Aidan's* bare feet? There's something so intimate about seeing this larger-than-life man's masculine toes resting on the heated wood floors. For some reason I'd rather not explore right now, I don't mind them all that much.

He must see the look on my face because a deep chuckle rumbles through his broad frame. "I figured combining both of your favorite foods would make for a pretty daggum good birthday breakfast."

My mouth flops open like a fish, my eyes darting between the two handsome guys standing in front of me. "I had an alarm set to make birthday hotcakes for Crew..." For some reason, none of this is making sense to my sleep-fogged brain, but I know for a fact I set an alarm for six.

Crew's toothy grin is adorable as he grabs my hand, dragging me back to the bed. "I sneakeded in and turned it off so you could sleep in!

I huff and ruffle his wavy hair. "You *snuck* in, Crew-bug. And I'll let it slide this one time because you were doing something so sweet, but remember, we need to respect people's private spaces, alright?

He nods emphatically. "*Right.* Sorry, Lyly."

"Raptor, why don't we let Miss Lyla eat her breakfast and get ready for the day while you go get your shoes on."

Aidan glances at me with a shy quirk of his lips as his son sprints out of the room. "If you don't have any plans, Crew and I would like nothing more than for you to join us on a birthday trip to the aquarium."

Spending the day with Aidan and Crew would make for the best birthday I've ever had, so I readily agree. "Give me thirty?"

"'Course. Take as long as you need." Without a word, he stalks toward me and drops a gentle kiss on my cheek before ambling back out. Aidan moves to shut the door, but just before it clicks, he glances back at me under enviously thick lashes with a small but genuine smile. "Oh, and happy birthday, angel."

"Did you *see* how big that shark was, Lyly? It was bigger than our car!" Crew's enthusiasm makes me giggle, and I see Aidan glance at me with affection from where he sits in the driver's seat.

He's been glancing at me with these soft looks all day, and my resolve against dating is crumbling faster than a stale petit four.

"I did see it, Crew-bug! Were the sharks your favorite part?"

"Yes! The sharks and the stingrays. Did you see the baby stingray's legs? I don't really know why they have legs when they live in the water. And they're kinda funny lookin'."

I choke out a laugh as the wild six-year-old continues to recount every second of the last three hours from his booster seat, regaling his dad and me with exaggerated tales of his imagined underwater adventures.

Turning my focus to Aidan, I lower my voice so only he can hear me. "Thanks for inviting me today, Aidan. It means a lot that you wanted to include me in your last free day with Crew before the season starts."

He scoffs, keeping his eyes trained on the highway. "Are you kidding right now? Even if I hated being around you for some *unthinkable* reason, it would be a cold day in Arizona before Crew let me leave you out of a birthday activity. Or any activity for that matter. Like it or not, angel, you're stuck with us."

My cheeks flush crimson, but I'm saved from answering when we turn down our quiet street to see cars taking up nearly every available inch of curb space. Turning wide eyes to the man next to me, I see him grinning like the cat that caught the canary. Ever since meeting Sebastian, I haven't done well with surprises, so I'm worried Aidan has something planned and hasn't told me.

"Why are there so many cars lining the street?"

Aidan's grin turns mischievous, and he shrugs. "Oh, we have a little party for Crew's birthday every year. It must have slipped my mind with how busy we've been the last few weeks."

Something about his words ring false, but I can't imagine him doing something malicious, so rather than ask more questions, I do what I can to brace myself for whatever we're about to walk into.

It's midday, so at least everything is brightly lit and pleasantly warm for only being mid-March. Summer in the South can be brutal, so I like to enjoy the 75-and-sunny spring days while I can.

It takes less than five minutes for us to unload Crew and his new stuffed shark that's almost as big as he is, and instead of leading us through the garage as usual, Aidan hovers his palm just above my lower back and guides me around to the front door.

I raise an eyebrow at him, but he's got that damn grin

back on his face that makes me more anxious than I'm willing to admit.

"SURPRISE!"

My throat clamps down in abject horror when I see no less than thirty people milling around the living space, my oxygen momentarily being held hostage by my traitorous lungs. Crew knocks into me, squealing on his way to Wren's open arms. It's enough to open my lungs back up, and I quietly gasp for air.

Balloons and streamers are everywhere, along with an overly large banner that reads, 'Happy Birthday Crew & Lyla!' I try to use a calming technique my therapist taught me: naming five things I can see, four I can hear, three I can feel, two I can smell, and one I can taste, but the sheer amount of men in this room, along with all the eyes on me, is enough to allow the panic attack to fully take hold.

I choke out a strangled 'excuse me' and rush from the room, beelining for the furthest guest bath on this floor. It's tucked into a far corner of the house and doesn't have any windows, so the second I close the door behind me, dark silence engulfs me, settling the worst of my panic and hopefully stopping the bile that coats the back of my throat from coming up.

Turning the tap as cold as it will go and holding my hands under it usually helps when I'm having a panic attack. But this one was too bad, too unexpected, so I quickly splash the freezing water up onto my face and neck in an attempt to shock my body into remission.

I've got one cold hand cupped over the back of my neck and one laid flat over my sternum when the door swings open, sending renewed adrenaline skittering through my body as the ringing in my ears intensifies.

I don't even realize I've closed my eyes and braced

myself against the wall with my hands up until strong arms circle my upper body and *squeeze*. My hands are trapped against a masculine abdomen, and then he tucks my head into his chest, and all I can smell is Aidan. I've been picking up on it more the last week, but he smells like a summer day at the beach. Salty ocean air and just a little bit of citrus.

It takes a few seconds, but the panic ebbs enough that my hearing comes back online just in time to catch his murmured words. "*Shh*, angel, you're safe now. I've got you. I'm right here, and I'm not letting you go."

Aidan's warm, steady hand is a comforting weight on my head. Before I can even consciously process the action, my arms are encircling his trim waist, and I've buried my nose even further into his chest.

"That's it, angel. Use me however you need to. Can you try to copy my breathing, Lyla? I'm worried you'll hyperventilate if we can't calm you down."

It takes every bit of my focus, but I manage to do as he says and match my breaths to his. He's so much larger than me that I can't possibly breathe in for as long as he does, but it's the *trying* that gets my heart rate to decline.

I'm not sure how long we stand wrapped around each other in the tiny guest bathroom, but it's long enough that my breathing finally returns to normal, and sounds from the party start to float in around us.

A soft knock on the door startles me, but Aidan doesn't loosen his hold as a familiar head of curly brown hair pokes in.

"Hey guys," Rhodes says gently. "Wren is herding everybody outside, so don't worry about rushing out to entertain." His eyes scan me slowly before meeting mine with an understanding I'm not surprised to see from him.

Wren and Rhodes may not know exactly what happened to me back in Maryland, but Rhodes is perceptive and nosy as hell, so I'm positive he knows more than he should. Maybe even more than his fiancé. Normally, that might bother me, but I'm finding that more often than not, I've been grateful for his compassion and empathy.

After briefly checking with Aidan, he steps the rest of the way into the bathroom and sets a cold water bottle on the sink before hovering a careful hand above my shoulder. "You alright, Ly?"

I can't find it in me to be embarrassed when my body is shaking so hard I'm practically being held up by his best friend, *my boss*. So, rather than offer him false platitudes, I shrug with a shaky smile. The expression is minute compared to the smiles these men so freely offer, but it's genuine, and that's the best I can do right now.

Rhodes nods, but I can still see the concern shining in his eyes. "I'll go help Wren hold down the fort. Text me if you need anything."

Aidan lets out a sigh when the door shuts again, releasing one hand from the strands of my hair to open the water and hand it to me. "Little sips for now, angel. We don't want you getting sick when your adrenaline dumps."

The bridge of my nose burns at the gentleness in his voice. He witnessed me in one of my worst moments, and he's not running for the hills or making an awkward excuse to leave.

There's no way this man is real. He's too much like one of the heroes in those romance books Wren keeps making me buddy-read with her. Is he just biding his time like Sebastian did? Will I see a different side of him if I agree to accompany him this weekend?

He keeps one thick arm wrapped around my upper back as he pulls a white washcloth off a small shelf above the sink. Flipping the still-running water to warm, he waits for it to come to temperature before wetting the cloth.

With methodical movements, he wrings it out and brings it to my face, gently wiping under my eyes and nose before making a quick swipe over my forehead.

Green collides with blue when my eyes snap to his in awe.

Seriously, who wrote this man?

I've always struggled with anxiety, but whenever Sebastian caught me having an "episode," he would steer clear until I got over myself. His words, not mine. There's no way in hell he ever would have held me through it or cleaned me up afterward when I was covered in snot and tears.

"You alright, Lyla? You checked out on me again."

With a long sigh, I crash my head back to his chest, inhaling the scent that's uniquely him. "I was thinking about life before I came here and how much of a miracle you and Crew are."

Aidan stiffens slightly beneath me. Not enough that I think he's uncomfortable, but enough to let me know that I'm probably going to have to come clean to him about why I'm here and soon. His next words confirm it, the gentle care with which he says them bringing fresh tears to my eyes.

"Angel... I don't know what happened to you back home, but please know I'm here if or when you're ready to talk about it."

I nod against his chest, but a pit forms in my stomach when I think about telling him what happened. When I think about admitting to this perfect man how ashamed I still am that I allowed myself to get into that situation and allowed myself to stay for so long.

It's only a matter of time before Sebastian comes looking for me. And I don't know if I could live with myself if Aidan or Crew got caught in the crossfire.

11

Aidan

Lyla's whispered confession blares like a foghorn through my mind even hours later, and it has giddiness and anger fighting for dominance in my chest.

She and Wren are currently set up at a table in our backyard, painting the remaining kids' faces into different animals. Their squeals of joy bring a smile to my face where I'm sitting with a beer by the pool.

I've been nursing the same drink since just after we emerged from the bathroom two hours ago, but my mind has been racing too much to even enjoy it. Throwing a surprise party was clearly the wrong move on my part, and I feel like a class-A jackass for not thinking to check with her first.

For fuck's sake, Rhodes flat-out *told me* she had likely been through something traumatic, and here I am tossing her into a room full of strangers with no warning.

The only saving grace here is that after a half hour of reassuring words and co-regulation, Lyla seemed to come out of the panic attack relatively okay. The second she was steady on her feet, her focus turned to Crew and making sure he had a great party, so I left her to clean up and finally greeted our guests.

Luckily, said *guests* consist only of guys on the team and their families, so they were all really cool about the whole thing and politely didn't ask questions.

Wren, however, almost cried out of guilt. I tried to reassure her, but it's pretty hard when I feel just as guilty, if not more so. If my mom weren't in Seattle visiting my younger brother, she'd be reading me the riot act.

"Hey man." Rhodes slides into the deck chair next to me, sipping a juice box. I scoff, raising a questioning brow, to which he just shrugs. "What? I'm driving, and I've got precious cargo. Sue me for drinking fruit punch."

I just shake my head with a chuckle. He's always been a cheesy bastard, but his entire demeanor has changed since Wren made her way back into his life last year.

Some selfish part of me hoped they would want to have kids right away so I'd have friends in the parenting boat with me, but no dice. They're happy being dog parents, and though I was a little bummed at first, I truly couldn't be happier for them.

"So," Rhodes starts quietly. "How are things going with Lyla anyway? You two seem a lot closer since the last time I saw you together."

One other thing about my best friend? He's as gossipy as an old woman after Sunday service.

"Lyla is incredible with Crew," I say wistfully. "I know I wasn't doing a *bad* job raising him before, but he's an entirely different kid since she moved in. He's doing regular schoolwork and is on a set schedule, which means he's sleeping better and hasn't been as emotional when I have to leave."

He looks over to where Lyla is helping Crew eat a

cupcake the size of his head and laughs. "He seems really taken with her." From the corner of my eye, I see him studying my profile, but my gaze is so riveted on my son and his nanny that I can't be bothered to return his stare. "But it seems like he's not the only one."

I fight a blush and sigh, scrubbing a palm over the back of my neck. "I asked her to come with me to New York this weekend... *without* Crew."

Rhodes nods in understanding, but he doesn't look surprised, so I'm pretty sure Wren already told him. It's nice to talk to someone about this without worrying about how they'll perceive it. "And is this a date? Is it just a fling? I mean, you've only known her a month, and just a couple weeks ago, you were worried because you didn't know anything about her."

Shrugging, I take another pull from my lukewarm beer and grimace, setting it to the side.

"I guess I still don't know all that much about her. But it's the little things that have sucked me in, like the way she wakes up early and sits with me while we drink our morning coffee and how it's easier to talk to her than it has been with anybody else, maybe ever. Or the way she takes care of me, even when she doesn't have to, either by making me special macro-friendly meals so I don't have to eat reheated food every day or by asking me how I'm doing and caring about the answer."

My gaze strays to where she's chatting with a pretty redhead I think might be here from a local bakery. Crew stands at her side, still eating his massive cupcake, and my smile grows when Lyla pauses their conversation to wipe some frosting off his face with her thumb.

"When she's working with Crew on his schoolwork, she scrunches up her nose in this adorable way that makes me want to squish her cheeks and kiss her all at once, and she has a crazy obsession with cherries that I think is absolutely precious. And her laugh? Good god, Rhodes. That woman laughs, and every molecule in my body stops to soak in the sound."

I sigh heavily. "The truth is, she hasn't done anything groundbreaking to draw me to her. It's every little detail I've learned and all the things I haven't that keep me helplessly in her orbit. The fact that it's all wrapped up in such a gorgeous package definitely doesn't hurt either."

With each hurried word that falls out of my mouth, Rhodes's smile grows bigger, eventually getting so wide it's almost unsettling. I don't think I've ever seen someone's molars when they smiled before. He keeps on smiling and not saying anything for long enough that I start to squirm uncomfortably, and defensiveness has me straightening in my seat.

"What?" I grouse.

He barks out a laugh, and it seems like that breaks the dam. Soon enough, he's forcing out words between bouts of laughter. "Fuck, Aidan. I owe Wren a hundred bucks."

That wasn't anywhere on the list of things I expected him to say. Raising a brow, I glance between him and Wren, who's currently telling what looks to be a wild story to Lyla and the redhead.

"Wanna explain? Or should I just go jump off the dock? Because that seems like it would be about as helpful as you are right now."

My best friend finally gets control of himself as his laughter subsides, and he shakes his head at me. "Wren also bet me you'd fall for her by the end of her first month as Crew's nanny. I thought you'd hold out at least three."

My jaw drops, but I shouldn't be surprised. In our

friend group, someone always has some inane bet going. Though I'll admit it's usually Wren and me betting about the stupid things we can get Rhodes to do.

"Y'all made a bet about Lyla, even knowing she was coming off of something traumatic?"

That thought fills me with indignation because nobody should be making bets about my girl.

Woah. My *girl?*

"The bet wasn't about Lyla, you ass. Honestly, I wasn't sure about this whole arrangement in the first place. You didn't see her back when she first moved here, but she was as fragile as fine china. Every sound made her jump, and she didn't go more than ten minutes without checking her surroundings or looking over her shoulder like she was expecting somebody to jump out at her."

He takes a breath and scratches his elbow, casting a sideways look at the woman in question, who's laughing at Crew as he drags her over to the face-painting station.

"I didn't know her as well as Wren because men still made her extremely uncomfortable back then, but the difference between Lyla a year ago and Lyla now? It's jarring. If working for you is what's putting that look on her face? I think you should keep up whatever y'all are doing."

His words simultaneously break my heart and light it up because I can picture Lyla then, alone and so scared of her own shadow she'd feel the need to constantly be on alert, but she's not now.

She's changed so much, even from just a month ago, and I know I'll do everything in my power to keep breaking down her walls and building up her confidence in men. In *me.*

I don't get a chance to say anything else because Lyla makes her way over to us with a huge smile on her flushed face. She looks so pretty today that it's honestly distracting. Jean shorts that would be criminal on someone of average height hit the tops of her thighs in an entirely too enticing way, and she's wearing her very own dinosaur shirt that Crew insisted we buy for her birthday.

Of course, she didn't wait even a minute before putting it on, and he's been on cloud nine all day because of it. Her reddish-brown hair hangs down to her waist in big, shiny curls, and I can't help but notice that every week, her hair takes on more of a red tint.

"Hey there, cowboy. Having fun over here?"

I look to my right and am surprised to see Rhodes is nowhere to be found, but when I glance behind Lyla, I catch his wink aimed my way from where he's standing with Wren and Crew. Ignoring him, I turn back to the gorgeous girl in front of me.

"Hi, angel, having fun?"

She blushes right on cue and takes the newly vacated seat next to me. "I've never had a birthday party like this before. I didn't realize what I was missing. And those cupcakes are *divine*. I know you're on a strict diet, but you need to have at least a bite of one."

Her voice is full of childlike excitement, and my heart expands in my chest. She could ask me for just about anything, and I know I'd give it to her. Her words niggle at me, though.

"You've never had a birthday party like this before? So what were your parties like then?"

Lyla's eyes widen like she didn't mean to say that, but she surprises me when she elaborates. "My birthday parties were always treated more like... let's say *networking events*, for my father. They were all crudités and champagne and petit fours in place of an actual cake. It's fine for a charity event or a formal dinner party but for a kid's party?"

She shakes her head with a sigh. "I honestly can't remember a single birthday I ever enjoyed until this one."

With a covert glance around, I don't see anyone paying attention to us, so I take a risk and thread my fingers with hers. "As long as I'm around, the rest of your birthdays will be even better than this one, Ly."

Her unique eyes sparkle in the afternoon sunlight, pulling me further under her spell. I watch her chest rise and fall as she takes a deep breath, and then she knocks my carefully balanced control off its axis.

"Does your offer for this weekend still stand?"

My lips part in surprise even as my heart soars. "You want to spend the weekend with me?"

She bites her bottom lip and nods shyly. "I like you, Aidan. I've been trying not to because I really love this job, but everything you do makes me like you a little bit more. But if it doesn't work, you're sure I can stay on as Crew's nanny, and it won't be weird?"

I start to respond, but she cuts me off. "This is a non-negotiable for me. I don't want to be another person that leaves him," she finishes on a whisper.

My mind and heart fill with affection as I squeeze her tiny hand in mine. "I promise, Lyla. I have no expectations here. If you don't want to pursue a relationship at the end of the weekend, we go back to being boss and employee like nothing happened. Think of it as a trial run where you have all the power."

Her breath hitches, and I watch the panic flare in her eyes. "Why would I need all the power?"

I roll my eyes a bit but catch myself and instead momentarily let my own demons out from their reinforced cage. "I know what it looks like to be afraid of someone who isn't around anymore. Constantly looking over your shoulder, holding your breath when you round a corner, learning to live with the physical and emotional damage they left behind."

My callused hand cups her cheek with as much affection as I can possibly pour into the small gesture. "I'm here when you're ready to tell me, but I won't push. All I ask is that you come to me if you need help."

My pulse races as emotions fly across her face too fast for me to decipher, and suddenly, I'm worried she's about to back out of her agreement.

The thought of letting someone else in after what Crew and I have already been through, first me with my father and then both of us with Mia, is terrifying enough. But we're adding in a whole new layer of unknowns with whatever trauma Lyla is hiding, too. She offers a hesitant nod, and that will have to be enough for now.

The tender smile she gives me melts some of the indecision surrounding my heart, and for the first time in seven years, I find myself wanting to confide in someone about my father. Just as I open my mouth to reassure her with *something*, a battle cry interrupts us from the back door.

"Raptor attack!"

The screeched words are the only warning we get before my boy barrels between us, diving onto Lyla's chair with her and causing it to tip abruptly into mine, nearly knocking us both over. Lyla is fine and laughing with arms full of a sticky six-year-old, so I take a second to daydream about what this scene would look like if she were here as more than just the nanny.

And the thing is, I think she might want that too.

12 Lyla

I'm nearly finished packing for our early flight to New York when my phone rings. The sound of *Wild Things* by Alessia Cara blasts through the room, letting me know exactly who's calling.

"Before you say anything, I swear to God, Ly I didn't say a word to Aidan." Wren's voice is frantic on the other end of the phone, and it's almost enough to make me smile, but the subject brings me back to being annoyed with my best friend.

The bite to my tone is unintentional, and I'm sure I'll feel guilty later, but I can't find it in myself to care at the moment. I feel like a caged animal with eyes on me all the time since my last conversation with Aidan.

"Then who did tell him, Wren? Because nobody is *that* perceptive. It makes me feel like all of that therapy was for nothing if somebody who was a complete stranger only a month ago can see things about me I've worked so hard to push past."

"Did he say or do something that made you uncomfortable?" Her voice sounds like the crack of a whip through the spacious room as I pick up my phone and move to the window seat facing the water.

With a sigh of resignation, I put the phone on speaker and cross my arms over my knees, bringing them to my chest so I can rest my head. I can already feel a migraine building behind my eyes. "Yes. But that's more of a me issue than a him issue."

I can practically feel her sympathetic grimace through the phone. "I get that. I didn't meet you until after I had started therapy again, but I kind of stopped dealing with all the negative shit for a while after Derrick cheated on me, and it took thinking I was going to lose Rhodes to stop running from my problems."

Wren and her fiancé, Rhodes, had been best friends and secretly in love with each other since college even after she got married and moved away. It took her ex-husband publicly cheating on her for them to finally admit their feelings last spring, and aside from the incident she's talking about, they've been inseparable ever since.

The hidden meaning in her words hits me full force, and I snort, glaring at the phone and hoping she can feel it on her end. "He told you?"

"I don't know what you're talking about, babe. If Crew is spending the weekend with his pseudo-grandparents, that's between them and the lord. I had absolutely nothing to do with it."

I wish she could see my eye roll.

"I can hear you rolling your eyes, and sassy is not a good look on you, Ly."

That finally brings a smile to my face, but I quickly sober. "What if he doesn't want me anymore after finding out about my past?" I whisper fearfully. The anxiety that's had a grip on my very soul since Aidan asked me out earlier this week is stifling. "I'm terrified I'm going to end up dragging him and Crew into my mess."

She's quiet for a moment before clearing her throat. "Aidan knows you're running from something, babe. He doesn't know what or *who*, but he does know, and he's fully prepared to deal with the consequences of starting something with you. I know he'll wait for you to tell him your story, but you need to know that you have a lot of people here and ready to help if you'll let us." After a minute of silence, Wren cackles suddenly, startling me.

"Oh man, just *wait* until Copeland gets ahold of that info. He'll be chomping at the bit to get started on the little sleuthing thing he does."

My brows raise. "What do you mean? And remind me which one Copeland is?"

Wren snickers. "He's been out of town with some family thing, so I doubt you've met him yet. But he's got pretty black hair and is covered in tattoos and metal. Looks like he belongs in some sort of emo rock band."

I chuckle at her description because I remember seeing pictures of him with Crew in the hallway, and now I know exactly who she's talking about. I remember thinking he looked like Andy Biersack, so her description is spot-on.

"Anyhow," she continues. "Cope can find out anything about any*one* if given enough to go on. I swear he must have been a detective in a past life."

I think about everything she just told me about running from her problems and then take a moment to truly consider what she's saying right now before coming to a decision that I hope will change things for the better. "Wren?" I interrupt her rambling.

"Yeah, Ly?"

Taking a deep breath, I lay down the first card in my hand. "What all does Copeland need to start digging?"

A quick inhale is all I hear for a second, followed by Wren's whispered voice. "Lyla, are you sure?"

"You're right. I'm letting him control me, and I don't want to live that way anymore. If this weekend goes well, I have two more people to think about when it comes to their safety. So what does he need?"

I can hear her tapping away in the background like she's typing on her phone, and it's a fifty-fifty toss-up on if she's texting Copeland or Rhodes. "All he needs is a name."

With terror freezing me to the spot, I give up my first secret and pray it won't doom us all.

———

"I could've flown separately, you know. I didn't need to fly with you guys."

I'm in a large, comfortable seat on the team jet with Aidan seated next to me while Wren and Rhodes, who are currently sitting in front of us, beam at us like proud parents sending their kids off to prom.

Wren scoffs. "As if we would have let you fly alone. Plus, Aid is a nervous flyer, so now you can hold his hand." She winks at him, a sly glint in her ocean-blue gaze.

I don't know what they put in the water here, but I swear everyone in their friend group is freakishly gorgeous. Even Rhodes' parents look like they should be playing lawyers on TV, not in actual courtrooms.

Aidan turns pleading eyes to me when the engines

fire, and I feel my own widen in response. "Wren is yankin' your chain, but she wasn't lying about the nervous flyer thing. I hate airplanes and usually latch on to the person next to me. It was Cope, then it was Rho, and now..." he trails off.

With a resigned sigh I don't mean, I grip his giant hand and twine our fingers together. "And now I guess it's me."

Rhodes snickers in front of us and finally turns back in his seat as the flight attendant flips on the seatbelt sign.

My seat-mate shoots me a grateful smile, his belt already locked and as tight as humanly possible across his lap. I filter through my mental Rolodex of distraction techniques, but it's hard because most of them are designed for children.

Turning in my seat slightly, I try to catch Aidan's eye and think of the most ridiculous question I can. "Have you ever seen *Charlie and the Chocolate Factory*?"

He snorts in amusement, but the slight green pallor to his skin nearly has me reaching for a barf bag. "The original or the remake?"

I use my free hand to tap a finger on my chin. "Both."

"I've seen both more times than I care to admit. Crew went through a candy-obsessed phase. His fourth birthday? Candy factory themed."

That makes me laugh and his coloring is starting to look better, so I keep going. "Okay follow-up question then: which did you like better?"

Apparently, my question is ridiculous because it earns me an eye roll and a look that clearly asks, "Are you serious?"

"The new one, obviously. I don't know what it is

about that movie specifically, but Gene Wilder's version of Wonka creeps me the fuck out."

I snort with laughter. "I literally couldn't agree more! I loved him in other things, but that movie? Ugh, I get chills just thinking about it. And *not* the good kind."

Aidan smirks and shakes his head at me, squeezing my hand the slightest bit. "Was there a specific reason you asked that?"

"Nope. Just wanted to distract you until we were comfortably in the air." I shrug, letting go of his hand briefly so I can pull out my laptop.

When I glance back, his mouth is gaping open, and even the nosy couple sitting in front of us is staring at me in shock. It makes me feel slightly defensive, so without thinking, I snap at them. "What?"

"I don't think he's ever gotten through a takeoff that easily before," Rhodes whispers in awe. "One of us is normally holding a barf bag for him or losing feeling in our fingers from his meaty paws squeezing the life out of them." He leans over the back of his seat and offers me a high five, which I proudly return.

"Thanks," I smile smugly. "I learned that in one of my child psychology classes."

That has our friends howling with laughter in front of us, earning us a glare from one of the flight attendants. If this is any indication of how this trip is going to go, I can't freaking wait to get there.

Aidan
13

I've never been this nervous for a game in my life, and as someone who's been to the playoffs multiple times in his major league career, that's saying something.

This won't only be Lyla's first time watching me play but her first baseball game *ever*. I'm both honored and antsy as hell. I've been unconsciously bouncing my leg for the last ten minutes, making the metal bench rattle.

"Dude." Copeland hits me with a vicious side-eye from his spot next to me before reaching out to rest a hand on my knee. "What the fuck is up with you? I haven't seen you this nervous since your rookie year when you puked on coach's shoes."

The reminder makes me cringe. "Who was it that convinced me taking shots of Fireball would help me relax?"

Several of the guys overhear and snicker, sending Cope into a fit of laughter. "You smelled like a sorority house the rest of the day." He gets a faraway look in his eyes, making me roll mine.

Of course, he would conveniently leave out that he's

the one who supplied me with the liquor and assured me it would help the pre-game jitters. I can't even look at cinnamon-flavored things now.

"Really though, is there something I should know? I need you on your game out there today, Preach. New York is going to be our toughest series this year, and we need to hit them hard in the preseason to rattle them a bit."

Copeland is our starting pitcher and has been my partner in crime on and off the field since I was drafted to catch for the Raptors seven years ago.

He and I have both received trade offers from other teams over the years, but my best friend has been set in his ways ever since he broke things off with his ex, and I wanted Crew to have as much stability as possible.

I turn to face the broody bastard next to me with a sigh. "You know how I hired a nanny for Crew last month?"

His eyes narrow suspiciously. "Yeah, I saw it in the group chat, but what..." he gasps, squeezing my thigh hard enough to give me a Charlie horse.

I curse and slap his hand away, massaging the sore spot as he crows. *"You didn't.* Did our little Preacher finally break his celibacy with the hot new nanny? Talk about sex on tap without the hassle of commitment."

That fucking nickname. You get caught celebrating *Palm Sunday* a *couple of times,* and suddenly, you're branded Preacher for the rest of your career.

In my defense, Crew was a baby, and I was too tired to go out and find some random hookup, so I took advantage of my roommate being out to relieve some tension. How was I supposed to know he'd come back early and catch me with my pants down?

"No!" My cheeks heat and I know I'm probably red with a mixture of embarrassment and anger. The anger wins, and my next words come out as a threatening growl. "And don't talk about her like that. Like she's some cleat chaser who doesn't give a shit about us."

Cope's jaw drops as he stares at me in shock. I can count on both hands the number of times I've snapped at him over the years, and I'm fairly sure all of those were when I was bone tired after Crew was born. Guilt quickly follows on the heels of the anger as it dissipates, and his kicked-puppy look makes me feel like shit.

"Aidan... I didn't mean anything by it, man."

Dropping my head to rest on my knees, I murmur, "I know. I'm sorry I snapped at you." Turning my head to the side, I give him a pitiful look.

"Oh shit," he laughs. "The first girl you like in six years, and it's Crew's nanny?" He shakes his head with an amused look, but I see the concern swimming in his dark green gaze.

I drag my hands down my face with a groan. "It's the way she treats Crew that got me first. Not a single person I've ever hired before has treated him like he matters beyond the job. And then she started asking about *me*. She noticed when I wasn't okay, and she told me I didn't have to be. I mean, for fuck's sake, Cope. She distracted me with one question before we took off on the flight here, and the next thing I know we're cruising at altitude, and I'm totally fine!"

His dark brows nearly hit his hairline. "You made it through a flight sober, unmedicated, and you didn't have a single minute of panic?"

I don't think I stopped staring at Lyla once until we got to the hotel in New York last night. I've never liked flying, but ever since Crew was born, it's gotten a thousand times worse.

All I can think about is how many planes go down during takeoff and landings, and it's enough to send me spiraling into a full breakdown until we're back on solid ground.

With one single well-placed question, my guardian angel was able to distract me enough that I actually had *fun* during the flight, which is something I've absolutely never said before. Honestly, if I didn't know any better, I would think she's a witch, not an angel.

"See what I mean? It's only been a month, and she's turned our world upside down. She's got this whole homeschool program going for Crew, and I swear to god, I thought that kid was smart before, but now? He's doing math like it's second nature."

I trail off, momentarily lost in thoughts of the pretty brunette. "I asked her to go on a date with me this weekend."

Those brows that had been raised furrow in concern. "What if it doesn't work out?"

I shrug. "I've wondered that too. But we agreed to one weekend, no expectations. If it doesn't work out or she isn't feeling it, we go back to being boss and employee with no hard feelings. She can stay on with Crew, and I'll be professional, or she can find another job, and I'll write her a fantastic recommendation. I think she could be worth the risk, Cope. And not just for me."

He opens his mouth to respond, but our head coach, Benny, claps his hands and starts his pregame pep talk, effectively pausing the conversation. We do our team chant, and then I'm in the dugout searching the stands for a head of long brown hair.

Lyla is fucking tiny, so it takes me a minute to spot her next to Wren and some of the other wives and girlfriends, but when I do, my peripheral vision goes dark, and the breath is knocked from my chest.

She's in my goddamn jersey.

Lyla Taylor is sitting in the WAG section looking like a fucking knockout with the number 23 and *my* last name plastered across her back, and I think I might be having a stroke.

I don't hear Coach coming up behind me until his sun-weathered hand clamps down hard on my shoulder. He follows my gaze and whistles loudly when he sees my girl turn around.

"Boys!" he shouts gleefully. "Looks like Preacher here finally caught himself a WAG! Do you know what that means?"

Some of the newer players are kind of confused since they haven't been around for a wife or girlfriend introduction yet, but all the veteran players grin like the smug assholes they are.

It's an unspoken general rule that you don't give a partner your jersey or invite them to sit with the wives and girlfriends unless things are serious or you're top over tail for the poor thing, so having Ly out there in my jersey is going to be a bigger deal than she probably knows.

The opening notes to *Beautiful Soul* by Jesse McCartney play over the field speakers on our side, and the Raptors fans go wild. New York is only a two hour flight from South Carolina, so a surprising amount of the fans here are ours, and they know exactly what this song means. They're no doubt waiting to see who leaves the dugout first.

Benny hands me a bouquet of fake roses in the signature

Raptor blue, making me roll my eyes dramatically. I'd bet my right hand Wren tattled to the team about Lyla being here.

Rhodes was the last guy to get a serious girlfriend, but she works for the organization, so they didn't have to deal with this, and Wren has been dying to see it in person.

Coach approaches me with a twinkle in his eye and hands me a family access pass before patting me on the back. "Well," he grins. "Best get on out there, Black. Wouldn't want to keep them waiting."

I groan and take the stuff from his hands, nearly stomping out to the field like I'm not secretly thrilled at the idea of claiming my angel so publicly.

The fans absolutely lose it the second I come into view. I feel kind of bad bombarding Lyla like this on our first date, but I'm also looking forward to seeing that adorable blush on her cheeks again.

And if I put a little extra swagger into my step, who's gonna know but me?

I realize with satisfaction that the girls are, in fact, sitting right behind home plate, which will give Ly a clear view of my ass all game. I make my way over to them, and the closer I get, the more I can see the bright, mildly confused grin taking over my girl's face.

Her cheeks are flushed pink as she watches me make my way to the only short part of the fencing right next to the home team's dugout. I see a few players I recognize on my way past and send them a wink, earning me loud laughter and plenty of ribbing.

Hopping the gate, I finally make it to Lyla and crouch at her feet, offering up the flowers first with a sneaky grin. "Heard it was a gorgeous girl's first baseball game."

She bats her long, dark eyelashes at me with a way too

innocent grin. "Who, me?" she asks with a fake yawn. "Nah, I go to these things all the time. Honestly, this one has been pretty boring so far."

That pulls a bark of laughter from me. I can tell she's been spending way too much time with Rhodes' fiancé if the sudden burst of sass is anything to go by. A crazy idea hits me, and I couldn't stop my smile from spreading if I tried. "Wanna make it more interesting?"

Lyla raises an eyebrow in question, but she's still grinning. "What did you have in mind?"

She's so short when she sits down that I'm still eye level with her while crouching, so I use the angle to my advantage and slide my hand around the back of her neck, gripping firmly. Her smile is wide, like she thinks I'm going to make a joke, but I don't.

Leaning in so our mouths are nearly brushing, I whisper, "I was thinking something like this."

And then I kiss her.

You know those disgustingly cheesy movie moments where the main characters kiss for the first time and everything stills around them? Kissing Lyla Taylor is like that.

The roar of thousands of fans and all the constant noise in my head. The fears that I'm not doing enough as a father, brother, and friend, and the overwhelming weariness of everyday life. It all goes silent the second my lips touch hers.

I try to keep it short and sweet since I'm painfully aware more than fifty-thousand people are watching us, but as I go to pull away, she licks her lips, making that sweet tongue brush against my mouth, and for the hundredth time since I met this woman, my control snaps.

I yank her mouth back to mine with an intensity I'm confident I've never felt for another person.

My tongue invades her mouth, swallowing the breathy gasp that tries to slip from her sinful throat until the cheers and catcalls around us become impossible to ignore. We pull apart, both of us breathing heavily. Her green eyes are glossy and dark with desire, making my cock throb painfully inside the protective cup I have on.

I'm totally going to have an imprint of the damned thing on my dick later, and I don't even fucking care.

"Wow," she whispers quietly, her gaze locked on my mouth. Her gaze is locked on my tongue as I lick my lips. Just to let her know she wasn't imagining it, I roll the ball of my tongue piercing between my teeth as subtly as I can and wink at her when her eyes widen.

Wren is grinning like a menace next to us, and I discreetly flip her off where my angel can't see. Ly looks just as stunned as I feel, and as much as I want to stay and kiss her some more, I can hear the guys calling my name, and I know I'm probably going to catch a hefty fine for delaying the game.

That kiss was worth every fucking dollar.

Lyla

14

"Sooo," Wren sings next to me. "How was your first major league game?"

I snort, linking our arms together as we walk down the hall towards the locker room. Apparently, most of the player's families meet them here after games, and even if I weren't about to go on a date with the incredibly sexy catcher, I would still be welcome because I'll usually have Crew.

My smile is wide, and any panic I thought I'd feel is suspiciously absent as I recall the way Aidan effortlessly hopped the fence to get to me. I have to fight the urge to swoon when I think about the kiss—*our first kiss*. It was nothing short of a movie moment, and with his blond hair and perfect smile, he reminded me of Prince Charming.

Yeah, if Prince Charming had a perfect ass.

Turning to my best friend, I grin. "It was alright, I guess."

She howls with laughter, pulling the attention of the entire room. Most people just smile or shake their heads, so I'm guessing they're used to Wren's brand of boisterous laughter.

"*Alright*," she says. "Yeah, I'll bet getting up close and personal with Aidan's surprise hardware and getting to stare at your soon-to-be boyfriend's perfectly toned ass the whole game was such a hardship for you, Ly-bear."

I snicker and shrug because I can't even deny it. The tongue piercing was a surprise, alright. A freaking hot one.

I tried really hard to focus on the girls when they tried to explain the rules of the game to me, but then Aidan would catch my eye and wink, or crouch down in those damn pants, or my mind would drift, wondering what that particular piece of jewelry would feel like on other parts of my body. Either way, now I get why some women are so obsessed with baseball players.

It's gotta be the pants.

"Slow down there on the labels, Wren. We literally haven't even started our first date. And what if it's terrible? Then we have to try and pretend it never happened and go back to being reluctant boss and employee for Crew's sake."

My best friend gasps dramatically, clutching perfectly manicured hands to her chest. "Don't say that. You'll jinx it!"

"What's the new girl going to jinx?" Brandy, one of the wives, pops up like a dang jack in the box next to us, startling a squeak out of me.

Her blonde hair is professionally highlighted and styled, and her makeup expertly applied. Her outfit looks to be designer, and the handbag she's sporting is worth more than a used car. Or it would be if it was real.

Wren flips a switch, her once happy smile turning a

little sharper. "Oh, nothing," she laughs lightly, waving the other woman off. "We were just talking about an exam she still doesn't have the results for yet."

Brandy's obviously fake smile falls slightly at the fabricated story, the glint leaving her eyes as her overfilled lips pull up into a sneer. "Oh, well then. I'm sure it was fine! Never would have guessed Aidan was so desperate for company that he'd stoop to high school jailbait." She flicks my hair that I threaded into a loose braid during the seventh-inning stretch.

A scoff of indignation leaves Wren's lips, but I hold my hand out, trying to reassure her with my eyes that I could handle it. I may have been sheltered from boys growing up, but I sure as hell wasn't sheltered from spoiled rich bitches. Slapping on my tried and true "I know something you don't" grin, I rest my chin in my hand.

"Oh dear," I sigh sadly, returning her gesture and playing with a strand of her pin-straight hair. "I know it's hard to believe, but some of us are blessed with excellent genetics and don't need filler or highlights to look younger. I can tell it's hard for you to watch a younger woman encroach on what you seem to think is your territory, but don't let a twenty-something threaten you so much that you insult one of your husband's teammates, darling. It's not a good look."

She gasps, a look of indignation shining in her eyes. But before she can speak, I lean in close enough to smell the Chanel on her collar. "And hey, I have a friend at Dior if you're interested! She might be able to get you a good deal on a sample piece, so you don't have to keep carrying around a fake bag," I whisper, flicking the tassel on her purse.

Brandy stomps off after emitting a quiet scream of frustration, and normally I would laugh but instead, guilt slithers around my stomach and wraps it in a vice.

I promised myself when I left Maryland that I was leaving that life and the person I was behind, but one negative word about Aidan and I slipped right back into that skin like it was made for me.

I don't ever want Crew to see me be this person, especially after hearing bits and pieces about what his mom was like from passing comments Aidan, Rhodes, or Wren have made.

Loud clapping behind me yanks me out of my pity party and back to the present. I fight to keep my face blank as I turn around to see not only Wren staring at me with wide eyes, but Rhodes, Aidan, and who I'm guessing is Copeland as well.

Copeland is the one clapping with a huge grin on his striking face. He's maybe only slightly taller than Aidan, but that's where their similarities end. His hair is jet black and shaggy around his forehead but shaved on the sides, and his eyes are a dark emerald green.

With cheekbones that could cut glass, multiple facial piercings and dark tattoos on every inch of visible skin, he very much fits the image of the emo rock band leader Wren recently compared him to.

He clamps a hand down on Aidan's shoulder with a loud laugh. "I like this one. Can we keep her?"

My date hasn't stopped staring at me like I'm a stranger, and it's making the vice around my stomach clench even tighter. I think I might actually be sick if he doesn't say something soon. My cheeks heat, and in my quest to avoid eye contact at all costs, my eyes land on my best friend and her fiancé.

Wren is nearly bursting at the seams she's so excited, and Rhodes seems to be holding back a laugh. Rolling my eyes, I send them both a mean glare, making Rhodes hold up his hands in surrender.

"Is it just me, or was that weirdly hot?" Aidan's voice has me whipping my head around in shock.

He shrugs innocently at my astonished stare. "What? You defended me, and it was sexy as hell."

The dam finally bursts, and everybody breaks into hysterical laughter at the bewildered look on their catcher's face. I'm fighting off a smile of my own until my phone pings with a text message that drains all the blood clear from my face.

Bile burns my throat as I read the words on the screen, thanking my lucky stars we are out of the state and away from Crew.

> **UNKNOWN**
>
> You looked so pretty on the TV today, darling, and so very close to home. We'll be together again soon, Little Bunny.

"Angel? Everything okay?" Aidan's concerned voice cuts through the static buzzing in my ears and I quickly block the number before deleting the text.

I clear my throat and force a smile. "Totally fine!" The words sound strained even to my own ears, so I swallow hard, hoping I sound normal with my next words. "So, what do you have planned for tonight?"

I can tell he doesn't want to let it go, but the man clearly knows how to read a room, so he does, offering me a small, reassuring smile. "It's a surprise, but you'll need a jacket."

"Oh my god!" I squeal into the microphone attached to the large headphones resting over my ears. "When you said I needed a jacket, I never would have expected this! What happened to being afraid of flying?"

Aidan had a hired car waiting outside the field's staff entrance to take us to a private airstrip just outside the city, and he had me bundled into a helicopter before I could protest.

We've been in the air for over an hour now and the views are absolutely stunning, but I'm slightly anxious about the direction we're headed. I haven't been this close to my home state in over a year, and a small part of my brain is terrified we'll run into Sebastian somewhere.

He laughs, intertwining our fingers and placing a sweet kiss on the back of my hand before he brings them to rest on his muscular thigh. "I'm terrified of airplanes. You're in a giant metal tube thirty-thousand feet in the air with hundreds of other people breathing recycled air. Helicopters are totally different."

He trails off, a shy smile lighting his handsome features. "Plus, this was the fastest way to get to our destination. And I don't want to waste a single moment with you."

I can't find the words to express how that makes me feel, so I squeeze his hand tightly. His shy smile transforms to a blinding grin when I do, making me feel breathless. He's easily the most attractive man I've ever seen.

"I guess since we're already above the city, I'll tell you we've got reservations in Washington DC for this evening." One side of his pillowy lips pulls up into a smirk. "But I'm not telling you for what until we get there."

The last fifteen minutes of the flight are incredible as the sun descends in the sky, casting a golden glow over the devastating man next to me.

I should be in awe of the way his icy eyes turn transparent in the waning light or the way his hair glows and creates a halo of light above his head, but how can I be in awe of his looks when Aidan continues to prove he's also golden on the inside. Over the last month, there were so many times he could have cornered me about my past or the inconsistencies in my story, but he didn't.

Aidan Black is kind, smart, beyond attractive, and such an incredible father. I can't help but feel like me and my issues are going to drag him and his sweet son down to the gutter with me when this blows up in my face.

I want to believe I can make this work. I want so desperately to take the happiness and family Aidan and his son are so freely offering. But how can I when I know Sebastian will never let me go?

When I realize what I'm going to have to do, my thoughts are so consumed by turmoil and sadness that I don't even notice when we touch down until Aidan squeezes my hand tightly. I paste on a smile, unwilling to waste even a minute of the time I get with this perfect man being sad.

"You ready for this, angel?" he asks with a wide grin after hopping out of the now silent helicopter.

The way he reaches for me as he uses that nickname brings a genuine smile to my face, even as I make a mental note to ask him where it came from later. Taking a deep, steadying breath, I grab his much larger hand and let him help me out. "As ready as I'll ever be."

Aidan

15

Seeing Lyla bathed in the golden light from the sunset on our helicopter ride with her hair all wild around her face was a goddamn religious experience. She doesn't know it yet, but I snuck a picture of her when she was looking out at the Washington skyline, and if I thought it wouldn't creep her out, I would make it the background on my phone in a heartbeat.

I keep a tight hold on her hand as we stroll around the Tidal Basin, enjoying the smell of the cherry blossom trees. We went on a murder mystery dinner cruise on the river and had the best time, taking us both out of our comfort zone. Seeing Ly open up and have fun with me is a core memory I'll never forget.

Not to mention that hot-as-hell British accent she pulled out of nowhere for her character. I'll definitely be asking her to role-play with that sometime soon. She sounded like a sexy boarding school teacher.

Needless to say, I've been painfully hard since dinner. "So," I murmur, placing my lips against her ear. I track the shiver that runs across her body with immense satisfaction, even as her cherry perfume threatens to undo me.

Lyla can sometimes be so hard to read with how she locks her emotions down, so seeing physical evidence that I affect her is a great feeling.

"We can either fly back to New York tonight and stay at the hotel with the team..." I trail off, skimming my lips over her neck lightly, loving the tiny gasp she gives me.

"Or?" she breathes.

"Or, I can have the driver take us ten minutes down the road, where I have a reservation for a suite at Sofitel." I pull her to a stop and move us off the main pathway, backing my sweet angel up against the nearest cherry blossom tree.

"There's no pressure here, Ly. I know we said one weekend, but that doesn't have to mean anything more than us going on a couple of dates and getting to know each other. If you're uncomfortable with how fast things are moving, pull the brakes. *You* are in control, always."

Her eyes are slightly glassy from the themed drinks we had at dinner, but her response is clear as day and has me going from rock-hard to nearly busting in seconds. "I think... I think I want to lose control with you, Aidan. I mean, it wouldn't be a real trial run if we didn't try *everything*, would it?" she whispers with a shy grin just barely tinged with nerves.

I groan, watching her teeth dig into her plush bottom lip, and yank out my phone to text the driver, ushering her over to the meeting point as fast as I can without looking too eager.

I'm not saying I've been a saint or anything since Crew was born, but it's been nearly two years since I was last with a woman, and I'm genuinely worried I might embarrass myself here.

Her quiet giggle does nothing to help the uncomfortable situation behind the zipper of my jeans right now, so I reach down to adjust myself as discreetly as possible.

My tongue ring clicks against my teeth when I clench my jaw, and a dirty smirk crawls its way onto my mouth thinking of all the ways I can make this as good for her as I know it will be for me.

We make it to the hotel and up to our room in record time, and not one minute goes by that we aren't touching or sneaking heated kisses. The second the heavy door closes, I grip her face between my hands and back her up against the door, slanting my mouth over hers with a sigh.

The scent of her perfume surrounds me as I sweep my tongue into her hot mouth. A loud groan emanates from deep in my chest when I realize that somehow, she tastes even better than she smells.

My angel tastes like cherries and looks like temptation.

"Goddamn, Lyla," I huff, trailing kisses down her neck and collarbone. "If that's how good your mouth tastes, I can't imagine how good you'll taste in other places."

Her moan is sweet and breathy, and it drives me to the brink of madness. Scooping her up in my arms, I encourage her to wrap her toned legs around my waist so I can carry her to the master bedroom down the hall. I'm completely oblivious to our surroundings as wind-swept hair and lust-darkened green eyes steal my attention.

Setting her down next to the bed, I step back and take a seat. "You sure this is what you want, angel?" She nods, but I need more, so I grip her chin between my thumb and forefinger, pulling her in to meet my eyes. "I need words, sugar."

"I'm sure," she promises. "I haven't been with anyone since... well, in over a year. And I can't think of anyone I would want to take this step with more than you."

I release her with a smirk and sit down on the edge of the bed, leaning back on my elbows. "Then strip for me."

I wouldn't necessarily say I'm a dominant man by nature, but the way my little angel's eyes darken as she rushes to follow my command has my cock thumping behind my zipper, making me wince slightly.

Lyla isn't even *trying* to be seductive, but seeing her in nothing but my jersey is so fucking sexy that I can't stop myself from pulling my length free from my slacks and stroking it slowly, being careful not to wind myself up too much.

When she drops the jersey to the floor, standing in front of me in nothing but a thin lace bra and panties, my chest tightens in anticipation. Crossing an arm in front of her stomach, she stares at me, biting her lip anxiously. Her eyes darken even further as her gaze follows the path of my hand.

"Your turn," she murmurs.

We don't break eye contact once as I slowly unknot my tie, letting it fall to the bed. I watch her pupils expand as I unbutton my shirt and take a small step toward her, making quick work of the rest of my game-day suit. The look on Lyla's face as she examines my form is worth every second spent sweating my ass off in a gym or on the field.

Her tiny finger sweeps across the tattoo of Crew's birthday on my left pec before leisurely tracing the divots in my abs with a wistful sigh. A shiver races down my spine and sends goosebumps skating down my arms. At this point, I could probably come from this alone.

She squeals when I scoop her up and toss her on the bed, tracking her every move like a predator hunting its prey. I'm ready to do a little exploring of my own.

I don't hesitate to crawl over her and trap her in my arms. A look of panic flashes across her eyes, but it's gone so fast that I'm not sure if I'm imagining things. "You still good, angel? Remember, you say no, and we stop right now. No hard feelings."

Eyes I see every night in my dreams snap up to meet mine, determination filling them and replacing any lingering doubts. "I want this, Aidan. I want *you*."

The quiet words are all I need to take her mouth in a searing kiss that's so good I don't know if the whimper that escapes comes from her or me. "For someone who looks so much like an angel, you sure do taste like fucking sin," I murmur against her soft lips.

She pulls back with a moan, and I take that as my cue to continue, raining kisses down her neck. I stop briefly to nip at her collarbone, groaning when she clenches her thighs around my hips.

Continuing the line of kisses down her body, I stroke my tongue leisurely over her rosy nipples, sucking first one and then the other into my mouth until they're hard peaks.

Ly's quiet mewls of pleasure are noisy in the otherwise silent room, spurring me on. Her fingers thread through my hair, tugging slightly when I lower my mouth to hover over her mound and the trimmed strip of hair there.

"Aidan," she gasps. "It's okay, you don't have to—"

A primal sound rumbles from my throat. "We never got dessert earlier, and I suddenly have a desperate craving for cherries." The first swipe of my tongue along her slit has her back bowing off the bed.

"Oh, god!"

With each lick, I make sure to scrape the stud in my tongue across her clit, loving the sighs and moans falling from her sweet lips. Her fists tighten in my hair, and she yanks my face further into her heavenly pussy, the prickling pain from my scalp making my cock leak on the sheets beneath us. "Fuuuck," I groan against her clit. "That's it, angel. Use me like I know you want to. Ride my face with your perfect pussy."

Bringing my hand up, I slide a finger inside her and quickly add a second when I realize she can take more. I curl my fingers just a bit, searching for that spot that will make her scream.

"Aidan!"

There it is.

She chants my name over and over as I bring her to the edge, but I stop before she can fall.

"Aid!" she whines. "I was so close."

As quick as I can, I snatch my wallet off the floor and roll on a condom I stashed in there just in case. "I know, baby, but I want the first time you come for me to be on my cock. We have plenty of time for you to come on my tongue later." Lyla's cheeks are flushed with pleasure as I line myself up at her entrance.

Meeting her eyes, I slide in with one long thrust, taking a steadying breath when I bottom out. She's so goddamn tight I worry I'm about to embarrass myself.

She writhes under me, and I grip her hips tightly to hold her still. "Give me a second, or this is gonna be over a helluva lot sooner than either of us wants it to be, angel," I growl out through gritted teeth, shaking my head when she bites her lip with a mischievous look in her eyes.

She clamps down on me, making me curse. "Lyla, I swear."

The smirk she gives me frays the thin thread of control I'm barely hanging onto, but when she swivels her hips, I'm fucking done for.

I snap my hips into her, basking in the way she cries out for more. I thrust hard and fast, bringing my thumb up to her mouth and pressing it against her bottom lip.

"Suck."

She does, swirling her pink tongue around my finger like I imagine she would do to my cock. Yanking my thumb free, I bring it down to circle her swollen clit, smirking when she yelps at the contact. I'm dangerously close to losing it, and I need to get her there first.

I lean down and use my free hand to capture her jaw as I press our foreheads together. "Look at you taking my cock so well, angel. Such a good girl, takin' me like you were fuckin' made for me." Her walls flutter around my shaft forcing a grunt from between my clenched teeth.

"Aidan, I'm close," she pants out.

Leaning down, I pull her into another intense kiss, using the angle to my advantage to thrust as deep as I can. "Good. Come for me, Lyla."

I circle her clit with renewed pressure, and she falls into an orgasm, triggering my own. It's so intense that black spots float across my vision, and my breathing is so heavy you would think I just played a double header.

When I can see clearly again, I pull out, whispering

an apology when she lets out a pained whimper. I carefully tie off the condom before disposing of it in the garbage can next to the bed, and then I grab a soft cloth from the bathroom and wait for the sink to run warm.

Wet cloth in hand, I return to the bedroom only to see my pretty girl curled on her side on the bed, breathing shallowly.

Concern spikes through my chest but quickly turns to anger when she flinches at my soft touch. I'm not angry at her. I could *never* be angry at her. But I'm pissed as hell at the motherfucker that sent her running to South Carolina. "It's just me, angel. Can I clean you up?"

She nods, relaxing slightly. I make quick work of it and toss the cloth in the corner of the room before sliding into bed next to her soft, warm body. She doesn't tense up when she feels me at her back, so I take a chance and wrap her up, holding her to me as tightly as I dare. "What's going on in that complicated mind of yours, Ly?"

Heaving a deep sigh, she turns in my arms so we're face to face. "I just needed a moment," she murmurs, gently scratching her nails over the thin layer of scruff covering my jaw. My eyes close, reveling in the intimacy of her movements.

I had my fair share of hookups over the years, but they were always quick and meaningless and left me feeling kind of empty. I wasn't ready for a relationship and all the things that went with one back then, but I forgot how damned good it feels to connect to another person like this. The little touches that show affection and make you feel wanted.

With a kiss to her slightly sweaty forehead, I breathe in her sweet cherry perfume that's even more potent now. "Wanna talk about it?"

"I've been going over it in my head all week since you asked me out." Her words drop to a whisper against my chest. "I just don't see a way that we can make this work past this weekend, Aid. Not right now, anyway."

My heart cracks, and I don't even care that I probably sound like a pathetic loser. "But... was it something I did? I went too fast, didn't I? Fuck."

I run my hands through my hair in frustration before dragging them down my face. I knew this was a possibility, but I wasn't expecting it to hurt so goddamn much.

"No! Aidan, no. I just... I promised to always make Crew my top priority. There are things in my life that might make us being publicly linked unsafe for both of you, and I couldn't handle it if you or Crew were caught up in my mess."

I hear the undercurrent of fear in her words, and her sudden reluctance makes sense. I knew one date probably wouldn't have her spilling all her secrets but I won't lie, I'm still pretty disappointed she's calling things off before we even have a chance to start them.

Holding back a sigh, I force my eyes down to meet her determined ones. That one look is enough to tell me pushing her for more right now will only solidify her decision to end things, but that sure as hell doesn't mean I have to stop trying to win her over. A plan forms in my mind, and the first step is to finish the weekend we promised each other.

"Finish out the weekend with me?" I beg, capturing her soft hands between my calloused ones. "If this is the only time I get to feel what it's like for you to be mine, I want to keep that feeling as long as I possibly can."

Lyla exhales with a sad smile. "I guess I did promise..."

I fight to keep the victorious smile from playing across my face. My girl may not know it yet, but I can be a relentless bastard when I want something. And if her heart is on the line?

There's no chance I'm playing fair.

Lyla

16

I have a bad feeling I started a war with my boss by trying to end things last night. I hid it well, but I got several more thinly veiled threats from blocked numbers during our date, and it spooked me.

I'm sure Aidan can handle himself, but Sebastian is a nightmare and I can't let Aid be romantically linked to me unless I can guarantee that he and Crew will be safe.

Several texts arrived this morning while Aidan was in the shower. I think he could tell something was up when he came back in the room and I freaked out and almost tossed my phone. All the texts came from different numbers, each scarier than the last.

> **UNKNOWN**
>
> It's cute that you thought running would save you, little bunny. If you think I'll let some other man touch what's mine, you're in for a rude awakening.

> **UNKNOWN**
>
> I can't wait to see my marks on your creamy white throat again, Lyla. Diamonds don't hold a candle when you've got a necklace of bruises in the shape of my hand.
>
> I'll be seeing you soon, future wife.

Shudders wrack my body as I once again block the numbers, but this time, I save screenshots of the messages just in case.

The fear that would have sent me spiraling only a few weeks ago is at a manageable level even after reading the texts, and I can't help but think it's partially because of the family I've found here in Charleston. Or the strength I feel every day from Aidan.

Honestly, I should have said no to this whole weekend trial he suggested in the first place, but clearly, I'm a weak woman when it comes to pretty blond men because one smile had me brushing aside every reason there was to say no. Okay, that's not entirely fair. I wasn't *weak* for Sebastian. I was naive and afraid of disappointing my father.

My stomach churns with guilt thinking about my dad. I haven't seen or spoken to him in nearly a year, and the more time passes, the worse I feel.

When I left Maryland, I wasn't just running from Sebastian. I was running from my life as Lyla Kingsley. Growing up and only being known as Colin Kingsley's talentless daughter was incredibly isolating, and he never once seemed to notice or care.

South Carolina was my chance to start over and be known as Lyla Taylor and nothing more, but I can't help but wonder if I should reach out to my dad. Does he even care that I'm gone? Or will he be angry I messed up his business deal with Sebastian Senior?

I pull out my phone, discreetly making sure I'm still alone in the friends and family box before unlocking it. I'm pleasantly surprised to see I don't have any new messages, either.

Taking advantage of the first moment alone I've had all weekend before the box fills up for this afternoon's game, I make sure my number is blocked before quickly dialing my father's personal line. Anticipation makes my hands shake so hard I have to try multiple times to get the number right.

My heart is in my throat, but as each ring passes with no answer, sadness begins to eclipse any hope I had of hearing his voice. When a robotic voice picks up letting me know his voicemail box is full, my eyes burn with tears. I know he likely ignored it because I blocked my number, but that doesn't make it hurt any less.

"What's up, Ly-bear!" Wren's hand on my shoulder startles me so bad I nearly fall off the high stool I'd taken up for my failed attempt at reconciliation. I look up in time to see alarm flash in her bright blue eyes as she grips my wrist to pull me upright. "Woah there, killer. You okay?"

The innocent nickname is the last straw on the camel's proverbial back, and I lose it, a harsh sob breaking free. My panicked best friend pulls me into the private bathroom and flips the lock before whirling around to sweep me into a tight hug. Her sweet apple and honey perfume tickles my nose where it's pressed into her collarbone.

"Lyla, I need you to breathe, babe. If you pass out on

this disgusting floor, I'll be forced to spray you with bleach before I let you in the rental car."

Her ridiculous threat has a choked laugh escaping me between sobs, but with a little effort, I do manage to pull in a full breath. It's only after I do that I realize my vision is spotty, and I'm lightheaded. A hard knock on the door sends a choked squeak from my aching throat.

"Wren? Lyla? You guys in there?" Copeland's deep voice has both relief and anxiety flowing through my tense frame, and I sag back against the concrete counter.

Wren's worried gaze tracks the movement but with my nod of assent, she lets him in the small bathroom. Copeland Hawthorne cuts an intimidating figure.

At maybe an inch taller than Aidan, Copeland towers over me, and every inch of his visible skin is covered in colorful tattoos from his fingertips to the top of his neck. Toss in the piercings in his ears, eyebrow, and apparently, his tongue, and he looks like someone you wouldn't want to meet in a dark alley.

In other words, he's kind of scary.

Everyone has assured me he's really a giant marshmallow underneath his rough exterior, but I don't know him well enough to tell one way or the other. I think if Wren weren't here, I'd be on the verge of running out the door.

As soon as the door slams shut behind him, Copeland's eyes lock on mine. I cringe knowing how red and puffy I probably am from crying so hard.

"What the fuck happened?" he demands gruffly.

"What are you doing here? Shouldn't you be warming up?" Wren scolds him.

He shrugs, holding his palms up. "I came to find you. Rhodes wouldn't shut the hell up about his pre-game kiss.

But don't change the subject. Why is Lyla crying?" He turns to me. "Did something happen?"

Wren already gave him Sebastian's name and some of the basics, so I decide to come clean about everything. The sooner this is taken care of, the sooner I can beg Aidan for a second chance after shutting him down yesterday. Heaving a breath, I hold up a finger so I can step into one of the two stalls and grab some toilet paper to blow my nose.

Wren snickers at the noise, but Copeland still has a terrifying scowl on his face. Shoring up my reserve, I meet both of their eyes.

"Something did happen, but I think I should start from the beginning. My name isn't technically Lyla Taylor," I pause. "Well, I mean, it is. But my full name is Lyla Taylor Kingsley. Daughter of Colin Kingsley and almost-heiress to the Pennington family fortune."

My voice takes on a haughty tone with the last sentence, but my attempt at levity falls flat when Wren lets out an exaggerated gasp and Copeland chokes on air. "*You* are the missing Pennington fiancé? Is that why you had me digging up dirt on Sebastian Junior?"

I sigh out a heavy breath of relief, my shoulders relaxing for the first time in a year. Sebastian didn't call the police. The rest of his words register, and I wince.

"They said I went missing? God, I bet Bas has women all over him trying to comfort him. His dad is probably spinning it to secure sympathy from his investors," I murmur bitterly. Their confused and angry stares prompt me to explain, so I do.

"Almost three years ago, my father introduced me to Bas at an industry party. He used a technique I now know is called love bombing to make me fall for him quicker than I thought possible. It was all flowers, jewelry, sweet words, and elaborate gestures until he convinced me to move in with him after only a few months together. Then he started making cutting remarks and doing little things to control me."

A shudder wracks my shoulders as memories from that time come back in vivid detail. "He started restricting my food intake and monitoring my weight *because he cared*. Every time we left the house, I had to be meticulously made up, or he would punish me for it by ignoring me or flirting with other women in front of me. And then he proposed, and I was young and naïve and afraid of disappointing my father, so I said yes. That's when he started getting physical."

I ignore the angry growls and curses from the two people in front of me, studying my chipping nail polish instead.

"The day I left, he had accused me of cheating on him during the two hours I was alone after I had spent the day watching his sister's kids, all because the living room was still messy. When I told him I had been doing homework, he choked me, hit me, and nearly snapped my wrist. He tried to drag me up the stairs with the intent of teaching me a lesson, but he kept a bat in the hallway…"

"I panicked and hit him. I knocked him out, and when I was sure he wasn't dead, I packed a bag and got the hell out of dodge. I haven't seen or spoken to anyone from my old life in over a year. The breakdown you just saw was the result of too many things happening at once."

Two wide-eyed gazes meet mine when I finish up my tragic tale, but I'm not expecting Wren to break out into hysterical laughter. "Oh my god!" she screeches. "My little Lyla, who was working under the table for a *pottery painting shop* when I met her, is a millionaire who was almost an heiress to a multi-*billion* dollar company." Her blue eyes are shiny with unshed tears from how hard she's laughing.

Sighing in exasperation, I roll my eyes at her, and she finally pulls herself together. "Sorry, I'm not trying to make light of the situation. I just love you so much. And I think I might be in shock."

Copeland pins me with an assessing stare, but he doesn't seem angry. "So this is what you've been keeping from Aidan? That you were a victim of domestic violence and did what you had to do to get away? Forgive me if I sound like an asshole, but why bother keeping it from him at all? Why reject him when it sounds like things were going really well?"

I shouldn't be surprised he told them, but it makes this part that much harder to admit. "I have to protect Aidan and Crew. Sebastian is a vindictive asshole who doesn't take no for an answer, and I fully believe he would hurt them to get back at me. To punish me for leaving him, for landing a hit on him and marring his cosmetically perfected face."

Embarrassing tears sit on my eyelashes, but I've done enough crying for the day, so I dam them back. "I would willingly go back to him before I let Crew or Aidan get hurt."

The intimidating man's whole face softens with a small but genuine smile, transforming him from scary as hell to the marshmallow everyone says he secretly is. "That's all I needed to hear."

Huh?

"Needed to hear for what?"

Copeland smirks. "For this," he says smugly, handing

me a small flash drive he pulls out of his pocket. "I have a friend at the FBI, and we have a meeting with him in three weeks to hand that over. I did some digging and found out that both Sebastians are into some pretty shady shit in their business and personal lives. Funds that were allocated to the business or their charity are being used in... let's just say, less than legal ways. Add in all the lewd services and people they've paid off to look the other way? They're looking at some pretty serious federal charges."

My heart threatens to beat right out of my chest, and my eyes widen so much that they start to burn. "You're serious?" I choke. "Will he actually go to jail?"

He barely starts to nod before I'm tackling him in a giant hug. "I don't know how I can ever repay you."

"Just love them how they deserve to be loved," he murmurs, surprising me when he hugs me back even harder.

"Now," he pulls back. "Why don't you let Wren help you fix the raccoon thing you have going on here." His hand waves in a general way over my face, making me snort. Glancing in the mirror, it's obvious he's not exaggerating.

There's mascara running down my cheeks and all around my eyes, making it look like I've never slept a day in my life. Copeland leaves, and Wren, the angel that she is, hands me a small bottle of makeup remover and reusable wipes from her work bag. I stare at her in wonder when she digs around, pulling out a new tube of mascara and some gum.

"Has anyone ever told you you're kind of like a fairy godmother?"

She laughs. "No, but now I'll make sure they do," she says with a smug smirk.

I clean up my face and take several deep breaths, preparing myself to face a crowd. The relief coursing through my veins is so intense that I feel like I could lie down and sleep for a full week. I know I should probably talk to Aidan about everything, but I think it will be safer to wait until after the meeting with the FBI, just in case.

Once I know Sebastian won't be a problem anymore, I'll do everything I can to let Aidan know I want to be in his and Crew's lives in any way they'll have me.

17

Aidan

We're on our flight back to Charleston, and normally, I would be spiraling, but right now, I'm exhausted and trying not to panic. For our last night in New York, Rhodes, Wren, Copeland, Lyla, and I all went out to this tiny place someone had recommended and ended up with food poisoning, effectively shredding any hope I had left that I could convince Ly to give us a chance before we return to reality today.

I got away with only some mild symptoms, and I didn't want my girl suffering alone when it hit because Wren was with Rho, so I brought her back to our room so I could take care of her.

For whatever reason, it hit Lyla and Copeland harder than the rest of us, and they've been commiserating since we got back from dinner. I don't know if it was sharing a bathroom floor with him for most of the night or just them bonding over feeling awful, but they've been inseparable all day.

In any other circumstances, I would be out of my

mind jealous watching the girl I like be so friendly with another man, but it's kinda cute seeing them bond. Cope is such a standoffish asshole most of the time. It's funny to see him making friends with such a sweet girl. God help the woman that willingly takes on his moody ass.

Lyla thankfully fell asleep almost the second we sat down for the flight and hasn't moved since, but she's been squirming in her seat for a few minutes, and her face is still really pale and sweaty.

Suddenly, she shoots straight up in her seat, clapping a hand over her mouth. "Oh no," her muffled words are barely out before the tiny thing is up and stumbling down the aisle to the bathroom at the back of the plane.

Copeland lifts bloodshot eyes my way and widens them slightly, waving a hand in my direction. My brows furrow, and he scoffs. "Go take care of her, you fucking moron. You want to prove yourself to her? Hold her hair back and wipe her face or something. Just be there so she's not alone."

I offer him a chin lift, but before moving to go take care of my girl, I hand him a barf bag and order a ginger ale from a passing flight attendant. My parental instincts kick in when I see how bad he still looks.

Sometimes I forget that before his ex Carly stomped on his heart, my best friend was one of the sappiest motherfuckers I'd ever met. Copeland Hawthorne is a grump with a short fuse, but once you make it past that prickly exterior, he's as loyal as they come.

Coming to a stop in front of the pocket door, I knock gently. Lyla's hoarse voice calls out occupied, but the door isn't locked, so I slip in behind her. The bathroom is just barely bigger than one on a commercial flight, so it's a tight squeeze with her curled up on the floor and me towering over her.

She barely lifts her head off the balled-up sweater she's resting on to look at me, immediately letting out a long groan. "Ugh, please go away. You don't need to see any more of me being sick."

Ignoring her grumbles of irritation, I carefully step over her shaking form to run some paper towels under the tap, wringing them out so they don't get her shirt too wet.

One glance around the bathroom nearly has me huffing in frustration at the small space. I want to take care of her without *literally* being on top of her and making her feel worse.

I take a chance and get down on one knee behind her, doing my best to ignore the shiver wracking her body when I sweep her long hair up and off the back of her neck. There's a ponytail holder on her thin wrist, so I gently take it off and pull her long hair up into some semblance of a bun on top of her head before laying the wet towels on her neck and forehead to cool her down.

Lyla moans on the floor beneath me, cracking her tired, bloodshot eyes open just enough so I can see the tears that want to spill over.

"Even if we aren't together, I still care about you, Ly. You could be nothing more to me than Crew's nanny, and I would still worry. You're important to him, which means you're important to me. No matter what. But angel? You are and always will be more to me."

I watch her resolve crumble with quiet satisfaction, hoping she won't fight me again while she's feeling so bad. "Do you want to stay in here or try to go back to our seats, angel?"

"I just want the world to stop spinning, Daddy."

My whole body tenses at her garbled words because *what the fuck?* Why would she call me that? More importantly, why the hell did it turn me on? I've had plenty of people call me Daddy Aidan since Crew was born, but I've *never* reacted like this.

One glance down at myself shows me I'm not imagining things. I'm hard as a rock at the worst possible time because Lyla called me *Daddy*.

She's obviously half delusional and probably won't remember saying it, but I sure as fuck won't be forgetting anytime soon. Definitely a topic to broach later, preferably not when she's just spent fourteen hours vomiting and *after* she gives up on the whole 'I can't be with you right now' nonsense.

Up until she got sick, Lyla had been doing her best to put distance between us, and even though I promised things wouldn't be weird if she called it off, they've been a little weird. How can they not be when her breathy moans have been playing on a constant loop in my mind since the first one I heard fall from those pretty pink lips? Or when every time I look at *my son's nanny,* I see her bent over with that perfect pussy in the air, begging me to fuck her.

Shaking off the lustful memories of our night together, I smooth back a few errant strands of hair that escaped her messy bun. She's basically asleep on the floor now, so I scoop her up, being extra careful not to jostle her too much. I don't think I'm all that successful because she whimpers, a single tear escaping and tearing my heart wide open.

"I'm so sorry, angel. I'm going to bring you back to our

seats and if you need to throw up again you just tell me, okay? Trust me to take care of you."

Her lack of response makes my throat tighten with anxiety, and as soon as I get her buckled in, I'm using the plane's wifi to message our group chat for advice.

ME

> Do you think doc would take a look at Ly if I bring her in when we get home?

FUTURE MRS. GRAY

It would have to be unofficial, but yeah probably. Everything okay?

WREN'S STALKER

Why would she need to see Doc? You haven't been sleeping together long enough to knock her up... right?

ME

> She's still really sick, and I'm worried she's dehydrated. I just had to pick her up off the bathroom floor and carry her back to our seats

> And no, I didn't get her pregnant, you dick.

FUTURE MRS. GRAY

Oh my god, do you need help? I can swap seats with Cope for the rest of the flight.

And ignore Rhodes, he's got baby fever and it needs to go to hell.

ME

> She's sleeping now, and Cope has actually been really helpful... you know, when he's not throwing up too

> **WREN'S STALKER**
>
> But Starling, imagine how cute a mini us would be!
>
> **FUTURE MRS. GRAY**
>
> Absolutely not, Rhodes Colter. The only reason you want a baby is because you saw Coach's granddaughter trying to eat her own foot and thought it was cute. Finn ate your favorite socks last week and your exact words were "thank god we aren't adding a human to this mad house."
>
> **ME**
>
> I love y'all, and I'm with Rho on team baby, but this wasn't helpful
>
> **FUTURE MRS. GRAY**
>
> Sorry, Aid. I'll text doc and have him meet us at your house with an IV kit. And if you want a baby so damn bad, go have one of your own. Crew is cute as hell and I bet he'd love a little brother or sister.
>
> **ME**
>
> Lol thanks, darlin'. But better make it two IV's, Cope still isn't doing too hot either.

Relief loosens the vice grip on my throat enough that I can finally take a deep breath, and I studiously ignore the thought of knocking Lyla up with my baby. That's just a little too much insanity for this early in the morning.

Turning slightly, I bury my nose in Ly's hair where her head rests on my shoulder. I don't know how it's possible after all the sweating and lying on multiple different bathroom floors, but she still smells like sweet cherries and vanilla.

Her scent haunts my dreams almost as much as her moans do.

The last half hour of our flight is easy, and nobody gets sick again, which feels like a win after the last twenty-four hours. The minute we're off the plane, I'm herding Lyla and Cope to my truck, ignoring his protests in favor of getting an IV in him back at the house.

I open the back door for Cope, and he grumbles as I help him get settled, but his threats don't hold much water when he passes out the second he sprawls out across the seats.

Lyla, my sweet, sick little angel, is propped up against the passenger side door, looking like death warmed over. So I scoop her up and deposit her gently into the passenger seat with a plastic bag, just in case she gets sick again.

Making my way around to the front of the truck, I turn it on to get the air going and then turn to inspect Ly and make sure she's still okay. I almost chuckle when I find her asleep with her mouth hanging open.

Quiet puffs of air are the only thing letting me know she is, in fact, still breathing. I place a gentle kiss on her sticky forehead and shift into drive, getting us one step closer to home.

"Aidan, I'm telling you, I feel fine! That IV and a full night's sleep did wonders, and I want to make breakfast."

After forcing fluids into both her and Copeland all day yesterday and sending him home late last night, Lyla woke up at our normal time this morning and forewent her usual cup of coffee for a mint tea. She joined me on the swing in spite of my insistence that she go back to bed.

Rhodes's parents were kind enough to keep Crew again last night so we could get some rest after not sleeping the night before, and from their constant updates, it sounds like he had the time of his life. They should be bringing him home in a couple hours, and I can't wait. As much as my night with Lyla was worth being away, I'm missing my boy something fierce.

Stroking a gentle hand down her messy hair, I sigh heavily. "Lyla, you were so dehydrated you were delirious, and we almost had to take you to the hospital. If the doc hadn't been able to get the IV in you when he did, there could have been a serious problem."

I know I'm being stubborn, but *fuck*, seeing her so sick twisted something inside of me, and I haven't been right since. I've seen the guys, Wren, and even Crew sick plenty of times, but never so sick that they couldn't open their eyes or hold their own heads up. I had to pull over for her to throw up five times on the way home, and each time, she seemed a little weaker and a little more out of it.

I was so tense by the time the team doctor got here that I developed a raging headache I'm still struggling with today. The concern in his eyes as he examined Lyla did exactly nothing to ease my worry for her, and that moment solidified what I already knew. I'm completely gone for this girl.

"But he *did*, and I feel much better today. I swear, I wouldn't lie to you after seeing how worried you were when I woke up yesterday. I even skipped coffee to give my body a chance to rehydrate properly. And I haven't gone a day without coffee in like... eight *years*. There's nobody else I would give up coffee for just to ease their worry, Aid."

Even though it's dumb, my chest swells with pride, knowing she cares about my opinion so much that she's willingly giving up her beloved caffeine. Even if it's just for one morning, that still means more to me than she'll ever know.

"And I appreciate you making such a hefty sacrifice to alleviate my worry, Ly, but I can't just turn it off. Not after seeing you completely out of it on the floor of a cramped airplane bathroom."

She brings her hands up to cover her flushed cheeks, and I instantly feel like a dick. I didn't mean to embarrass her or make her feel bad. I just want to make sure she's taking this seriously.

"Aidan, I'm sorry you had to see that, and I'm even more sorry you had to take care of me in that condition after literally one date, but it's not like it was some life-threatening illness. It was *food poisoning*. And yeah, it got kind of bad, but I'm almost back to normal today, and I would love to forget it ever happened."

I start to get frustrated because she's just not *listening*, but I shove it down. "Lyla, you weren't awake when the doctor was examining you, and I don't think you realize just how bad off you actually were. Do you remember me carrying you to and from the truck to puke up stomach acid on the way home? Do you remember your legs going out from under you on our way to the front door after you insisted you could walk?"

Her eyes widen with each new thing I list and it's clear she doesn't remember a single one of them. "I'm sorry if it seems like I'm being an overbearing prick, but Jesus Christ, Lyla. You weren't okay, and seeing you like that scared the hell out of me! I've had enough people die on me. I really don't need to add another person to the list because you insist on not taking care of yourself!"

My chest is heaving by the time I finish, and the room is eerily silent. Lyla's eyes are wide, and her pale lips are parted in shock, but I can't bring myself to stick around and hear whatever she has to say. Panic is turning my blood to ice, and I need to get out before I lose it.

"I'm going to go for a run in the basement. If Dom and Kaci show up early, let me know."

I know I'm being rude, but I can't seem to find my rational thoughts at the moment. Too many things about this situation remind me of Mia and even of my father, and it's messing with my head to the point where I know I need to get away from Lyla, or I'll say something I shouldn't.

I don't even bother changing out of my shorts and muscle tee before making my way down to the home gym I had built in the basement, knowing this is pretty much what I work out in anyway.

An incessant itch under my skin drives me to run, push, and *forget* the memories clawing at the locked metal box in my brain where I keep them for my own sanity.

Skipping my typical warmup, I hop on the treadmill and start at a dead sprint, knowing the pain and exhaustion it will bring are my only chance of pushing the demons back right now. Sweat pours down my forehead after only ten minutes, and I regret not stopping to put on my headband.

When my eyes start to sting from the sweat, I huff and pull the safety cord to bring the treadmill to a stop before using one hand to grip the back of my shirt and rip it over my head. A quiet gasp catches my attention as I'm mopping my face with the shirt, and I look up to see Lyla's heated gaze staring back at me through the wall-to-wall mirrors.

Without taking my eyes off hers, I drag the sweaty tee down my chest with a smirk, letting my knuckles graze my abs on the way down. I work hard for the body I have, and if my girl wants to admire me, I'll do whatever I have to to encourage it. Especially if it helps keep the memories at bay.

"See something you like, angel?"

Her cheeks flame immediately, making my smirk stretch into a full-blown smile. Now that most of my earlier frustration has drained away, I owe her an apology. Just as I go to speak, however, she surprises me.

"I'm sorry for not being more appreciative of everything you did to take care of me, Aidan. Growing up, any illness was downplayed or brushed under the rug, so I'm not used to anyone caring enough to be upset when I don't take good enough care of myself."

So many things about the last few weeks start to make sense when she tells me that, and though it's a relief to learn more about her, it pisses me off that she had so little support growing up. What kind of parent doesn't take care of their sick child?

Moving slowly, I approach her with my arms open, leaving the choice up to her if she wants to hug me or not.

I can't contain my sigh of relief when she willingly walks into my arms and wraps hers around my back. With her nose buried in my chest, I can smell her perfume, and it calms me further.

"You never have to apologize to me, angel. I was lucky and had my mom who constantly fussed over my brother and me when we were sick, but I was ignored in pretty much every other aspect of my life unless I was playing ball. I know what it's like to be swept aside, and I promise you'll never feel that with me. Whether we're friends or more."

My next words are a risk, but I never claimed to be smart.

Leaning down close so my lips meet her ear, I put myself out there and pray this doesn't backfire. "And if you want to take a break and have somebody take care of you for a change? Well, let's just say I'm happy to be Crew's dad and your *Daddy*."

18

Lyla

At Aidan's murmured words, a memory comes rushing back from our time on the plane, and my cheeks heat to inferno-levels of hotness. I don't think I've ever been this mortified in all twenty-three years of my life.

I called Aidan Daddy. In an airplane bathroom. While I was completely delirious from dehydration after puking all night.

I've always been intrigued by that sort of dynamic in some deep, dark corner of my mind, but I've never acted on it with anyone. At first, it felt too taboo, then I didn't want to bring to light my obvious daddy issues, and then Sebastian was an absolute nightmare and would use anything he could against me.

Burying my burning face further into Aidan's chest, I try to will the ground to open up and swallow me whole. "Jesus, Aidan. I'm so sorry! I can't believe I called you... *that*. Do you accept verbal resignations, or do I need to write one up and slip it under your bedroom door before I run as far as humanly possible in the opposite direction?"

His husky chuckle rumbles through his chest, and one

muscular arm tightens around my lower back as he lifts the other to cup my cheek, bringing my face to his.

"Lyla, if you really want to quit, you already know you have my support and a letter of recommendation. And if I've made you uncomfortable, I'm truly sorry. But if you're embarrassed by what you said, you don't need to be. It was a surprise, yes, but not an unwelcome one."

Peeking up at my boss's sparkling blue eyes, I see nothing but honesty and desire staring back at me. My teeth dig into my bottom lip as I think about how to respond. "Aidan..." I trail off.

There's so much sadness hiding behind his smile, and I don't want to add to it with my drama, but I think I was right before, and he's going to make resisting this pull between us nearly impossible.

"There are things you need to know about me, but I don't know if I'm ready to tell you yet. In the interest of transparency, Copeland is using some of his legal contacts to help me resolve the situation, but it could be another three weeks before things even begin to iron out. I want you, but I don't want to add any stress to your life when you already have so much going on."

His eyes widen when I mention Copeland, but he quickly schools his expression into something neutral. I expect Aidan to question me about the secrets I'm keeping from him, but instead, he surprises me by pivoting completely.

With a nervous look on his handsome face, he grips my hand in his and attempts to smile reassuringly. "Will you come somewhere with me? And then we'll swing by and pick up Crew on the way home."

I don't even have to think about it before nodding in agreement. If there's one thing my life has taught me, it's that truly good people don't come along often. Yet somehow, I've managed to find myself an entire family of them here in Charleston. And I think it's about time I allow myself the grace to carve a permanent place here in this little slice of happiness just for me.

Fifteen minutes later, we're turning onto a dirt lane that's so overgrown I never would have seen it if Aidan hadn't made the turn. It looks like nobody has been down the road for months, if not years.

Sending a questioning glance to my left, I see tension written into every line of Aidan's face, and it puts me on high alert. Whatever we're about to do isn't something he *wants* to do, and that has every nerve ending in my body standing at attention.

After a few hundred feet, he pulls his truck into an even more overgrown clearing of sorts, only this one has a clearly marked footpath right in the center, leading to what looks to be a set of headstones rising out of the tall grass.

I unbuckle and grab the door's handle, thinking we're visiting someone's burial site, but Aidan takes my hand in his and squeezes it tightly, not saying a word.

Sensing he needs a few minutes, I release the handle and wrap both of my hands around one of his, offering whatever comfort I can. When he's still quiet several minutes later, I raise the center console and slide across the bench seat so I can press myself to his side.

If being here didn't feel so ominous, I think I'd be enjoying myself. It's a dreary, overcast day, but a storm is coming, and you can feel it in the atmosphere. It's like the air is electrified, charged with endless possibilities, and the knowledge that the coming storm has the potential to wash away anything unwanted.

It's more than ten minutes later when Aidan finally speaks. "When I was eight years old, my father told me I would never go anywhere in life. That I would end up just like him because we were one and the same."

I stifle my noise of surprise and wrap my hands around his bicep, clinging to him. My mouth opens to speak but he gently shakes his head and uses one finger to close it back.

"My father was a bastard, Lyla. He was a mean drunk who couldn't hold down a job and took his anger issues out on his kids and wife. When I was eight years old, he told me I would grow up to be just like him, and then when I was eighteen, I watched him die in front of me, and I didn't do a damn thing to stop it."

Tears cloud my vision for a young Aidan who was dealt such a terrible hand in life. "Aid…"

He shushes me. "Please, let me get this out."

I nod, and he continues.

"My father was notorious for driving home from the local bar when he was too drunk to function. We lived in a shitty, run-down, one-bedroom trailer on the opposite side of town that only had enough hot water for one shower a day. And that hot shower never went to me or my younger brother, Wesley, unless our dad was passed out drunk. He drank so much it's a wonder the alcohol could still have any effect on him by the time I was eighteen, but it did. He still had awful anger issues, and by that point, he knew he couldn't get a hit on me or Wes because we'd fight back, so he'd taken to beating up on our mom when we were at school or practice when we couldn't do a damned thing to stop it."

Aidan takes a deep, shuddering breath before continuing his story, and my heart cracks straight down the middle. He's mentioned his mom on several occasions, so I know she's still alive and well. But it's obvious that whatever he still has to tell me is tearing him up inside, even after so many years.

"One day, I came home early from a two-day baseball tournament to find him slapping my mom around. Wesley was still at his own tournament, so he thankfully wasn't around to see it go down. But the image of my mama on the floor curled in on herself while her husband beat her black and blue is so burned into my damn brain no amount of alcohol could wash it away. I lost it, Lyla. I got so fuckin' angry I attacked my father. One good hit sent him to the ground, but it was like eighteen years of pain just bubbled up and finally overflowed."

I squeeze his hand hard as he talks to remind him that I'm still here, and he sends me a grateful look.

"He came to a few minutes later mad as all hell and took off for the bar. I helped Mama patch herself up and settled in for what should have been just like any other night. Only it wasn't. You see, the bartenders in that part of town didn't give a shit what their patrons did after last call. One of those 'you don't have to go home, but you can't stay here' type of establishments. Little did I know the sheriffs had been cracking down on this particular bar for letting their patrons get behind the wheel after being cut off, so the bartender took dads keys and called me to come pick his drunk ass up."

His voice lowers to a whisper, and the more upset he gets, the more his accent thickens.

"Maybe if I'd refused, the sheriff woulda brought him home, and he'd still be alive. But that's not what happened. We didn't have a second car, so I walked the three miles to the bar, and when I got there, he was drunker than I'd ever seen him. Slurring his words and stumblin' all over the damn lot, rantin' about his miserable life. I got the car keys, loaded him up, and took off like a bat outta hell. It was three in the morning, I had school in just a few hours and was exhausted. We lived on a deserted back road in the middle of nowhere, South Carolina, so you really had to concentrate on navigatin' the road safely, especially at night."

I grip his arm even tighter, knowing now where this is going.

"Dad was up in arms about me driving and kept tryin' to open his door, but he was three sheets to the damn wind and didn't realize I had set the child locks before we left. He got pissed, turned to me, and grabbed the wheel in a fit of rage."

Aidan turns to me with tears in his eyes, and the amount of guilt shining back at me nearly knocks the breath from my lungs.

"The car swerved, and we hit a massive tree stump. It all happened in less than ten seconds. One minute, I was shoutin' at my dad to knock it the fuck off, and the next, we were upside down with a tree nearly splittin' the front of the car in half. The officers who responded to the call told me we likely hit the stump and flipped over it, sending the car careening into another tree. I lost consciousness, but I have no idea how long I was out. Long enough for Mama to call me a dozen times. But my phone was on the roof of the car so I couldn't reach it. Against my better judgment, I looked over at my dad, but he was so still. And there was so much blood. But... I waited. I managed to use my pocket knife to cut myself out of the seatbelt and get out of the car, but I waited to call for help."

His voice grow more ragged as he tells the story, and I can tell without even asking that this is the part that eats away at him, the part that drowns him in guilt every day.

"I wanted him to die, Lyla. I waited to call for help because I was hopin' he wouldn't make it out alive."

My heart breaks for this man who was dealt such an awful hand by fate. One who's spent his entire adult life taking care of people to atone for his perceived wrongdoings.

"Aidan... your father wasn't a good man. There's no way you can know that waiting for help caused him to die. But honestly, even if it did... you may have saved your mother's life."

He snorts derisively and wipes his nose on a napkin he pulls out of the glove compartment. "You know what's ironic? It's been eight years, and I still beat myself up about it to this day, wondering if anything would have been different if I called the second I woke up. But the asshole died on impact. He didn't suffer. He wasn't hanging upside down, bleeding out while I sat there sobbin' like a scared kid. His neck snapped and severed his spinal cord, killing him instantly."

A strangled gasp escaped my throat, and I climb into Aidan's lap, resting my back against the steering wheel. Using my hands to cup his face, I angle my head to meet his watery gaze. "Listen to me, Aidan. You did nothing wrong. It's tragic that your father died so traumatically, but there was not a single thing you could have done to change it. You can't possibly think you deserve punishment for something you didn't even do."

His large hands cover mine on his cheeks, and he uses the contact to pull me closer so he can bury his head in my neck. He's so much taller than me that it's almost comical how far he has to bend to make it happen.

I stroke my hands through his shaggy hair in what I hope is a soothing motion, trying to reassure him without words that I don't see him any differently after his confession.

"I've never told a single soul about my part in what happened that night. They know about the crash and that my dad died on impact, but they all think I was passed out until I called 9-1-1. And I didn't correct them. How could I admit to my mom and brother what I'd done? What kind of person waits to call for help, hoping their parent dies before anyone arrives?"

My hands continue their soothing motion in his hair as I pull him even closer. "A teenager that had been repeatedly brutalized by the one person that's supposed to love them more than anything. Someone who had to watch his mom and younger brother be tortured at the hands of a monster who used his family to exercise his demons."

Taking a deep breath, I offer him another small piece of my truth. "I know what it's like to feel powerless at the hands of someone who's supposed to love you. That's how I know you did nothing wrong."

He lifts his head to meet my eyes, unanswered questions thick in the air between us. I can see in his eyes he wants to ask, but I also see the moment he decides against it. I can't hide my sigh of relief.

Aidan takes the opportunity to press his forehead to

mine. "I need to know soon, Ly. Even if you decide you never want to be more than friends, I need to know what kind of danger you're in so I can keep you and Crew safe."

Guilt squeezes my chest, and my eyes sting with the imminent threat of tears. Aidan was brave for me, so I swallow the bitter taste of my fear and dig deep for some of the bravery I had when I left Sebastian and started a whole new life hundreds of miles away from home.

"I was born and raised in a small-ish town in Maryland by a rotating horde of nannies hired by my famous father. I don't remember my mother or even know who she is. All I know is she wasn't there."

Understanding dawns in his eyes, and I'm sure some of the things I've said are starting to make sense, but I keep going so I don't chicken out.

"Shortly after I turned twenty, my dad introduced me to an associate's son, hoping we would hit it off." Aidan growls, and I grimace up at him. "To make an incredibly long story short, we did. We dated for a few months before he proposed and convinced me to move in with him."

Aidan pulls me to his chest with a hand on the back of my head, and his beachy scent calms the storm raging in my mind. "My ex wasn't a good man, Aid. He hurt me in so many ways, and one day, I couldn't take it anymore. During his last blow-up, I managed to knock him out by sheer luck, so I took what I couldn't live without and ran. I took the first bus out and landed here. I met Wren a week later, and the rest is history."

My eyes lock on his, and I hope he knows how much I mean my next words. "I promise I'm doing everything I can to keep you and Crew out of it, but when I started getting threatening texts, I finally caved and accepted the help Wren offered on behalf of Copeland. He got in contact with the FBI and managed to help build a case against my ex, but they can't meet to exchange information for another three weeks."

I finish my explanation with a huff as if the weight of all the events from the last year suddenly dropped off my shoulders now that someone else knows. For the first time in months, I feel like I can breathe for a moment without looking over my shoulder.

A strong hand tilts my chin up, and the sight of Aidan's understanding gaze makes my earlier tears spring back to the surface. I've kept so much from him, and the fact that he's able to look at me with anything but anger is more than I ever could have hoped for.

"I'm going to want a name eventually, angel," he grumbles roughly.

Raising a brow, I stare at him skeptically. "Why?"

He growls, shifting to grip my chin tightly between his thumb and forefinger. "So I can kill the son of a bitch who thought he could lay hands on you and get away with it."

My breath catches at the conviction in his voice, and I know in that moment he means every word. If I gave him Sebastian's name right now, he wouldn't hesitate to hunt him down. I've never had someone defend me so fiercely before, especially for something that happened before he even met me.

Aidan eyes me like he's worried I'll panic over the threat of violence, but it seems to have had the opposite effect, and whatever he sees in my eyes has a pained groan leaving his throat before he yanks my head forward and kisses me.

19
Aidan

Every good intention I had of respecting Lyla's wishes goes out the goddamn window the second I see her eyes heat with desire after I threatened to kill her piece of shit ex-fiancé. The conscious thought doesn't even float through my mind before I'm roughly pulling her in for a fierce kiss.

Our teeth clash but it doesn't deter either of us; instead, it seems to spur the moment on even more. She tastes like her favorite cherry vanilla lip balm and something else distinctly *Lyla*. The combination is downright addictive. If I'm not careful, I could get lost in her flavor and the way her lips mold to mine.

"Lyla," I murmur between brushes of our lips. "We don't have to do this. I know you said you weren't ready."

She groans, nipping my bottom lip *hard*. "Aidan?"

In spite of my rational words, I can't stop myself from dropping kisses down her soft neck. "Yes, angel?"

"Please shut up and fuck me."

A husky chuckle escapes me before I can stop it because even when my girl is being bossy, she's still polite.

I tuck my face down and smile into her neck before lightly biting at the soft skin between her neck and shoulder. "Yes, ma'am."

Moving back just far enough so I don't accidentally elbow her, I reach up and grip the back of my shirt, nearly ripping it in my haste to get naked. I'm thankful the cab of my truck has so much space, otherwise this wouldn't be possible.

The way Lyla's appreciative gaze roams over my bare chest has my dick jumping behind my zipper, and I push a hand down over it to alleviate the ache. I don't think there will ever be a day when this girl doesn't turn me on like nothing else ever has.

With practiced movements, she shucks off her shirt and bra, leaving me staring at her gloriously bare tits. They're on the smaller side and a perfect handful. I go to cup them in my hands and grunt at the feel of her stiff nipples scraping against my palm. She moans, and it's like a siren's call, leaving me powerless to resist her.

I dip down and take one of the stiff peaks in my mouth, sucking and nipping until she's squirming in my lap.

"Dammit, angel. You taste like I'm gonna need to go to church and beg for forgiveness next Sunday."

The way she giggles as her nimble fingers go for my belt and zipper has me thrusting into her hand before she even gets my pants undone, and suddenly, I can't go another minute without tasting her.

She already had the center console flipped up, so I band one arm around her back and flip us so I'm lying over top of her across the bench seat.

Lyla shrieks, making me chuckle, but her surprise turns into breathy moans when I tuck my fingers into the waistband of her leggings and yank them down, barely stopping long enough to get them off her feet. I kick the driver side door open and drop to my knees on the sideboard, so I'm at the perfect angle to toss her legs over my shoulders.

Her gaze is hot on mine when I glance up, and I don't wait another second before diving in. A ragged groan escapes my throat when I get the first hit of her flavor, and I lose all sense of time and place.

Forget baseball, I want to spend the rest of my days worshipping at this angel's alter.

Dragging my tongue along her drenched core, I circle her sensitive little clit and dip a single finger inside her, curling it up to hit the spot I know drives her crazy.

Right on cue, her hips buck up and bring her even further into my mouth, and I make sure to vocalize just how much I like it.

Pulling back for air, my words are barely more than a gasp. "Fuckin' love it when you use me, angel. Ride my face like it's your own personal toy."

She moans loudly and cries out when I suck her clit between my lips, giving it just enough pressure to feel good but not enough to offer any relief. I use the stud of my tongue ring to keep a smooth pressure along the underside of her clit. Toying with her this way might become my new favorite game.

"Daddy, *please!*"

Oh, fuck. If I had any thought in my mind that the first time she called me that was a fluke, it was *gone*. My cock just went from hard to a steel fucking pipe in half a second, and I know I'm dripping precum into my boxer briefs right now.

With a hoarse moan, I dive back in and add a second

finger to Lyla's sweet cunt, pumping them in and out at a swift pace, keeping my fingers curved to hit that little spot behind her pubic bone. With my other hand, I unzip my pants and pull my dick out, nearly hissing at the friction of my hand against it. I haven't even been inside her yet, and I'm already close.

I move my mouth to the side and bite the inside of her thigh, growling like a fucking animal. "You gonna be a good little sinner and come for Daddy, dirty girl?"

She cries out when my tongue returns to her clit, her pussy clenching around my fingers as she detonates. "That's it," I praise her. "That's my good girl. Come all over my fingers, and then you can come on my cock."

Lyla whimpers, scrambling back slightly when I don't let up the pressure on her clit. I gentle it just a bit, but I want her close again when I impale her because I know I won't last, and my angel deserves *at least* two orgasms for every one of mine.

"Ah ah ah, angel. Did I say we were done?"

Her eyes are wide and unblinking as she stares at me, but then her eyes drop to where my hand is still wrapped around my cock, and her mouth parts, giving me a glimpse of her tongue. She doesn't answer me or act like she heard me, so I land a gentle slap over her clit to get her attention, loving the whimper it gets me.

I keep my words firm, reminding myself we'll need to go over rules and expectations later if we're going to keep this dynamic in our relationship. Even if it's only confined to the bedroom. Or, in this case, my truck. "I asked you a question, Lyla. Did I say we were done?"

She shakes her head this time, letting me know she did, in fact, hear me. "N-no, Daddy."

A smirk finds my mouth easily because *fuck*. I love

that so much more than I ever thought I would. "Good. Glad we understand each other."

Without giving her a chance to respond, I grip her hips in my hands and flip her over so she's on her knees, facing the woods outside the passenger window. We're far enough away from the road that I'm not worried about someone seeing her, but if they did, at least they'd know she's mine.

Is it fucked up that I just ate out my son's nanny in the cab of my truck next to my father's dilapidated gravesite? Probably. Do I care? Not in the slightest. I hope dear old Dad looks up and knows his life goal of fucking me up beyond repair failed.

Well, mostly. I did just devour my girl in a graveyard, so I might be a little bit fucked up after all.

Shaking myself back to reality, I place a hand around Lyla's throat and pull her up so her back is pressed firmly against my chest. "You with me, Ly?"

She nods. "Mhmm. I'm with you, Aid."

I breathe a sigh of relief, grateful I haven't pushed her too far. "Good, then listen to me, okay? This is a new dynamic for both of us, and I don't want you uncomfortable. So if I say or do something you don't like, you say stop. You say stop, and everything stops. No questions or complaints. Okay?"

"Yes, Daddy."

All the air in my lungs evaporates, and the lack of oxygen in my brain is the only excuse I have for what I do next. Taking the barest second to line us up, I thrust into Lyla's heat and curse at how fucking *right* it feels.

There's no build-up, no slow start to get her used to my size. Two little words from her sinful lips, and I'm thrusting into her savagely like I'll die if I have to go one more second not being inside of her.

"Goddamn, angel. You feel so fuckin' good. I'll never get enough of you."

Her breathing is labored, and every other breath comes out as a moan, and just when I think I can't possibly take anymore, she places her palms flat on the center console and bounces back into me, sending a thump through my balls.

Without warning, I pull out and drop back down to the seat, picking her up so she straddles me before I impale her on my erection again. She wastes no time starting up a steady rhythm, bouncing on my cock, and playing with her clit like she was made to ride me.

"Fuck, Aidan. I'm close."

I grit my teeth to hold off my own orgasm and knock her hand away from her pussy, licking my thumb and replacing her fingers with it. "I know, angel. I want you to hold off and come with me. Can you do that?"

She nods emphatically, and thankfully, I don't have to wait long. After a few more rough thrusts, I pinch her clit gently, and with the first clench of her inner muscles around my cock, I explode. Shooting rope after rope of cum into her. Somewhere in the deep recesses of my mind, I hear Wren's text from the plane about having my own baby, but I ignore biology and focus on helping Lyla come down from her orgasm.

Our lips meet in a sweet caress, and the grin she gives me when we separate is blinding. "Wow," she whispers softly. "I guess my staying away from you plan didn't exactly pan out, huh?"

I snort a laugh and lift her off my oversensitive shaft, setting her cute little ass on my thighs. The second I do, I feel something drip onto my leg, and we both look down in shock.

The reality of what I just did smacks me in the face, and I look to Lyla with what I'm sure is a mixture of horror and desire written all over my face at seeing the cum dripping down her silky, toned thighs.

She finally looks up and chokes on a laugh when she sees my expression, reaching up to press my mouth closed from where it had fallen open. "Relax, Aid. I have an IUD, and I trust you."

Biting her lip, she keeps her eyes trained where our bodies meet. "I've never had sex without a condom before... it's so much better than I thought it would be."

Well, in that case...

Leaning back, I move one of my hands off her hips and gently swipe two fingers over her pussy, keeping my eyes locked on hers as I lick them clean. My eyes roll back in my head at the taste of us combined, and this time, it's *her* jaw that drops in shock.

Lyla's eyes are hooded and filled with heat again, but the surprise is still evident on her pretty face. "Well fuck," she whispers under her breath. "Why was that so hot?"

With a smirk, I pull her to me so her head rests comfortably under my chin. I just need a second to breathe her in and remind myself that she's here and safe.

I know we need to clean up and get on the road to pick up Crew, but a quick glance at the clock shows it's barely 8 a.m., so he's likely not even awake yet. I have time to just hold my girl as I figure out a plan to keep us all safe from her walking dead ex-boyfriend.

Because whether she's ready to accept it or not, Lyla Taylor is *mine*.

Rhodes's parents have known me since he was drafted five years ago, so I'm fully expecting the Spanish Inquisition when I pull up with sex hair and Lyla in the front seat next to me.

Don't ask me how they'll know I have sex hair when their own son was a virgin until last year. Just trust that they do and that Dominic will most likely put his foot in his mouth about it.

Ly is fidgeting in her seat, and I can't figure out why, so I pull off to the side of the road and park just before we make it to their house.

"Hey, why are you stopping?"

Turning in my seat, I grab one of her small hands in mine and stare into her beautiful green eyes. "Why do you seem nervous? You've met Kaci and Dom plenty of times before. Nothing's changed, and you know they love you."

She sighs and leans back on the headrest with her face tilted towards me. "I know they like me, and they're always so nice whenever I see them. But what if they figure out something happened between us?"

I snort because it's too late for that. "Angel, they knew something was going to happen between us the minute I asked them to watch Crew for the weekend."

Her mouth gapes open in the most adorable way, and I can't help but lean in and nip her cute bottom lip. "Don't act so surprised. They know you've been working for me, and they also know you went to New York with us from the pictures I'm sure Wren sent them. In case you forgot, your bestie has a big mouth."

The panic in her eyes only recedes the tiniest bit, but

I'm not sure what else I can say to reassure her. If she's this nervous to be around Rhodes's parents, I can't imagine how hard it'll be when I bring her home to meet Mama and Wes.

"Ly, what's the real issue here?"

Lyla heaves a deep breath and shakes her head, scooting to the middle seat so she can lay her head on my shoulder. "I worry they'll think I'm not good enough for you. Or that I'm taking advantage of you for your money. Obviously, I'm not, but that's what my ex-fiancé's mother used to say when she thought I couldn't hear."

That fucking family. I need to get names from Lyla or Copeland as soon as possible so I can fuck up some lives. After all, what's the point of having money if I can't use it to help the people I lo—am closest to?

Too soon for the l-word, Aidan.

"Angel... first of all, if anything, I'm the one who's not good enough for you. You're a smart, sweet, incredibly brave woman, and I am in awe of you every day. You've made our lives so much better since you came in and did your thing. Crew is sleeping better, he's learning more every day, and his separation anxiety is nearly gone. Have you ever wondered why I call you angel?"

She nods slowly, her eyes glossed over with tears.

"I call you angel because to us, that's exactly what you are. You're our angel, Lyla. And I'll do anything I can to make sure we get to keep you."

I don't give her a chance to respond before continuing our drive, and within three minutes, we're in Kaci and Dominic's driveway. Giving Lyla's hand one last comforting squeeze, I hop out of the truck and run around the front to open her door. She seems shocked every time

I do this, and it makes me hate her ex even more for being such a piece of shit.

We haven't had 'the talk' about what we are, but it doesn't stop me from threading my fingers through hers on the way to the door. Though I do go against every fiber of my being and let go once we ring the bell.

As much as I want to claim Lyla as mine and show her off to the world, I don't want to throw another big change into Crew's life when he's so happy and settled the way things are now.

The front door opens, and Kaci's smiling face greets us. Her smile is a little too wide and a little too knowing. "Hey, guys! Crew literally *just* woke up, and he's already asking about you, Lyla."

I grin at Lyla and raise an incredulous brow. "It seems I've been replaced."

Her answering smirk is cute as hell, and I see Kaci's eyes widen just as a small blond mass comes hurtling at us at top speed.

"Lyly!"

Crew dives into Lyla's legs, and I instantly move behind them to catch her slight form as she starts to topple under the weight of my enthusiastic son. I shouldn't have worried, though, because she instantly drops to her knees and envelops Crew into the biggest hug I've ever seen.

I'm honestly speechless at the display, and when Lyla looks up at me with those beautiful eyes and smiles, I'm seconds away from saying "fuck it," and kissing her right here out in the open.

I think a little family fun day might be in order.

"Really? You want to spend the day here?" Lyla asks incredulously.

After picking up Crew from Rhodes's parent's house, I told Crew and Lyla I was taking us out for a surprise fun day together and refused to say a word about where we were going.

When I pulled up outside the Charleston Fun Park a minute ago, my pretty passenger looked at me like I was insane as Crew squealed in his booster seat.

My grin is so big it feels like it might split my face, and I can't hold back a chuckle. "Oh, ye of little faith. This may look silly to you, but I've found there's no better way to bond than by kicking each other's as—*butt's* at go-karts."

She snorts and shakes her head, placing her hand on the handle to open the door.

"Don't!" My shout startles her, and I grimace in apology, hopping out on my side so I can open both of their doors. Leaning down next to her ear, I whisper my apology. "Sorry for shouting, angel. But my girl doesn't get her own door when I'm around. You sit your pretty ass in that seat and wait for Daddy to come to you."

The flush that covers her cheeks is perfection, making me smirk as I stealthily kiss her cheek and go to grab Crew from his seat. The kid learned how to undo his buckles ages ago, so he's standing up and waiting to jump into my arms the second I open the back passenger side door.

"Alright, y'all. Let's go battle it out on the track!"

Lyla 20

"Lyly, can you come with me to get some water?" Crew's sweet voice reaches my ears, and at the same moment, he tugs on my hand. I'm taking a break from our activity for the day to catch my breath because going around the small track so many times made me dizzy.

A cursory glance around shows me Aidan is on the phone. When I catch his eye, he uses his thumbs to gesture a texting motion and points to me. Taking the hint, I check my phone to see a couple of texts from him waiting for me.

> AIDAN
>
> Sorry, angel. This is my agent, so I have to take it. Can you hang with Crew for a few minutes?
>
> I promise I'll be back to kick your ass on the track as soon as possible 😉

Him threatening to kick my ass shouldn't make me blush, so tell me why my cheeks are hotter than the surface of the sun?

CROSSED UP

Turning back to Crew, I smile and grab his hand. "Of course I can, Crew-bug." I noticed a concession stand on the way in, so I lead us both to it, grateful there don't seem to be many people milling about.

There is a man and a little girl in front of us in line, and when the girl notices Crew, her face widens into a huge, gap-toothed grin. "Crew, hi! Daddy, look, it's Crew!"

The man turns around, and his eyes widen when he sees me holding Crew's hand. I watch his gaze dart to my clearly visible left hand, and when he sees my lack of a ring, he smiles.

He's classically handsome, with dark brown hair and eyes that glitter in the midday sun, but something about his gaze makes me nervous. It's completely opposite to how I felt when I met Aidan.

Holding his hand out to me, his smile turns into a smirk. "Hey, I'm Colton. We've seen Crew and his dad around here plenty of times, but I know for a fact I would remember a gorgeous face like yours. Are you Crew's mom?"

That nervous feeling turns to discomfort when I shake his hand and he tightens his grip, holding on just a bit too long to be friendly.

Still wanting to be polite because he hasn't done anything outwardly threatening, I offer a small smile in return. "No, I'm not Crew's mom, but I am his nanny." Crew tugs on my hand, and I'm shocked to see his eyes watering, so I quickly excuse us.

Only Colton grips my bicep before I can go. "I hope this isn't too forward, but could I possibly ask for your number? I'd love to take you out sometime."

I fight to keep my smile from turning to a grimace as I

extricate myself as politely as possible from his grip. "I'm sorry, but I actually have a boyfriend. If you'll excuse me, we really do need to be going."

I hustle Crew to an abandoned table tucked away in a small alcove around the corner and sit down, helping him onto the seat next to me. Big crocodile tears cascade down his cheeks as he looks at me, and I gape.

"Crew-bug!" I pull him into my arms and pet his hair in the motion I know soothes him. "What's the matter?"

He sniffles, burying his face in my neck as his arms twine around my neck. "Why can't you be my mommy?"

It takes every ounce of willpower not to let the shock show on my face at his question, but I do pull him tighter against me. When I don't say anything, he keeps going.

"All of my friends have Mommy's and Daddy's, and you sleep at our house, and take care of me and Daddy. And I love you. So why can't you be my mommy?"

My heart *shatters* with his quiet, raspy words. Tears spring to my eyes faster than they ever have before, and I pull back just slightly so I can see the tear tracks running down Crew's pink cheeks. "Crew..."

I feel like I'm walking a tightrope made of fishing wire. One wrong word, and I could set him up for heartbreak if Aidan and I don't work out. Not to mention, it's not my place to tell Crew anything, especially when I don't really know what the heck is going on between me and his dad.

With a sigh, I stroke my fingers through his soft, wavy hair. "Anybody would be lucky to be your Mom, Crew-bug. You're the coolest kid ever, and you make every day so much fun."

Aidan's concerned face appears in front of us, and I decide that my next words are as much for him as they are for his son. "I really hope I get to be a Mommy someday, sweetie. Especially to somebody as smart and kind as you. But for now, being your nanny is the best thing that's ever happened to me, and I don't plan on leaving anytime soon. Okay?"

He perks up with a small smile at my words and throws his deceptively strong arms around my neck, squeezing so tight I have to remind him to let me breathe.

Aidan finally approaches, his eyes a little glassy, and drops down to the bench next to us with a soft smile as he runs his large hand over his son's back.

"Hey, you two. I was wondering where y'all ran off to." His gaze roams over where Crew is snuggled into my arms and the glossiness increases a fraction, just shy of actual tears gathering on his lower lashes. "I'm pretty tired. What do you say we head home and have a movie night? We can get pizza?"

At the mere mention of a movie night, Crew gets a second wind and hops off my lap to do hot laps around the small table. "Yes, a sleepover! Daddy, can we do another fort? *Pleeease*? I promise I'll help Lyly clean it all up tomorrow!"

The handsome man next to me snickers at his son with a fond smile, raking a hand through his messy hair. "Of course we can, raptor. And I think we should just leave the fort up, since you like it so much."

Crew stops to stare at his father in awe. "Really? We can leave it up all the time?"

Aidan glances at me for confirmation, but I just shrug with a smile. It's not *my* house.

"We sure can, raptor. Now, let's get a move on so we can swing by Joe's and get some pizza before they get busy."

As we're making our way to the truck, I lean into my boss just the slightest bit and lower my voice, keeping my words just for him. "You're a really good dad, Aidan. I don't know many parents who would willingly let their six-year-old indefinitely take over their living room with a blanket fort just to make them happy."

He tosses an arm over my shoulders but keeps his eyes on Crew as he answers me. "I did it for you, too, angel. I saw the way your eyes lit up whenever y'all were in the fort. If it makes the two most important people in my life happy, then who gives a hoot if it's a little messy?"

I melt into a puddle on the cement at his sweet words. "The two most important people, huh?"

Aidan peeks at me from the corner of his eyes with a smirk. "Yep. Sometime during the last five weeks, this sweet woman I hired as a nanny wormed her way into my heart. A place no other woman has been before." He grabs my hand and pulls me to stop next to the passenger door of his truck.

Just before I go to climb in, he rests a hand on my hip and leans down to murmur next to my ear. "And if I have it my way, a place no other woman but her will ever be again." Checking on Crew, who's happily chattering away in the backseat, he smacks my ass before lifting me into the passenger seat, earning a squeak from me.

His smirk is sinful and promises wicked things but his next words knock me off kilter. He picks up the seatbelt, reaches across me to fasten it, and takes the opportunity to nip at my ear. "Unless, of course, that sweet woman of mine lets me knock her up, and we have a daughter."

This man is insane. Absolutely off his damn rocker. We've barely known each other a month, and here he is talking about wanting to knock me up.

Goddamnit. Why does that turn me on? It's the 'Daddy' thing all over again.

Maybe that's it. I've dreamed of being a mom since I was a little girl, so maybe seeing Aidan being such an amazing dad is triggering both my daddy issues *and* my desire to be a parent and rolling them all into one big amalgamation of confusing attraction. It's probably the same thing for him. Just biological impulses triggered by seeing me care for his son.

The fact that we've now had unprotected sex should freak me out, but I trust Aidan. He's proven time and time again that I can rely on him for just about anything. Even so, I'm still not sure I'm ready to take that final leap into a relationship with him. There's too much up in the air with Sebastian, and this case the FBI is supposedly building against the Pennington family.

I don't even realize I've zoned out until a soft hand on my shoulder startles me out of my thoughts, and I see Aidan staring at me, concern darkening his pale blue irises. The car is off, and we're parked in the center spot of the three-car garage. He always parks here so I can park in the spot closest to the door with the SUV.

"Hey, gorgeous. You okay? You checked out again."

Feeling guilty for worrying him, my smile feels more like a grimace as I lay my hand over top of his. "I'm fine, just thinking."

He nods in understanding, his eyes tracking over my face, trying to detect any hint that I'm not okay. "Lyla, I think—"

"Daddy! Lyly! Hurry up, I wanna watch *Tinker Bell!*" Crew's voice interrupts whatever Aidan was about to say, and I breathe a sigh of relief. At least until I notice him track the movement and narrow his eyes.

"We need to have a conversation soon, Lyla. I know you're worried about things with your ex, but if that's the only thing holding you back, it's a nonissue. There's an entire team of guys willing and able to help us at the drop of a hat if it comes down to that, and from the sounds of it, Copeland already has things well in hand on the legal end."

His sigh is loud in the quiet of the truck's cab, and guilt slithers through my belly at the disappointment on his face. "But if there's something else, another reason you aren't ready to give us a chance beyond sex, then I need to know now before I get more invested, before Crew sees something he shouldn't and gets his hopes up even more than they already are. Because that little boy in there is in love with you, and losing you would devastate him just as much, *if not more*, than it would devastate me."

"Our original deal still stands, Ly. If you don't want this, that's okay. No harm, no foul. You can stay on for Crew, and I'll be completely professional. We can still be friends if you're open to it. Or I can help you find another job, either with someone on the team or another family who'll be almost as grateful to have you as we have been. The ball is in your court, sugar."

Without waiting for a response, he gets out of the truck and heads into the house, his face instantly transforming the second he walks through the door. From this angle, I can see how his cheeks bunch with his wide grin and the little crinkles in the corners of his eyes prove his smile is genuine.

Aidan has a point. I need to figure out where my head is at and what I want before any of us fall deeper into this family dynamic we've blended into so seamlessly.

Choosing to remain in my seat for just a bit longer, I pull out my phone and text Wren.

> ME
>
> Hey, you busy? I could use one of your famous heart-to-heart chats right about now
>
> WRENNY
>
> Never too busy for you, Lyla-boo. Text or call?

Flashing a quick look around the cavernous garage, it seems like the boys are still inside, so I respond by asking her to call me, and she does not even thirty seconds later.

"What's gotcha down, girlypop?" Wren's peppy voice soothes some of my jagged edges, and I let out a long sigh that makes her chuckle. "That bad, huh?"

I shake my head even though she can't see me and reach over to open my door so the breeze from the open garage door can cool my flushed cheeks. "It's not *bad* per se... but... how did you know you were ready to make things official with Rhodes?"

After a few minutes of silence, she hums quietly, but I don't rush her. One thing I love about Wren is that she always gives you her full attention and is thoughtful with her answers.

"Well, the situation with us was different. We'd been friends for so long, and even though I married his teammate and moved away, there were always feelings there. They just got put on hold for a while. We jumped into things really fast because our history made the transition of going from friends to more feel as easy as breathing."

I slump down in my seat, dejection taking root in my chest. Rhodes and Wren were almost a *decade* in the making. My history with Aidan is five weeks of sleeping down the hall from him and some hot sex.

Wren's voice interrupts my pity party. "But Lyla, sometimes you just know. In some cases, especially when there's a child involved, things move faster than polite society might consider proper or 'normal.'"

The emphasis around the word normal creates air quotes that are practically palpable in the air, and I find myself snickering. Even when she's not trying to, Wren has a way of making everything feel a little less heavy. The woman is a ray of freaking sunshine, and sometimes I need that.

"I really like him, Wrenny. And I've completely fallen in love with Crew. I'm terrified that things won't work out with Aidan, and we'll hurt Crew."

"Is Crew the only one you're worried about getting hurt?"

I go to answer, but she interrupts me. "Really think about it, Ly. You escaped your ex, went to therapy, and did the work to heal, but you're only twenty-three. And this is only your second serious relationship. It's natural to be scared. But I also know you've said on multiple occasions your dream is to be a mom. Seeing you fall into that role with Crew won't come as a surprise to anyone who knows you. And Aidan has *never* been like this with a woman before."

"So yes, it's okay to be scared. But you've been through more in twenty-three years than most people go through in a lifetime. I say fuck being proper and grab hold of both of those boys and don't let go."

Her words hit their mark, so I'm only a little bit surprised to find tears trailing down my cheeks. "So you really don't think this is a bad idea? Even knowing what you know about the situation with Sebastian?"

Wren snorts, and I hear masculine chuckling in the background. I groan. "For the love of God, please tell me y'all at least have clothes on."

The silence on the other end of the phone is answer enough, and I fake a gag.

Their combined laughter has me rolling my eyes and fighting a smile. Whenever Wren and Rhodes are home together, they're rarely clothed. I learned that the hard way last year and now before I'll enter their house, I send a preemptive text *and* ring the doorbell. Usually a few times, just to be safe.

"Sorry, Lyla. But full disclosure? We've been betting on this since before you moved in." Rhodes's words are completely unsurprising. If there's one thing the those two are known for besides their inability to keep their hands off each other, it's their bets.

I am curious, though. "Who won?"

Wren snickers, giving me my answer. "I told Rhodes y'all would be in love in less than three months."

I choke on my own spit and launch into a violent coughing fit. "We're not *in love*, Wren. Jesus. It's been a month."

She scoffs. "Whatever you say, Taylor."

Oh, shit. She only ever calls me Taylor when she's in PR mode.

"Go tell your man how you feel and remember what I told you. Time means nothing, and fuck being proper."

A full-blown laugh finally makes its way out of my throat, and I shake my head. "Right. Fuck being proper. Love y'all. See you at the game next weekend?"

"You know it. Love you, Ly."

We hang up, and for the first time in weeks, I feel centered. Wren's words grounded me and made me feel like I'm not doing anything wrong by wanting Aidan this soon.

I might not ever be completely ready to make the jump into a new relationship after my experience with Sebastian, but I know there's nobody else in the world I would rather take a chance on than Aidan and Crew.

21
Aidan

Lyla walks into the living room with a serene smile on her pretty face and a relaxed air to her that's been absent for most of our time together. Not to say she's uptight, because she's not *at all*. Her stress levels have just been obvious since our relationship progressed past friends and into the "more" category.

This calm countenance, however, makes me nervous. She was zoned out the entire drive home from the fun park, and I could see the panic building behind those gorgeous eyes, but that's part of why I said what I did.

I'll wait for her as long as she needs me to, but I also need to know if she's all in or not, so I can take myself out of the headspace where I'm calling her mine.

She stops in the wide doorway that separates the mudroom from the kitchen, moving toward us slowly. Her grin spreads the closer she gets, but the only thing I can focus on is the way her hair swishes around her hips as she walks.

I can't say I've ever been turned on by someone's *hair*

before, but I'm pretty sure Lyla could just breathe in my direction, and I'd pop a boner.

"Are we sleeping in the fort tonight, boys?"

Crew pops his head up from where he'd been arranging pillows in front of the couch as a back rest. Whereas the fort he made with Ly a few weeks ago was just big enough to fit their small frames comfortably, the one he and I are building makes that one look like a dollhouse.

Alaskan King sheets are spread out and rigged up with fishing wire I snagged from our gear on the back porch and twin top sheets that Crew refuses to use are clipped to wire as well to form an enclosed space facing the large portable movie screen I brought up from the theater room.

Movie nights have always been my favorite way to spend my downtime. It was one of the only times my piece of shit father would shut up and leave me be for a few hours. First, I shared the tradition with my brother, and then after I was drafted with Copeland, and now with Crew, so nearly every room in my house is equipped with a high-quality projector on the ceiling for times just like these.

I look her way nervously and beckon her closer, taking her tiny hand in mine to help her into the mountain of blankets my son has assembled. I try not to focus on how right her hand feels linked with mine, but it's nearly impossible when it's just another in a long line of things that feel right with this woman.

"Raptor and I were thinking it would be nice to have our movie night here and then just sleep downstairs. This is my last free week before the season opener, and some quality fam—" My eyes widen when I realize what just came out of my mouth, and I cough before finishing my thought, hoping Lyla didn't notice my little slip-up calling this family time. "Some quality time with y'all to get my head on straight for another busy season."

If she noticed me sticking my foot in my mouth, she's polite enough not to say anything. Instead, she plops herself down next to Crew and smiles at him, running her hand over his head. "Did you already pick our movie, Crew-bug?"

He nods emphatically, and I do my damndest to focus on his words and not the way Lyla so effortlessly shows my son affection. "I did! Daddy said it could be anything I want."

She laughs, shaking her head with a sidelong glance my way. "He did, huh? And does that mean we're watching *Tinker Bell* again?"

"No, I wanna watch *Tarzan* tonight."

Lyla's eyebrows reach her hairline, and I can understand why. Crew's been on this *Tinker Bell* kick for *months* and hasn't wanted to watch anything else since she came to live with us, so the sudden switch-up is jarring.

My son goes uncharacteristically quiet, curling in on himself in a way that has me nearly lurching forward with concern. But when his meek voice hits my ears, I can't stop the flood of moisture that assaults my vision.

"Nana Kaci says Tarzan's mommy has to leave, but then he gets a new mommy that loves him a lot, and it makes him really happy. Maybe if I watch the movie, I can see how he got a mommy, and I can do it, too."

I clear my throat several times, but my voice is still

choked when I try to redirect him. "Alright, raptor, why don't you go get washed up, and then we'll eat dinner before we start the movie."

He's back to his normal perky self as he sprints up the stairs, but in spite of the high ceilings of our living room, I feel like the room is closing in on me. Tears sting my eyes, and I mutter a husky "excuse me" before I hightail it out of there and into the first room I find, slamming the door.

I'm only alone for a few seconds before the door is being pushed open, and when the scent of cherries hits me, I nearly groan. I don't need her seeing me like this. When I'm on the brink of a meltdown over a comment my six-year-old probably won't even remember tomorrow.

Lyla doesn't say a thing, instead wrapping her delicate arms around my waist and squeezing as tight as she can. Her head only reaches my chest, but when she takes one of my hands and places it over her heart, I realize she's attempting her own version of co-regulation.

The sweet gesture finally releases the torrent of emotion I've been shoving down for weeks, and ragged sobs force their way from my throat.

"Oh, Aidan. It's okay. Let it out."

And for the first time, maybe ever, I do. I don't worry about what anyone else needs in this moment, or what Lyla thinks about me breaking down like this. I just focus on the mess of feelings coursing through my chest and the feel of my angel's heart beating steadily against my palm.

Lifting the other hand to grip the back of her head, I pull her to me even tighter and relish in the way her comforting smell surrounds me. Cherries and sweet vanilla invade my nostrils and soothe some of the roiling emotions currently holding my mind in a hostile takeover.

I know I really don't, but a big part of me feels like I owe Lyla an explanation for why I reacted the way I did to Crew's words.

Even with those conflicting thoughts, all of me understands she has the right to know about Mia. If not as my girlfriend and a potential mother figure for Crew, then as his nanny.

This is going to hurt, but definitely not as much as telling her about my father. I was never hung up on Mia, as terrible as that sounds. She was a one-night stand who was never meant to be more. And she had absolutely nothing on the woman in front of me.

Steeling myself for my second painful conversation today, I launch into the story of how my little boy came to be.

"And she really just left her newborn baby at the hospital with strange nurses and a man she slept with one time and spent a week in his guest room. I mean, no offense, Aidan. You're a wonderful father. But *still*. I could never... I'm so sorry you had to go through that on your own," she trails off, looking distraught.

Crew fell fast asleep between us in the fort a little while ago, and our conversation quickly turned back to Mia. I think Lyla was still processing from everything I told her earlier, so the fact that she has more questions doesn't come as a shock.

I nod, grimacing at the memories racing to the forefront of my mind. "Here I was, this not even twenty-two-year-old kid, newly drafted and still struggling with the loss of his own father, and a nurse comes in to tell me this fragile, tiny human is now solely my responsibility."

My hands shake in a visceral response to the emotions I remember feeling in that moment, but then Lyla slips her soft hand in mine and the tremors ease. Releasing a shaky breath, I give her a wobbly smile in thanks.

"I didn't know the first goddamn thing about being a parent or taking care of a baby. But when I was sitting there in that rock-hard recliner in the NICU with this little one-and-a-half-pound-baby that looked more like a baby bird than a human, I took one look at him and knew I would do anything, *be anything,* for him. No matter who his mom was, or how shitty my own example of a father was. It took three seconds holding his tiny body to my chest for my entire world to change."

My breath stutters in my chest. "Suddenly, I wasn't just Aidan Black, catcher for the Charleston Raptors and son of an abusive, alcoholic asshole. I was Aidan Black, *father* to this perfect little boy. He became the love of my life in the span of one of his small, labored breaths, and I've never regretted it. Not for a single second."

Lyla's eyes are misted over with tears when I chance a look at her, and seeing the depth of her care for us is humbling. After growing up second best to my younger brother, having someone put us first has been enlightening, and I hate to think of how that will change if our relationship proves to be too much for her on top of dealing with her ex.

Her mouth opens to respond, but before she can get a word out, her phone starts buzzing like crazy on the couch. With a grimace, she mouths an apology before picking up the offending device, only when she sees the screen, her faces drains of color. Panic spikes in my chest at the sudden change in her demeanor, and I go to place a hand on her shoulder.

Lyla winces slightly when I reach for her, and it's like a knife to the chest. She stopped flinching around me weeks ago, so I can only assume whatever she's looking at either triggered or scared the hell out of her.

"Ly, what is it? What just happened?" My voice is slightly frantic, but the urge to protect her is nearly choking me.

Lyla

Aidan's voice sounds like he's speaking to me from above the surface as I drown underwater. My lungs refuse to expand to take in any oxygen, and the room is getting dark around the edges. The shaking in my hands increases tenfold as I read the headline and messages lighting up my screen again.

"Lyla!" The whisper-bark finally breaks through my frozen moment of panic, and I gasp, a hand automatically coming to rest over my throat. Logically, I know the bruises are long gone, but the phantom feeling of Sebastian's fingers wrapped around my neck makes me feel like I'm being choked all over again.

Large hands cup my face, and panic takes over until the scent of the ocean surrounds me seconds before Aidan's body heat meets my back. He picks me up effortlessly and carries me down the hall to his bedroom, not stopping until we reach his bed. I can hear the movie still playing out in the living room, and my mind immediately goes to Crew.

"Crew?" My voice is little more than a squeak, but thankfully, Aidan hears me anyway.

His eyes warm as he sits down next to me. "Crew is fine, angel. He's out like a light, and you know that kid can sleep through a hurricane."

I nod, the reassurance settling some of the worry in my chest. Warm fingers cover mine, and I'm surprised to find them wrapped so tightly around my phone that my knuckles are white. With a concentrated effort, I release the device, letting it drop into Aidan's hand. I stretch out my fingers with a sigh and direct an embarrassed look his way.

"Sorry I freaked out."

He shakes his head and scoots a few inches closer so our hips are touching. With one calloused finger, he lifts my chin so I'm meeting his icy blue gaze. "You never have to apologize to me, Ly. Do you want to talk about it?"

A month ago, the thought of talking about any of this would have sent me running for the hills, but after deciding to give a relationship with Aidan a real chance, I know he needs the truth when things like this happen. Even if he doesn't *know* that's what I've decided yet. Now isn't the time to tell him anyway.

Sighing, I point to my phone. "A news article came out today and was sent to me anonymously, along with some threatening texts I can only assume are from my ex."

His eyebrows shoot to his hairline, and he doesn't hesitate to unlock the phone and read through the many messages on the screen, his expression growing darker the further he scrolls.

CROSSED UP

> **LIVE** — breakyourownnews.com
>
> **BREAKING NEWS**
> **HOLLYWOOD DARLING MIA?**
> 21:04 — SEBASTIAN PENNINGTON JR. PLEADS PUBLIC TO HELP FIND HIS "TROUBLED" FIANCÉ

UNKNOWN

> I warned you I'd bring you back one way or another, little bunny. Dear old Dad was just heartbroken when I told him you suffered a bout of hysterics and took off. He'd do anything to find out where his precious little girl is.

> Come home and take your place by my side, or your little baseball friend will find out just how long my reach really is. This behavior is unacceptable for a Pennington.

> After all, it would be a shame if everyone had to find out just how mentally unstable you are.

> You have two weeks. Close your legs and get your ungrateful ass back home where you belong.

Aidan chokes suddenly, looking to me with wide eyes.

I roughly drag my hands over my eyes, knowing exactly what he's about to say. I'm likely smearing my ruined mascara even further down my face, but I can't bring myself to care. The man has seen me mid-panic attack. What's a little raccoon eyes?

"Lyla Taylor Kingsley? You mean to tell me your daddy is *Colin Kingsley*?"

The corner of my mouth turns up in a small smirk because he just sounds so *southern* when he's feeling big emotions. "I'm pretty sure we established *you're* my daddy. But yes, Colin is my father."

Realization dawns on his handsome face, and he grips my hand between his. "So the revolving door of nannies, being ignored when you were sick, the loneliness and aversion to social media?"

I nod with a shrug. "A byproduct of being the daughter of one of the most famous actors in the world while having no talent or notable skills of my own."

His expression freezes as he turns toward me on the bed, placing one knee up on the bed and grabbing my face in his hands. "Lyla Taylor, that is absolutely not true. You are one of the kindest, smartest, most generous people I know. And for someone who grew up without a reliable parent, you've become one of the most important parental figures in Crew's life. That, to me, is proof you're so much more talented than you think."

A smile easily emerges on my face at his words. "Thanks, Aid."

He returns the smile briefly before growing serious again. "As for your ex, I promise it will be okay. I won't let this motherfucker anywhere near you ever again. I know you don't know Copeland well yet, but when he decides he likes someone, he'll go to bat for them without question. And the man is as persistent as a leech after pond-swimming when he sets his mind to something, so having him on your side through all this is a great thing."

Sighing, I rest my head on Aidan's shoulder. "Getting off the bus in Charleston was the best decision I ever made."

22
Aidan

"I think I'm going to be sick."

My gaze flies to the right, where Lyla sits in the passenger seat of my truck, clutching the 'oh shit' handle for dear life. "Angel, you have nothing to be worried about. Mama is gonna love you."

I woke up holding Lyla in my arms this morning, both of us having crashed after we joined Crew back out in the fort, and for a few blissful seconds, I forgot that she wasn't really mine. I got to imagine I was waking up in our home with my girl wrapped around me for the first time and that Crew knew everything.

Her shooting up and out of my arms to the other side of Crew was a rude wake-up call I wasn't prepared for after the best night's sleep I've ever had.

She sighs exasperatedly. "Of course you'd say that. You have no reason to be nervous! She's *your* mother."

A snort escapes, and I give her a sidelong glance. "Have you ever met a southern mom, Ly? She'll be sweet as sugar to you and then turn around and hit me with the third degree the second she can get me alone. I promise Mama'll be so enthralled with you she'll try to have us married off before supper."

"Yeah, Lyly! Memama always says me and Daddy need a pretty girl around to keep us in line!" Crew chimes in sweetly, making me laugh.

Apparently, our words didn't inspire any confidence because her knuckles visibly tighten, turning white with how hard she's gripping that handle in her tiny little fist.

What woke me from my state of bliss this morning was my Ma calling me demanding we come to the house for lunch today so she could meet Crew's nanny. Little does she know she'll also be meeting her future daughter-in-law.

Or she will be if Lyla doesn't end up shooting me down after our little chat yesterday.

I'm still feeling pretty raw and emotionally wrung out after all the confessions yesterday, but as long as I don't let myself think too hard about what had her running in the first place, finally knowing Lyla's real identity is a huge weight off my chest. Learning what and *who* she's been so afraid of, though? That felt like being kicked in the thigh by a spooked horse.

The moment our tires hit the old dirt road, I grip her free hand and squeeze it, probably harder than I should. Her head whips around, and she stares at me with wide eyes but doesn't try to get me to let go.

"Aidan, what's up?"

I shake my head, heart pounding in a staccato rhythm against my ribs. Every time I make the turn down this road, nausea bubbles in my gut, and my heart threatens to expel itself out of my body through my mouth.

"Even though Wes and I pooled our money together to tear the trailer down and build Mama a nice little house, she didn't want to leave the plot of land where we grew up."

Lyla reads between the lines and gasps, her eyes darting frantically around the road before finally landing on the only piece of this place that still holds power over me.

The two small pieces of wood threaten to send me spiraling into a mess of flashbacks every time I dare make the trek to visit Mama. I've asked her repeatedly to take it down, but if there's one thing Shelly Black is firm on, it's Southern fuckin' hospitality.

So even though her piece of shit husband beat us all within inches of our lives on a regular basis, she won't dare touch the handmade cross our local pastor put up to honor his memory. It's not enough that the cross sits directly in front of the stump that we hit, but there's also a fresh goddamned bouquet of flowers every time I pass it.

Mama's never said outright if she was the one who left the flowers, but she also hasn't denied it. That cross is the reason Wesley refuses to come down here unless he absolutely has to, and because he's the prodigal son, she lets him get away with it and goes to him.

Whereas the one time *I* tried to get out of coming for Saturday lunch, she told Crew she couldn't wait to see him and forced my hand.

Lyla looks back to check on Crew and then moves the center console up so she can buckle herself into the middle seat. Resting her head on my shoulder, she places a small hand on my thigh. No words are said, but as we pass the spot where my father lost his life, I breathe a little easier than I ever have before.

Soon enough, we're bumping down the short driveway with the house clearly in view. Even though the land holds painful memories, I feel a sense of pride every time I see this house. Building our mother her dream home after she spent her entire life putting us first was something I never thought we'd be able to do, but it makes me even more grateful for the life I live.

"This house is darling!"

I smile over at Ly and place my hand on top of hers as we park. "When I was first drafted, I saved every cent I could in case I washed out of the majors and was left without a backup plan. I wasn't doin' too well in my college classes. I mean, shoot, I barely graduated high school. Thankfully, I didn't wash out. My rookie year was amazing, but then Crew showed up, and I had a whole new reason to save."

"At that point, Mama was still living in the trailer we grew up in with Wes, who was in his senior year of high school and being scouted by a few different teams. We got together and decided that if he was signed on with a decent contract, we'd pool our resources and tear down that godforsaken health hazard and build her somethin' real nice. She's been living here just over three years now and has the time of her life decorating it for every birthday, holiday, and season change."

Lyla laughs lightly, and it seems like her nerves have faded some, which I'm grateful for because Mama is standing on the porch, bouncing on her toes in excitement. Her silver-blonde hair is pulled back into a long braid, and it makes her look a good ten years younger than she is.

I offer a reassuring smile and squeeze Lyla's hand. "Just be yourself. I promise she's going to love you."

She takes a deep breath and sighs loudly. "Let's go."

Mama rushes to the bottom of the steps and sweeps my girl up into one of her famous hugs, rocking her back and forth.

Lyla visibly tenses for only a moment, and then she melts into the embrace.

Pulling back, my mom holds her by the shoulders, closely examining her face with a look of affection. "I hear you've been takin' real good care of my boys."

A blush heats Lyla's cheeks, and she shrugs. "I'm trying my best. They've been taking care of me too."

Mama nods sagely, wrapping an arm over my girl's shoulders. "Any woman who can wrangle my boys and make 'em this happy is good in my book. Welcome to the family, young lady."

Crew's squealing laughter brings a wide smile to my face at the same time I feel a presence at my side. Mama sidles up next to me with her own smile, watching Lyla chase Crew around the huge swing set.

"She sure is a pretty little thing, ain't she? Seems like Crew's really taken with her."

My smile gets wider. "He adores her. Hiring Lyla was the best decision I've ever made."

She nods. "Mhmm, I'll just bet it was."

Glancing over, I see her with a mischievous smirk on her sun-weathered face. "What's that look for, Mama?" I ask suspiciously.

"The way you look at her reminds me of those romance books Wren and I read for our monthly book club."

My eyes widen slightly, but I work to school my expression. "I don't know what you mean."

She snorts and smacks my arm. "Don't lie to your Mama, boy. I was there when you got your first crush, and hopefully, I'll be around for your last. Either way, I know when someone catches one of my son's attention. And like it or not, that woman out there has caught yours."

The sigh that I let out is heavy with the events of the past month and a half, and for the first time in years, I feel like confiding in one of my family members. "I really like her, Ma. I might even love her. But she has a lot going on, and I'm worried she's going to take off without giving us a chance."

I watch her face closely for any disappointment, but the only thing I see in her eyes is pride. Her arm goes around my waist, and she guides me to the small swing on the back porch, where we'll have a perfect view of Lyla and Crew as they play.

"Did I ever tell you about the man I almost married?

My head whips to the side, my eyes like saucers as I stare at my mother incredulously. "I thought Dad was your first boyfriend?"

She nods slowly. "And he was. But he broke up with me to go to college, and I started dating someone else. The man, Henry, was..." she sighs. "He was everything my parents wanted for me, and he was wonderful. He was kind, smart, wealthy, and incredibly handsome. I liked him quite a bit more than I expected to, but just a few short months into our courtship, I found out I was pregnant."

If I thought my eyes couldn't get any wider, I was wrong. "Wait, so Dad...?"

"Goodness, no. Unfortunately, David was your

biological father. I was nearly four months along when I found out, and Henry, the honorable man that he was, asked to marry me anyway. But I felt quite a bit of misplaced loyalty to David, so his father, your granddaddy, forced David to drop out of college. We were married in the courthouse two weeks later. I found out years later he was flunking out, and that's the real reason he agreed to come home so readily. Wesley was the product of a family wedding and too much tequila, and by that point, I didn't feel like I could leave."

The light in her eyes dims, but her gaze on me feels more affectionate right now than it has since the accident. "I could never regret you, my boy. But I know I haven't been a very good Mama to you the last decade. My entire identity was wrapped up in David, and once he died, I felt... an odd combination of devastated and relieved. It's taken me much too long to come to terms with the choices I made, and for that you have my sincerest apologies, Aidan."

My shoulders sag as I scrub a hand down my face and pull her into a tight hug. "I love you, Mama. I forgive you."

Her blue eyes are a little watery, but she looks relieved that I've accepted her apology. Wiping underneath one eye, she beams up at me. "And I promise to be much more present in your life from now on. Especially if I'm going to have a darling daughter-in-law to spend time with."

"Let's not get ahead of ourselves, yeah? She hasn't even agreed to be my girlfriend yet. She could still turn tail and run the other direction. After all, what fresh out of college twenty-three-year-old wants to hitch her wagon to a guy with a kid and a demanding career?"

Mama smirks and uses her pointer finger to turn my head towards the swings, where I see Lyla staring at me with a soft smile on her pretty pink lips as she pushes my son. "One that looks at you like *that*."

Lyla

23

"Crew-bug, we need to go!"

"I'm ready, Lyly!"

Wren decided to work from home today rather than attend the Raptor's last practice before the season opener this Thursday against New York, so Crew and I are heading over to play in their newly installed pool.

It's been a few days since I met Aidan's mom, and she's been texting me every day about all kinds of things. She also officially invited me to join the monthly book club she's in with Wren and Rhodes's mom, Kaci.

Crew comes bounding down the stairs in his neon pink swim trunks and white rash guard, making me smile. I told Aidan he needed to buy Crew a neon swimsuit if we were going to be in water at all, just in case, and it looks like he took my words to heart.

"You look so handsome, Crew-bug! I love the new swimsuit."

He giggles and does a little spin, showing off his trunks and the matching Crocs I didn't notice earlier. "You said you like pink, so I got the pink ones!"

My mouth opens in surprise, and my hand automatically comes up to hover over my chest. I made an offhand comment a few weeks ago that pink is one of my favorite colors, but I didn't really think he was listening since we were also watching *Tinker Bell* at the time.

"Crew..." I can't help the way my voice comes out all choked, and just like his father, Crew's eyes widen in a panic.

"Lyly! Why are you sad? Did I do something wrong? I'm sorry!" His eyes start getting watery, and he barrels into my legs, holding on so tight I belatedly wonder if he'll leave bruises.

I manage to dislodge him so I can drop to my knees and pull him into my arms. "I'm not sad, sweetie. I'm *so* happy that you picked my favorite color. You're the sweetest kid I've ever met."

When I pull back, he's back to smiling. "Love you, Lyly!" he chirps happily.

My heart threatens to explode inside my chest, but I quickly respond. "I love you too, Crew!" Clearing my throat, I grab my large beach bag off the counter and guide him toward the door. "Alright, little raptor. Let's go see Auntie Wren!"

His cheers are our soundtrack the whole way to their house, and Wren meets us at the car with their grey Newfoundland, Finnegan, trailing close behind. The dog is a massive sweetheart and never more than a few feet away from Wren whenever they're at home.

"There's my pumpkin butter! Gah, look at you! I think you've grown an entire foot since I last saw you," Wren exclaims dramatically.

Crew screeches with laughter as she tickles him, and he manages to answer her between breaths. "That's because I'm growing up! Lyly said I had a…" He looks to me for confirmation, and I mouth the words so he can say them. "Grow spit!"

I snicker. "*Growth spurt*, Crew-bug. But you were close!"

Making my way over to Wren, I pull her in for a tight hug. She stiffens slightly in surprise, but her smile is miles wide when she pulls back.

I think this might be the first time I've willingly initiated close contact like that with her, and I'm surprised at how much I liked it. I didn't come from an affectionate upbringing, and though there have been casual touches with both Aidan and Crew, they're really the only ones.

I've been friends with Wren for over a year now, but because I was still healing physically and emotionally from everything Sebastian put me through, I've always kept an intentional physical distance from Wren and Rhodes, especially Rhodes. He's a big guy and made me incredibly nervous despite his obvious kindness.

Wren must see the change come over my face because her expression softens, and she's quick to turn Crew towards the house. "Kaci is here, too, so we'll get him a snack if you need a second."

Gratefulness washes over me at her kindness, so I nod and do what she said, taking a second to sit on the front porch swing and pet Finn when he plops his head in my lap.

"I really do love Crew, Finny. But if I'm honest… I think I might love his Dad, too."

I know Aidan's at practice, but I send him a text anyway just so he knows I'm thinking about him. A snort escapes me when I notice his contact name. He must have gotten my phone and changed it at some point.

> ME:
>
> Love Crew's new swim trunks! :)

We really need to sit down and have that talk, but there just hasn't been time. And now, with the season opener only two days away, there likely won't be any time before then, either. I don't want to distract him before their first game against their fiercest competition for the World Series this year.

> DADDY
>
> I'm glad. This really hot girl told me he needed to be wearing neon colors for safety reasons, and she seems like she knows what she's talking about 😉

> ME
>
> *eye roll* *middle finger emoji*

> DADDY
>
> I see you woke up and chose violence today, angel. Do I need to fuck the sass out of you when I get home?

Holy shit. It's not that warm outside, but I'm suddenly flushed.

> ME
>
> You're welcome to try 😏

> DADDY
>
> Fucking hell, angel. Now I have to go back to practice and try to hide a raging hard-on. I want you in my bed when I get home tonight. Completely naked. Understand?

> ME
>
> Yes, Daddy.

> **DADDY**
> Goddammit.

Wren drops down next to me on the swing, making me squeak. "Jesus, Wren. You scared me," I say with a hand to my chest over my racing heart.

She snickers. "Yeah, 'cause you were so wrapped up in texting Aidannn." The way she sings his name has me rolling my eyes slightly, but I smile guiltily back at her.

"Sorry for leaving you guys with Crew. I just wanted to check in with Aid and let him know where we were."

Okay, so maybe I fibbed just a tiny bit. But Wren doesn't need to know her friend just threatened to fuck the sass out of me later.

Her shoulders lift in a delicate shrug. "You know I love hanging out with him. And if you need a minute alone, that's okay. Even better if it's a second spent talking to your boyfriend." She grins after the last word with a pointed glance at the cell phone still poised in my hand. She's enjoying this turn of events far too much.

"He's not my boyfriend," I grumble.

"Maybe not *yet*, but judging by the look on your face, it's only a matter of time."

A blush creeps up my cheeks, but she's right. "I left Maryland so I could start a new life away from Sebastian and out from under the influence of my father's fame. And that's exactly what I did! I've been supporting myself. I've been healing. I did the work on my own and built a life for myself here. It might not have been much, but it's mine."

Tears fill my eyes, spilling over with each blink. "I'm scared that by starting a relationship with Aidan, I would essentially be putting myself in the same position I was in with Sebastian, with no space or income of my own."

I'm expecting some words of wisdom or a classic pep talk, but she simply shrugs. "That's exactly what you'll be doing."

I stare at her blankly.

Wren rolls her eyes and takes my free hand in hers. "The biggest difference is you'll be with *Aidan*. The same kind, patient man who agreed to give my friend an interview when she needed a job just because I asked him. The same man who always puts everyone else first, even if it hurts him to do it."

Crew's bright laughter reaches us from inside, making both of us smile even as I wipe away tears.

"There's another very important difference this time, Ly," She says. "*You* aren't the same twenty-year-old naïve little girl anymore. You said it yourself! You went to therapy, did the work, and built a beautiful life with a brand new family that loves you unconditionally. You don't have to be alone forever, Lyla. Don't let the actions of one awful man make you doubt your judgment."

Taking a deep breath, I squeeze her hand. "You should think about being an inspirational speaker, Wrenny. You'd be great at it."

Crew must hear our laughter because he comes barreling out the front door and dives onto my lap, making the swing rock back against the house. "Woah there, little raptor! Let's not break Aunty Wren's swing, yeah?"

He giggles, settling himself on my lap with a proud grin. "Uncle Rho says it's not fun unless something breaks."

Wren cackles and Kaci's laughter joins the fray as she exits the house. She joins our little group with a shake of her head. "That sounds like something Rhodes and his father would say."

Her smile brightens when she notices me. "Hey, sweetie! You want to come join us in the pool? Crew here is ready and raring to dive in, and I set out snacks for all of us!"

I smile warmly at Rhodes's mom and tickle Crew, my smile growing with his happy squeals. "Absolutely! What do you say, Crew-bug? You ready to swim?"

He hops off my lap, nearly elbowing me in the stomach in the process. "Yes!"

The three of us laugh as he sprints through the house. Looking at these two women who took me in last year without question, I know Wren is right, and I don't have to be afraid to lose everything I've worked for. Dating Aidan will change things, but I have a feeling it will be for the better.

24
Aidan

The thump of my bat bag hitting the foyer floor sounds like a gunshot in the eery silence of my darkened living room. Nearly all the lights are off save for the small one over the stove that Lyla must have left on for me. It's after ten p.m now, more than three hours later than I should have been home, so I don't blame her for not waiting up.

With a sigh of exhaustion, I start going through the closing shift, checking that all windows and doors are locked and checking on Crew upstairs before making my way back down to my bedroom.

Fucking Daniels just had to shoot his mouth off at practice, and because his immature ass was in hot water for talking about the owner's daughter, the rest of us had to run the field for over a goddamn hour before hitting the weight room.

Lyla checked in a few times by text today, but the pictures of her and Crew were my favorite. Wren sent me one of Crew spider-monkeyed to Lyla's back standing next to the pool, and the way they were smiling at each other had my heart threatening to beat straight out of my chest. I immediately made it my phone's background, much to the amusement of Rhodes and Copeland.

Trudging back down the stairs, I pause when my bedroom door comes into view. There's low light coming from in the room, and any tiredness I was feeling dissipates, replaced immediately by anticipation as I recall my text exchange with Lyla earlier.

I'm more grateful than ever that I took a shower before leaving the training facility, so I don't have to stop and do that now, but when I push the door open, I see my girl asleep in my bed, only covered by a thin sheet.

I don't hesitate to strip down and slide in next to her, wrapping her warm body in my arms and taking a deep hit of her perfect cherry-vanilla scent.

All the tension I've been carrying since I threw down the relationship gauntlet a few days ago melts away at the feel of my girl safe in my arms, and I know that in spite of the things I said, I'll wait for her as long as she needs.

I don't remember falling asleep, but I wake what feels like minutes later to wet warmth surrounding my dick. Groaning, I thrust upwards, unsure if I'm dreaming.

The answering gag has my eyes flying open and my heart racing. Throwing off the covers, I see a sleep-tousled Lyla on her knees between my legs, my cock halfway down her throat.

A gravelly moan works its way out of my lips, and my hands fist in the sheets beneath us as I fight the urge to tunnel them into her long hair.

She backs off with a pop and shoots me a wicked grin

I can just barely make out in the soft moonlight flooding through the open windows. "Missed you."

My heart stutters in my chest when I hear the honesty in her voice. Sitting up, I pull her in for a soft kiss. "I missed you too, angel."

"So... I talked to Wren today."

I raise a brow in her direction, but I'm not sure if she can see it. "Odd topic to bring up when you're naked, but alright. And was this a good talk?"

She nods slowly. "I was going to wait until after your game on Thursday, but I don't feel like I can go another day without talking about this."

Fear grips my chest in a vice as my dick deflates, and I wonder if this is where she ends things. "Ly..."

"No, let me get this out. Please."

The pleading tone of her voice gets me, and I shut my mouth so she can continue.

"I've been so afraid that by agreeing to a relationship with you, I would be giving up every piece of independence I fought so hard for since I left Maryland. But today, Wren reminded me that it's okay to not be alone all the time, and that I'm not weak if I choose you and Crew. I'm still scared and I still have things to work on in regard to my past, but if you'll have me, I want to be yours."

My breath whooshes out as a wide grin overtakes my face. "Daggum, Lyla. I wasn't sure you would ever agree to be mine."

She smiles shyly and curls further into me. "Does that mean you still want me? Want this?"

I scoff, pulling her in for a deep, licking kiss. "I've never wanted anyone the way I want you, honey," I pause, contemplating my next words.

"It might be too soon, and I don't expect you to say it

back, but I love you, Lyla Taylor Kingsley. I love you because of the way you love my son and the way you treat me like I matter. You showed up in our lives and, in no time at all, became this person we can't imagine living without anymore. This new life we're starting is scary, yes, but as long as I have you and Crew by my side, I know it's going to be incredible."

She doesn't say she loves me back, but the look in her eyes as she smiles softly up at me is confirmation enough for now.

Lyla bites her lip as she trails a lone finger down my chest, and I'm instantly reminded we've been having this heartfelt talk buck naked.

"You know, I'm still feeling pretty sassy," she whispers.

My blood heats, and my erection pulses against my abs. "Oh?" I pull her even closer, adjusting her so she straddles my lap. Her wet heat brushes against my rapidly swelling cock, and I bite back a grin when she whimpers. Bringing my lips to her ear, I thrust against her ever so slightly. "Does my sassy girl still need me to fuck her into an attitude adjustment?"

She nods, grinding her dripping core over my dick and trapping it against my abs. "Please!"

"Please, what?" I growl under my breath.

"Please, fuck me, Daddy."

The last thin threads of my control snap, and I lunge, flipping us so Lyla lands on her back on the bed. "Such a good girl, asking so nicely. But don't think I'll forget about your little attitude so easily, angel."

Her breathing speeds up, causing me to fight a smirk. "Flip over and lift one knee up and to the side."

She raises an eyebrow but does as I say, and the new

position has me cursing up a storm. "Look at that pretty pussy on display for Daddy. Are you wet for me, too, angel?"

A nod is my only response, so I slap the inside of her thigh, making her yelp. "Words, Lyla."

"Yes! I've been wet for you since you told me to be in your bed when you got home."

"Hmm, I think I better check."

With that, I get down to my stomach and slide in so my face is even with her core. I can see she's already dripping, but I'm dying for a taste. Leaning in, I breathe deeply and release a guttural groan. "Sweet girl, it's been too long since I had my face buried in your perfect pussy."

My tongue gently parts her folds, and I moan at the taste. She squirms, nearly dislodging my mouth, so I band one arm across her pelvis to hold her in place. Circling my tongue around her clit, I revel in her muffled whimpers and glance up to see she's buried her face in my pillow in an effort to stay quiet.

"This room is soundproofed, angel. So move your face because I want to hear you screaming my name when you come on my tongue."

Lyla's cries increase in volume as I put more pressure on her clit with my tongue, and then I'm dipping two fingers into her slick heat and curling them upward. Her hips fly up, pushing her further into my mouth.

"Fuuuck, that's it, baby."

"Aidan!"

"You look so pretty when you're soaking my face, angel."

Keeping up the pressure on her clit, I watch with smug satisfaction as she shatters, her core pulsing around my fingers.

"Holy shit," she breathes. Her chest is heaving, and when she turns her head to the side, I can see that her eyes are sleepy, but I sit up and yank her closer to me.

"Did you think we were done already, Lyla? You asked me to fuck the sass out of you, and that's exactly what I plan to do," I growl the words against her spine between open-mouthed kisses placed on her warm skin.

Not wanting to waste another second with my girl, I slide inside her on one long thrust. Lyla whines as I curse. "It shouldn't be possible for it to feel this fucking good, Ly. I swear you were made just for me."

I shift her leg up higher toward her chest, and it puts me at a new angle that hits her g-spot every time, forcing a strangled cry from her lips.

"Fuck, I'm going to come again," she pants, turning her head into the pillow as she visibly shudders.

With quick movements, I flip her so she's on her back underneath me. "Need to see your face when you come on Daddy's cock."

"Oh, god!"

I growl under my breath and take her mouth in a fierce kiss. "Whose cock is inside of you right now, Lyla? Because it sure as hell isn't god."

"Daddy!"

My thrusts pick up speed, lightning licking up my spine the closer I get to release. "That's fucking right. Now come for Daddy, angel. I wanna feel you clenching around me when I come."

My words tip her over the edge, and she comes hard, screaming her release and doing exactly as I asked. She clenches around me so tight I have no choice but to follow her into oblivion.

After taking a few minutes to catch my breath, I pull

out with the intention of cleaning us both up, only the sight of my cum dripping out of her swollen pink folds stops me in my tracks. Placing my hands on her legs, I spread her even further apart to admire the sight in front of me.

"Fuck," I murmur. "I'm pretty sure I've died and gone to Heaven."

Lyla giggles beneath me, not doing a goddamn thing to hide herself from me. "Pretty sure what we just did is getting us both sent to Hell."

I shrug, my eyes still locked on my own personal wet dream. "With you? I'm pretty sure even the ninth circle of Hell would feel like the best kind of Heaven."

Dragging my fingers through our combined wetness, I push it back inside of her, biting my lip. "I know you have an IUD, but the thought of putting my baby inside of you gets me so fucking hard I can barely think straight."

Her eyes darken with want, making something in my body light up with excitement. Leaning forward, I stroke my fingers down her cheek and grip her chin. "Do you want that, angel? You want to have my babies someday soon and give Crew some little brothers and sisters?"

Biting her plush bottom lip, she nods slowly. "But that's crazy, right? We've only officially been together," she glances at the clock on my nightstand and snorts. "An hour."

I shrug for the second time in ten minutes. "If you're crazy, I should be locked up for the thoughts I've been having about you for weeks now. Who cares if other people think we're moving too fast? Last time I checked, our relationship decisions weren't up for a public vote."

Kissing her nose, I smile at her affectionately. "As long

as you and Crew are happy, I'm ready for everything with you, gorgeous. And that includes telling Crew about us."

Her eyes widen in panic, so I cup her face in my hands, doing my best to reassure her with my eyes. "It's going to be fine, Ly. You were there at the park and know Crew wants you to be his mom. He's going to be over the goddamn moon when we tell him."

Some of the panic recedes with a long sigh, and her body loses some of its tension. "I just don't want him to get hurt if we don't work out."

I roll my eyes at her and go in for a deep kiss, sweeping my tongue over hers and savoring everything that is *Lyla*. "That one's easy. There's not a single scenario in which we don't end up together."

Lyla

25

You know how some days are just awful from the start? And I don't mean waking up on the wrong side of the bed kind of awful. I mean waking up in a puddle of your own blood with cramps sent straight from the devil himself as your phone buzzes with texts from your crazy ex-fiancé. That's how my day is starting.

Aidan is still snoring quietly by the time I manage to shower and make it back to bed, but the stain on his sheets sends me into a tailspin. I wasn't due to start my period for another few days, but I should have known better than to sleep naked in his bed just in case.

His startling blue eyes flutter open, and he gazes at me with a sleepy smile until he sees the fear I'm sure is written all over my face. He shoots straight up in bed and scrubs his fists over his eyes.

If I weren't so worried about his reaction, I'd be gushing about how cute and boyish he looks when he does that.

"Angel, what's wrong?"

"I-I'm sorry. I swear I'll get you new sheets. I wasn't supposed to start yet and—"

"Lyla!" he barks.

It startles me out of my rambling enough that I'm able to turn wide eyes his way.

Aidan scoots off the bed slowly and crouches in front of me on his knees before cupping my face in his big hands. "Hush, baby. Take a deep breath and tell Daddy what's wrong."

A hiccup is the only sound I can make at first, but after an inhale and exhale to the count of five, I'm calm enough to speak again. "I started my period early, and I got blood on the sheets. I'm so sorry, Aidan. I didn't mean to, and wouldn't have fallen asleep in here if I'd known I was going to start."

His brows furrow in confusion, but instead of being annoyed or frustrated, he just sighs and pulls me to his chest. "Ly... why on earth would I be upset about something you have no control over?"

I shrug, leaning my cheek against his warm skin and tracing the tattoo of mine and Crew's birthday that sits over his heart. "I figured you wouldn't want to share a bed with me until I was done."

He stiffens against me, and his expression is thunderous when I lean back to look at his face. "Your period doesn't turn you into a leper, Lyla. There's not a single goddamn thing on this earth that would make me not want you in my bed, but especially something that's completely natural. For fuck's sake, I just told you I want you to have my babies, and you think a little blood is going to scare me off?"

Something clicks in my brain with his words, and I sag against him, burying my nose where his neck and shoulder meet. "I'm sorry," I murmur with a kiss to his neck. "I think I just found something new to talk about with my therapist."

He heaves a breath, softening minutely. "What did he do to make you so afraid of your own body, sugar?"

Tears spring to my eyes in record time, both at the term of endearment and from the reminder of life with Sebastian. "He made me sleep in a separate bedroom every month when I'd get my period. Only with the IUD, it's not always regular. So whenever it would show up randomly and catch me off guard, I would have to hide the evidence from Sebastian, my ex, so he didn't get angry and take it out on me."

Aidan's anger is so visceral he's shaking with the force of it, but knowing it's directed at Bas and not me eases the remaining fear I felt seeing my blood on his sheets this morning.

Blowing out a deep breath, he crushes me to him, his words sounding like they've been dragged through gravel on the way out. "Listen to me, angel. You never, and I do mean *never,* have to be afraid of my reaction to anything. Especially not something like this. You're precious to me, Lyla. Every single part of you. And if you think I'm going to be upset because of something that indicates you're healthy, you're dead wrong."

"I know. I'm not afraid of you, Aidan. I don't think I ever was. But this is one of those things I didn't realize would be a trigger until it happened."

"I know, baby. And we'll work through it together."

I open my mouth to thank him, but he shocks me when he places one of his warm hands directly over my uterus. "Are you in pain? How bad does it usually get?"

My mouth gapes, and I'm sure I look like a fish out of

water, but I can't seem to formulate a response. I shouldn't be surprised he's asking because Aidan is so purely *good*. Of course he's asking about my period symptoms.

Shaking off the shock, I smile softly. "The first day or two are pretty bad, but they're way worse without the IUD. That's actually why I got it in the first place."

He nods, a pensive frown covering his handsome face. I yelp when he picks me up suddenly and carries me into his massive en-suite bathroom. All the cabinets in here are done in the same sage green as the kitchen, and heated white tile floors and gold accents complete the modern design.

My jaw is still hanging partially slack when he sets me down on the cold countertop, but he just smirks at me and moves to the tub across the room, turning it on. I look on in stunned silence while Aidan prepares what looks like an epic bubble bath in his oversized freestanding tub.

He throws in bath salts that fill the room with the scent of eucalyptus and mint and enough bubbles that the mountain it creates would cover a grown man and absolutely *bury* me. When he turns back to me with an expectant look, I just raise a brow at him.

He rolls his eyes with a dramatic huff and stomps back over to me, picking me up bridal style and dropping me into the steaming water. The action reminds me so much of Crew that I have to stifle a laugh at his expense.

The bubbles completely overtake me, just like I thought they would, and Aidan's laughter booms through the space. His large hands part the bubbles like Moses and the Red Sea, and then I'm face to gorgeous face with my new boyfriend's wide smile and pink cheeks.

"You said you were in pain, and Epsom salt baths

always help me when my muscles are sore. Do you want some pain meds? I have regular and extra strength."

"Extra strength would be great, thanks. But you know you don't have to do all of this, right? I'm a big girl, Aid. I've been taking care of myself for a long time now."

Aidan meets my incredulous look head-on with a single arched brow, grin still firmly in place but softening the longer he studies my face. He lifts his hands to cup my cheeks and plants a gentle kiss on the tip of my nose. "I know you have. And you're probably the strongest woman I know. But one benefit of having a partner, a *family*, is that you don't have to do it all on your own anymore. You want my burdens? I get yours, too."

Another kiss, this time on my forehead. "Let me take care of my girl."

I nod silently, something akin to pain rolling through me at the sincerity in his tone. My entire life, I've been seen and not heard. My father was too busy to do the whole parenting thing, my nannies never treated me as anything more than a paycheck, and to Sebastian, I was a means to an end. A plaything.

And then along came Aidan. Aidan, with his sweet smiles and happy disposition. Who's selfless to a fault and is raising the most kind-hearted little boy I've ever met. The man who broke down every single one of my sky-high walls and implanted himself so deep in to my heart I can't foresee ever getting him out.

It's for all of those reasons I let my reservations go and offer a hesitant nod in response to his words. And when his eyes light up before he rushes off to get me pain medicine? I know I'd agree to just about anything to keep that look on his face.

After an obnoxiously long bath and a massage Aidan insisted on giving me, I feel as good as new and ready to face the day ahead. Today is Aidan's last day before the season opener, so he decided to skip their last optional practice and stay home with Crew and me so we can tell him about our relationship.

Thanks to our morning activities, I've just sat down with my coffee *much later than usual* when Crew comes flying through the French doors and launches himself onto the swing next to me.

He tucks himself into my side with a contented sigh and an exuberant, "Morning, Lyly!"

I toss an arm around his shoulders and kiss the top of his head, loving the smell of his watermelon shampoo. "Good morning, Crew-bug!"

Just then, Aidan joins us on the deck, his own coffee in hand and a nervous grin on his face as he sits down on the swing, propping a single knee up on the seat so he's facing us. "Raptor, do you know what a girlfriend is?"

My cheeks flame as my lips part in surprise.

Okay, guess we're diving right in then.

Crew's little face scrunches up in contemplation before he nods excitedly. "Uncle Rho told me all about girlfriends! He said I'll probably have one when I go to school. He said when you really like someone, you ask her to be your girlfriend! He also said sometimes boys kiss their girlfriends, but that's *gross*, Dad."

Aidan snickers at his son's shudder of disgust. I just smile because I love this age. Kids are so open and expressive with their emotions and opinions, and the thought of like-liking the opposite sex is still horrifying.

"That's right. When you're an adult and you find a girl you really like, you can ask her to be your girlfriend."

Crew just nods like this is obvious, but a suspicious look crosses his face that makes him look far older than six. "Do you want a girlfriend, Daddy?"

Aidan shakes his head slowly. "Actually, raptor, Lyla is my girlfriend now." He pauses to let the information sink in and check with me before his next words, and I nod. I'll go along with whatever he wants to tell him right now, and we can figure out logistics later.

"Is that okay with you? Nothing is going to change right now. She's still going to live here and be your nanny, but she's also going to sleep in my room sometimes, and you'll probably see me kiss her."

I'm bracing for a negative reaction to the bomb his father just dropped, but what I'm not prepared for is the undeniable hope shining back at me from wide, unblinking blue eyes.

"Does this mean you're going to be my mommy?" he whispers. The hope I saw in his eyes is reflected so clearly in his words that tears instantly fill my eyes to the brim before spilling over.

I have no idea how to answer him and I don't want to overstep so I look to Aidan for help only to see his own eyes glassy with unshed tears. I haven't even told him I love him back yet, and we're still so new.

He leans forward, enveloping us both in his long arms as he kisses Crew on the head. Ice blue irises flash with a determination that should make me nervous but instead fills me with a newfound sense of hope. Hope for us, for the future, and all the things I wanted so desperately growing up but was never lucky enough to have.

I pull Crew even tighter to my side without breaking

eye contact with Aidan and speak the words I've been too afraid to say until now. "I don't know if I'll get to be your mommy, Crew. But I think being your mom would be the best thing I've ever been lucky enough to do."

Aidan

26

A loud text tone startles us out of our little bubble on the swing, and when I see Copeland's contact name, I'm instantly on alert.

DETECTIVE COPE
> Hey man, are you guys home? I have some stuff to show Lyla and I assume you'll want to see it too

ME
> Yeah, we're home. Come on over

DETECTIVE COPE
> Be there in ten

The curiosity in Lyla's gaze turns to concern when she sees the look on my face, but I watch her push it down and focus on Crew. When he asked her again if she was going to be his mom, my heart broke into a million pieces and healed in a single moment.

I've never wanted something as much as I want Lyla, and to know that my son, the most important person in my life, loves her as much as I do? It's something I only imagined in my wildest dreams.

Which is why I'm so concerned about Copeland's text. Our little family is brand new, and the thought of anything happening to my girl terrifies me down to my damn bones. The fear of losing Lyla is on par with the fear of losing Crew. And just thinking about the effect that losing her would have on him has anxiety rising dangerously close to the surface.

Small hands trail up my sides and come to rest on my pecs, her left hand landing directly over the inked date on my chest. It doesn't escape my notice that the two loves of my life share a birthday. I was never a big believer in fate, destiny, or the universe, but I can't help but feel like Lyla was meant to be ours.

I heave a sigh, and she definitely doesn't miss it because her arms tighten around me. "What's going on, Aid?"

"Copeland texted. He's on his way over. Apparently, he has something he thinks we need to see."

Her body stiffens against my back, so I grip one of her cold hands in mine and pull her so we're chest to chest. My hands move to cup her cheeks in a gesture meant to reassure myself as much as her. "Whatever it is, we'll handle it together. Okay, angel? You're mine, and ain't letting some egotistical asshat anywhere near my girl."

A small smile breaks across her delicate features. "I love it when you call me your girl."

I take her mouth in a slow, sensual kiss. Our tongues tangling together in a dance that feels so natural you would think we'd been doing it for years, not weeks.

We're both breathless when I finally pull back, and I wrap one hand loosely around the front of her throat.

"Good. Because you are my girl, and I'm ready to make sure the whole damned world knows it."

The doorbell rings, interrupting our moment. "Do you want to start on breakfast? I'll go let Cope in."

I open the front door only for my surly best friend to shove his way past me, his face even stormier than usual and a small box ensconced in his hands. "Well, good morning, sunshine! What could we possibly have done to be graced with such a joyful disposition on this beautiful Wednesday?"

A vicious glare aimed my way is the only response to my sarcasm, and I have no doubt he would be flipping me off, too, if my son wasn't bouncing our way.

"Uncle Cope!" he shrieks. His voice is pitched just so that the shrill sound has my ears ringing.

Copeland's face brightens like it always does when he sees Crew, but the way his whole expression softens when he sees Lyla in the kitchen has white-hot jealousy roaring through my veins. Logically, I know I have nothing to worry about with *either* of them, but that doesn't change the fact I want to throttle my best friend.

"Hey, tiny, how ya doin'?" He greets her with a hug, and my jaw drops. When the hell did these two get so friendly? "I found this bakery that does chocolate cherry cupcakes, and I couldn't leave without grabbing you one."

Lyla squeals with unrestrained joy and pulls Cope back in for an even tighter hug that has my shoulders tightening with tension.

I wonder if I'd be released from the team for strangling my friend over a cupcake.

Cope sees my murderous expression and snorts before leaning down to whisper in Lyla's ear. A low grumble rattles in my throat, and she turns to me with surprise written all over her sweet face. He says something else too low for me to hear and gives her a gentle nudge in my direction before turning to the stove and taking over pancake duty.

Lyla approaches me slowly like I'm a cornered animal, but the second she's in arms reach I yank her to me and growl in her ear. "He's trying to get a rise outta me, and it's fuckin' working. I don't care if he's my best friend. Seeing another man's hands on my girl has me wanting to bend you over and fuck you so hard the only name you'll remember is mine."

Her jaw drops, desire quickly turning her mossy green eyes a stunning shade of emerald. Small hands land on my chest, and my attention is drawn to the soft pink polish on Lyla's fingernails. A vivid memory of those same fingernails wrapped around my cock last night flashes through my mind, forcing me to stifle a groan.

She lowers her voice to a murmur so low I can barely hear her. "Hmm. Are you sure your name is the one you want me to remember?"

I scoff, irritation flaring briefly, but she places her fingers over my mouth with a naughty smirk and yanks me down by the shirt so she can whisper in my ear. "Because if you bend me over and fuck me hard, do you want me to be screaming Aidan? Or do you want me screaming *Daddy*?"

There's no chance of suppressing my pained groan this time, and she giggles before moving back to the kitchen.

I'd think she was completely unaffected if it weren't for the delicate pink blush on her cheeks that I know from experience goes all the way down her chest to her perfect breasts.

Copeland snickers when she makes her way back over and holds his hand up for a high-five, making me roll my eyes. I take a seat at the breakfast bar next to Crew and ruffle his messy hair. "Whatcha doin', raptor?"

His gap-toothed grin makes my heart soar. He's been so happy since Lyla came to live with us, but knowing she and I are together and he might get to call her Mom someday has changed his entire demeanor. His separation anxiety is all but gone. He's sleeping better, eating more than just Mac n' Cheese and chicken nuggets, and learning new things every single day.

"I'm drawing a picture, Daddy. Wanna see?" I nod, and the picture makes my breath catch in my throat. There, in blue marker, are three figures and what looks to be a small cat. Crew enthusiastically explains the drawing, with the smile never once leaving his face. "It's a family picture! See? That's you with your mitt on, and Lyly is next to you. And that's me holding her hand with my kitten, Fish."

The cat is completely unsurprising. Crew's always wanted one. But the thing that has me fighting back waterworks is the messily scrawled "Mommy" above Lyla's head. Blinking away the sheen of tears, I look at my son. "This picture is amazing, raptor! Should we hang it on the fridge and show Ly?"

He nods enthusiastically, and Lyla is still chatting with Cope next to the stove, so I quietly stick the drawing to the fridge with a magnet and grab her hand to pull her to me.

Copeland looks confused for a second until his eyes track to the fridge, and they flare with understanding. He gives me the biggest grin I've seen on his face in years, making this feel all the more real.

My mama loves her, my friends have taken her in as one of us, and my son is practically begging me to marry her and make her his mom.

The only thing that could make this better is hearing Lyla say she loves me, too.

"Lyly! Look at my picture I drawed! Daddy put it on the fridge for you."

Lyla's steps slow when she spots the paper on the refrigerator, her gaze locked on the image. "The picture you *drew*, Crew-bug," she corrects absentmindedly.

Her eyes fill with tears in record time, a few spilling down her cheeks before she swipes them away. Her gaze darts to mine, and I hope she can see my love staring back at her.

Giving my hand a squeeze, she walks over behind Crew and wraps her arms around him, hugging him tight as she kisses the top of his head. "I love it, Crew-bug. Thank you for the wonderful drawing."

He sighs, his small body relaxing under the weight of our girl's arms. "Love you, Lyly."

The tears make a reappearance as she rests her cheek on his head. "Love you more, little raptor."

Copeland clears his throat from the stove next to a ridiculously large stack of pancakes. "Maybe we could eat in the living room today so the little dinosaur can watch a movie?" His unspoken words hang in the air between us, and I nod in agreement, forcing a smile on my face when Crew looks at me in question.

Lyla gets our boy settled at the oversized coffee table with his breakfast and *Tarzan*, and then the three of us open the sliding doors so we can see and hear Crew while we talk.

As soon as we reach the swing, I pull Lyla down so

she's sitting sideways in my lap, desperately needing the contact for whatever Cope has to tell us. She doesn't fight me or seem uncomfortable at all, letting me know she probably needs it as much as I do.

He watches us with a smile until we're settled, and then the expression slides off his face, replaced with something much more grave. "I'm not a baker, so I'm not about to sugarcoat this for you. The feds managed to arrest Sebastian Sr., but they lost his son."

My girl goes stiff as a board, her whole face draining of color, and I barely manage to stop myself from lurching forward. "What do you mean they *lost him?*" I snap.

He sighs, scrubbing a hand down his face. "That's exactly what I mean. The feds had eyes on him twenty-four-seven. When he was at home, work, clubs, parties. They always had someone on him. But then, one day, Sebastian went home after an evening event and just... didn't come out again. He's been MIA for almost a week. He just vanished. His car is at home, there's no charges on his credit cards, all of their planes and cars are accounted for, and his father is vehemently denying any knowledge of his son's whereabouts."

Lyla is shaking in my lap, but her eyes are determined. "Mike... sorry, Sebastian Senior, knows every detail about Bas's life. Has tracking on all of his vehicles and accounts. He was grooming Bas to take over the family business, but he didn't trust him as far as he could throw him. I don't know for sure if he knew what his son was doing to me, but all I can say is Senior's wife wears a *lot* of long-sleeved clothing."

Cope nods like this isn't new information. "From what my contact has been able to tell me, Mrs. Pennington has a concierge doctor on call, and he's made *numerous* trips out to the house for a variety of injuries. The man's NDA is so airtight you could use it to explore the Mariana Trench, which is why nothing has ever made it to the press."

"I didn't see the signs until well after we had gotten engaged, but Bas is just like his father. They're both controlling, calculating, and downright cruel if they don't get their way. During our time together, I'm pretty sure I heard 'That's how you run a billion-dollar business' more than I heard anything else."

"Tiny, I want you to be careful until they can find this bastard. If you have to go somewhere, be aware of your surroundings, and try to make sure you're always in a crowded place if you can."

My hand squeezes the back of my neck, anxiety spiking at the thought of Lyla or Crew in danger. "Should we hire security? How worried do we need to be, Cope?"

His eyes dart to the side, a tell he's had for years that what he's about to say isn't the full truth. "Nah, man. I think just being extra vigilant and not giving him the chance to catch you alone is the safest bet."

"Lyly, I'm done! Can you help me wash my hands?"

A smile lights up my girl's face as she goes to get Crew cleaned up, and I allow myself to watch her for a moment before turning a stern look to my best friend. "What aren't you saying?"

He sighs heavily, raking his hands through his hair. It's then I notice how... exhausted he looks. "Everything go okay during your trip home, Cope? You seem kinda run down."

His brow furrows in frustration. "For the most part, just more shit with my sister. You know how it goes."

I nod in understanding. Copeland's youngest sister,

Olivia, is a junior in high school and has been acting out since their dad died last year. Cope's been home as often as possible to help his mom out, but they live in Charlotte, so it's a bit of a drive, especially during the season when we rarely have more than a day or two off at a time.

He visibly shakes off the stress and steers the conversation back to Sebastian. "This guy is dangerous, Aidan. The feds found some majorly fucked up stuff in his house and office. Multiple restraining orders and assault allegations against him were all swept under the rug because Daddy threw money at the problems until they went away. You should probably hire security but don't tell Lyla. Have him follow her and hang back, just as a precaution. Because I don't see this guy going away quietly now that the feds are after him."

The idea of another man protecting Ly makes me nauseous, but her safety is undoubtedly in question, and I'm not willing to risk her or Crew over a bit of male pride. Now that the season is starting, it's even more important that we have someone around who can protect my family, even if it means hiding it from her.

If Sebastian tries to fuck with my girl, there'll be hell to pay. I've been fighting for what I want my whole life, and I'm sure as hell not going to stop now.

27 Lyla

UNKNOWN:

I warned you, little bunny.

You chose not to come home, so you've forced my hand.

Just remember, I didn't want it to come to this. If you'd behaved like a good little wife, we'd be honeymooning on a beach in Italy somewhere, but you had to go and be a whore.

See you soon, darling.

Shivers race down my spine at the blatant threat in Sebastian's texts, and I once again forward them to Copeland. Hearing that the feds couldn't find Bas threw me for a loop and threatened to send me spiraling, but Aidan's warm body underneath mine kept me from completely losing it.

We spent the rest of the day together after Cope left, and after we read Crew his stories, Aidan dragged me to his bed and held me all night long, stroking my hair and whispering assurances that everything would be okay. I know Copeland said we didn't need security, but I've considered dipping into my trust fund to hire someone anyway.

If I'm going to be out and alone with Crew, I want an extra layer of protection for him in case Bas somehow manages to get to me.

Crew is still sleeping, and Aidan is at the field already, so I take the opportunity to make the one call I've been dreading for over a year now. Each ring of the phone ratchets my heart rate higher, but I left my number unblocked, so I have a tiny sliver of hope that he'll answer.

"Hello?"

A sob catches in my throat when my father's deep timbre sounds over the line. He may have been absent for most of my childhood, but he's still my dad. "Dad?"

His quiet inhale acts as a balm to the part of my soul that worried he wouldn't care if I was gone. "Lyla, honey, is that you?"

Tears stream down my cheeks. "It's me, Dad."

"Where are you? Why does everyone think you ran out on Sebastian?"

Taking a deep breath, my words barely come out as more than a murmur. "Because I did."

"Why would you do that? Do you know how worried we've all been about you? You've been gone for *months*, Lyla Taylor. Where the hell have you been?"

"Dad, just stop for a second!" I rarely raise my voice so it has the desired effect, and he goes silent on the other end of the phone.

"A year and a half ago, Sebastian beat me bloody and nearly choked me to death. It wasn't the first time he'd hurt me, but I made sure it was the last. I managed to subdue him long enough that I was able to pack up the things I couldn't live without and get the hell out of dodge. I hopped on a bus with no destination in mind and ended up in Charleston, South Carolina, where I've been ever since."

The silence is deafening for a long moment, only to be broken by a growl. "Please tell me this is some elaborate joke, and you're just going through a delayed rebellious phase that made you want to run off to sow your wild oats."

At least it's not an outright refusal to believe me.

"I have pictures from each time it happened on a flash drive here. I have to hand them over to the FBI next week, but if you're ever in the area, I can show you. But please know they aren't pretty." I heave a sigh. "I just... I couldn't do it anymore, Dad. It took a year of intensive therapy to deal with what I went through, and now that I've finally found some happiness again, Bas is back and threatening to hurt my family if I don't come back to Maryland."

"I'll fucking kill him."

The line goes dead, and I'm left staring at the phone in shock. Of all the things I expected him to say, it sure as hell wasn't anything resembling anger on my behalf. I know my father, though, and when he sets his mind to something, he won't be persuaded otherwise.

The alarm on my phone beeps, reminding me I need to get Crew up and dressed for the game. The security guy I hired should be here within the hour, and he's going to tail us at the season opener today. The security guard already has season tickets, so it was a win-win all around.

When I reach his bedroom, Crew is already awake and halfway dressed, his features bright with elation about our plans for the day. He's been talking about this game for weeks now, and I can't wait to experience it with him.

"Well, look who's bright-eyed and bushy-tailed this morning!"

He giggles madly, his enthusiasm causing him to be even more wiggly than normal, resulting in his head being stuck in the arm of his shirt. "Lyly, help!"

I snicker and ruffle his hair when we finally manage to right his shirt, his smile never wavering. "We need to brush your hair and teeth before we can leave. Can you do that by yourself or do you need help?"

"I can do it by myself! Promise. I'll brush them real good."

Raising a brow at him, I lean down so we're eye to eye. "Top *and* bottom teeth? *Two* rounds of *Twinkle Twinkle*?"

His enthusiastic nod is answer enough for me, so I set up his toothbrush and let him at it so I can finish getting my own things ready.

Aidan told me he loved me again before he left this morning, and I think it's high time I tell him I love him, too. The glittery sign on the counter is finally dry, and Wren should have a bouquet of blue roses for me at the stadium.

I've kept my feelings for this man quiet out of fear of my ex finding us, but Aidan is showing me every day that I have nothing to be afraid of. Aidan Black loves big and loud, and he deserves the same from me, which is why I made a sign to hold up at the game today, just before the 7th-inning stretch.

I figure this way, even if we're losing, it might make him feel a little better and give him some motivation. Crew and I will be in the family box for most of the game, and then Wren will hang out with him so I can head behind home plate with my sign for the 7th inning.

I've got Aidan's jersey on again today, only this is his *actual* jersey—the very same one he's wearing out on the field today. I'm wearing it open over a white tank, and I paired it with some light ripped jean shorts and a pair of cherry-red Converse.

I took extra care with my hair and makeup this morning, knowing I would be seeing the WAG's again. The idea of being involved in another cliquish group like I was back home makes me anxious, but, save for Brandy, all of the wives and girlfriends I've met so far were really nice, and Wren assured me most of them are genuinely kind women.

The doorbell ringing saves me from delving any further down *that* rabbit hole, and after making sure it's the correct man at the door, I open it to see a real life giant. I interviewed this guy over the phone and he came highly recommended by my financial advisor, so I haven't actually seen him in person until now. I'd only seen his basic profile and headshot.

My mouth must still be hanging open in shock because he chuckles as he holds out a beefy hand. "Hello, ma'am. My name's Callahan Ward, but you can call me Cal. Are you Lyla Taylor?"

I grin back at him and shake his hand with a nod, noting absently how it dwarfs mine. It's almost comical how big this dude is. Aidan is 6'3, and I can tell just by looking at him Cal would make my boyfriend look average. "I am, and I really appreciate you taking this job on such short notice. I'm assuming you have questions before we head to the stadium?"

He follows me dutifully to the kitchen and declines

any drinks, choosing instead to jump right into it. "So it's you and the six-year-old I'm watching over, correct?" I nod. "Great. Now, in order to do my job, I need as much information as possible about the situation."

Blowing out a breath, I quickly launch into the story of Sebastian, giving Cal as much detail as I can. "So, just to recap," he begins, staring at his notes. "Sebastian Pennington Junior is the perp, and the feds are aware of the situation and actively looking for him? Are we assuming he's armed and dangerous?"

The question gives me pause as I consider, but eventually, I give him a slow nod. "I hurt his ego by leaving, especially after defending myself against his attack. I have no doubt he wants to hurt me back, and his texts have essentially confirmed as much."

Cal stays quiet, giving me a chance to study him. His expression is grave, but the smile lines around his mouth and eyes tell me he laughs a lot, and my gut is telling me I made a good choice in hiring him.

Crew comes skipping into the kitchen but stops short when he sees the giant sitting at our counter. His entire countenance changes in an instant as he backs away slowly, moving to my side and clinging to my leg. To his credit, Cal has a calm smile as he watches our exchange, and he slowly moves off the stool to crouch in front of us.

He holds his hand out to shake, never once quickening his movements or taking his eyes off Crew. "Hello," he says softly. "My name's Cal. Are you Crew?"

Crew nods slowly, his face belying his anxiety over meeting someone new. "Are you here to take my mommy?"

A quiet gasp slips from my lips, and I drop to my knees, pulling him into my arms. "Crew-bug, *no*. Nobody is going to take me, I promise. Cal is my friend, and he's going to keep us safe at the game today. Is that okay with you?"

With the threat of me leaving successfully quashed, his eyes narrow in suspicion. "You're not a bad guy?"

The large man's smile grows even more. "I'm not a bad guy, I promise. Actually, do you want to know a secret?" He pauses, and Crew nods hesitantly. "Up until a year ago, I was a GI Joe."

Crew's eyes go wide as saucers. *"Really?"*

Cal grins mischievously and shows us his phone screen. It has a picture of him with three other men, all in their fatigues, nearly blending in with the desert background. "See? Me and my friends catch the bad guys."

Squeezing Crew's shoulder, I grin at him. "Now that we know Cal is one of the good guys, can we get going? We're going to be late for your dad's game."

He jumps into action, and soon enough, we're on the road with Cal following in his own vehicle close behind. I meet the eyes of the sweet boy bouncing in his booster seat. "Crew-bug," I start gently. "You know your dad and I aren't married, right? So I'm not actually your mommy yet."

In a move eerily similar to his father, Crew rolls his identical blue eyes. "Daddy said he loves you, and you're his girlfriend. That means you're going to get married. And that makes you my mommy."

No hesitation, not a care in the world about formalities. In his six-year-old mind, his dad and I love each other, so that means I'm his mom now.

"Don't you want to be my mommy?"

Careful to keep one hand firmly on the wheel, I reach a hand back and grip his knee tightly. "Oh, sweetie. Of course I do. I would love to be your mommy and marry your daddy someday."

His grin is blinding, even through the rearview mirror. "So I can tell people you're my mommy now?"

"If it's okay with your dad, you can say I'm your mom."

The parking lot is a madhouse, so I circle around to park in the staff parking at the training facility next-door. I have to get Wren to call in clearance for Cal, so while I'm waiting, I send a warning text to Aidan so he's not blindsided by this new development later.

ME

> Hey, I know you probably don't have your phone on you, but I wanted to give you a head's up just in case I don't see you before the end of the game. Crew just started calling me Mommy, and I wasn't really sure if I should let him, but he's pretty adamant.

Aidan's reply comes within seconds.

DADDY

> Good.

Huh?

ME

> Good?

DADDY

> Yeah, angel. Good. He might as well get used to calling you that now

ME

This is insane, you know that, right? We've known each other two months. Been dating officially for a day. What happens if we don't work out?

DADDY

Hate to break it to you, Lyla, but that's not even a remote possibility. I love you, Crew loves you, and one day soon I'm going to put a ring on your finger and my baby in your belly. Ready or not, angel. You're a mom now.

My heart flutters inside my chest as I reread the words on my screen. I'm a *mom* now. These guys are my family. The one thing I've always known I wanted beyond a shadow of a doubt, and I somehow found it in the most unexpected place possible.

"Can we go inside now, Mommy? I wanna see Auntie Wren!"

I clear my throat and wipe my fingers under my eyes to clear away the unexpected tears. "Yeah, Crew-bug. Of course we can go inside." Cal rounds the hood of my car with a nod, his serious expression back in place. He's dressed down for the game in dark wash jeans and a black Raptors tee, but his size and the sheer power radiating off of him means he'll stick out like a sore thumb. Oh well, at least I know nobody will mess with us with him around.

Plastering a grin on my face to cover my nerves, I help him out of the car and hold his small hand the whole way into the stadium.

28
Aidan

"What has you grinning like you just landed a 70-pound Spottail Bass, Preach?" Rhodes's amused voice knocks me out of my giddy trance.

Tearing my eyes away from the phone screen is akin to torture, but we're minutes away from first pitch, and I'm more keyed up than ever before. Knowing Crew has completely accepted Lyla the way I have has my heart soaring in my chest.

Even if the words haven't actually left her lips yet, I know she loves me. Loves *us*. I don't even try to reign in my goofy grin when I meet my best friend's stare. "Crew called Lyla Mommy."

Rhodes's eyebrows hit his hairline as a shit-eating grin splits his face. "I owe Wren fifty bucks and breakfast in bed."

"How is that different from any other morning?"

A blush heats his cheeks and he clears his throat loudly before murmuring, "I have to serve it naked, wearing a bowtie... *not* around my neck."

A bark of laughter has us both turning to see

Copeland with a smirk. "Why do you bet her at all when you know she will always be right? And why the fuck would you agree to that?"

Rhodes shrugs. "I would've done it without the bet if it'd make her happy."

I just know we're wearing matching sappy ass grins and Cope shudders, faking a gag. "There's so much love in the air I'm practically choking on it." He drops down next to us and stretches his shoulders out, trying to hide a wince.

Warning bells go off in my head when I see his wince, but I don't want to stress him out before the game, so I file it away to bring up later. He hooks a thumb in Rhodes's direction. "I know why this idiot is being a sappy motherfucker, but what's the look on your face for, Preach?"

I couldn't contain my smile if I tried. "Crew started calling Lyla *Mommy* today."

His face immediately softens with a small smile. Coming from the broody bastard, a small, *genuine* smile might as well be him shouting his excitement from the rooftops. "I think she's really good for y'all. I'm happy for you, Aid."

Coach yells for us to take the field for opening ceremony, but I clap my friend on the back. "Thanks, Cope. Now all I need is for her shithead ex to be arrested and for her to tell me she loves me too, and everything will be perfect."

He snorts, punching me on the shoulder. "If you think she isn't head over heels for you, you're an idiot."

Opening ceremonies are over quick, and then the game begins. The Renegades chirp at us any chance they get, but there's tangible tension between their players, and it shows. Their plays are half-assed, and where their teamwork is usually tight and seamless, today, it just seems sloppy and stilted.

The first several innings pass quickly, and though we're up by two runs, they were hard-won. New York is our number-one competition for the World Series this year, and we're determined to bring the Commissioner's Trophy home to Charleston, where it belongs.

"Is it just me, or are the Renegades off their game today?" Rhodes asks from the fence next to me. Our goal as a team is to keep our focus on the pitcher and the ball at all times - whether we're on the field or in the dugout waiting to bat, so neither of us moves our eyes from the field as we talk quietly.

"I was just thinking the same, actually. The longer I watch, the more Rad seems to be the one at the center of all the tension." The Renegades shortstop, Conrad 'Rad' Ames, is one of the less douchey players in New York. I don't have any issues with the guy, and even Copeland, who's notorious for disliking most other people on sight, is relatively friendly with him.

Rhodes raises his hands to grip the siding in front of us. "You think he'll be looking for a trade soon?"

At that, my gaze whips to the side. "You think he'd come here?"

He shrugs. "Couldn't hurt to keep an ear to the ground. You know Daniels isn't going to last long here with the way he's constantly stirring up PR messes. And ever since the Derrick scandal last year, the league is being extra cautious with anything that could bring bad publicity."

Shaking my head, I recall the drama with Wren's ex. He's been trying to make amends with the couple for a while now, and to say Rhodes still isn't his biggest fan would be putting it lightly. "Can you believe he came out last month? Like, posted a picture with his boyfriend and everything."

Rhodes's eyes cut to mine briefly. "I'm happy for the guy, but it still doesn't excuse the shit he put my starling through." He grumbles in irritation.

Before I can do more than nod in agreement, a commotion pulls our focus to the field where two of the Renegades are in an all-out brawl on the field. "Oh shit!"

Our coaches and theirs rush the field, and it takes four of them and the umpire to break up the fight. Rad and the Renegades Center Fielder, Ryan Strand, are at the center of it. When the dust has settled, and everyone is forced apart, Ames and Strand are both ejected from the game, leaving the rest of us to wonder what the fuck just happened.

Coach storms back into the dugout with a scowl on his usually happy face. "What is this, social hour? We've got a game to win! Daniels, get your ass to the plate!"

The rookie hops to quicker than I've ever seen him move and somehow manages to run two bases on the first pitch. "Damn," I mutter. "Way to go, rook."

By the end of the top of the 7th inning, we're ahead by four runs and feeling good. There's always a chance New York could make a comeback, but they're a mess after the fight earlier.

Live While We're Young by One Direction starts playing, which is an unusual choice for the 7th-inning stretch, but Copeland walks up and points towards the Jumbotron with a huge smile on his face.

Glancing over, I do a double take when I see my girl holding up a glittery pink sign.

I LOVE #23

From the blush on her cheeks, I can tell she's embarrassed, but she looks cute as all get out up on that screen.

The words on the sign finally register in my brain, and my jaw drops. Guffaws sound around me, and Cope snorts. "Aaaand there it is."

My eyes dart around frantically, but Coach catches my eye and mouths, "Go get her," at me.

He doesn't have to tell me twice.

I take off at a dead sprint through the tunnel leading out of the dugout and into the locker room, only to find Lyla already standing right outside with a shy smile on her gorgeous face.

I don't say a word, storming toward her, scooping her into my arms, and cutting off her giggles with a scorching kiss. My erection presses painfully against the cup in my sliders when her tight little ass grinds down, but I grin and bear it.

"I can't believe you just told me you love me on national T.V. *Fuck,* I love you so goddamn much, angel."

Without even consciously deciding to do so, I've led us to one of only two other doors in this hallway. "I need you, Lyla. Right now."

She gasps, her hands digging into my hair and tugging hard. "Here? Anyone could see."

My smirk is wicked as I move one hand off her ass and open the door her back was pressed against, quickly locking us in an equipment room. "Any other objections?"

Her eyes are wide and glittering in the low light coming from under the door. "No, Daddy."

I groan loudly and set her down, spinning her around and bending her over a tall stack of folded backstop mats. "Fast and hard, baby. We have five minutes max."

The look in Lyla's eyes when she looks over her shoulder at me nearly has me coming in my cup, and the reminder of the offending item has me shucking off my pants as fast as I can and sighing with relief.

My girl watches me the whole time with a mischievous grin, biting her lip when she notices the hard plastic hit the floor.

"No," I growl.

Her eyes snap up to mine, an indignant look replacing the lustful one she wore seconds ago. "What do you mean, *no*? You dragged me in here!"

Moving forward, I slide my bare erection between her thighs and kick her legs together so they press in around me. The action must give her some friction against her clit, because she rocks against me with a pitiful whimper. One hand comes up to tangle in her long hair, allowing me to pull her head back so I can trail kisses down her neck.

"I said no because you looked like you were seconds away from dropping to your knees for me, and we don't have time for that right now, you needy little thing. So bend over, shut your mouth, and take Daddy's dick like a good girl."

She moans loudly so I lean forward and place a palm over her mouth while the other works to unbutton her shorts. As soon as they're undone, she helps me by shoving them down her legs and stepping out of them. I back up to admire her briefly, running a hand over the smooth globe of her ass.

"You ready, angel? Fast and hard."

My hand is still over her mouth, but her mumbled agreement is enough for me. One hard thrust has her crying out as she stretches to accommodate me, but I don't give her any time to adjust, setting a brutal pace to the sound of her muffled moans and whimpers. "You want me to play with your clit?"

She nods frantically.

"Then I need you to keep quiet when I move my hand, baby. Can you do that for me?"

"Yes, Daddy," she whispers.

I reward her with gentle passes over her swollen clit. "Good girl," I purr.

My pace begins to falter when her pussy flutters around my length, letting me know she's as close as I am. I curse. "Fuck, angel. Are you going to come for Daddy?'

Another nod, followed by a quiet whine. I circle her clit with firm pressure and use my free hand to pull her back flush to my chest, pinching one peaked nipple. The change in angle has her crying out in the small room as she detonates, and I quickly follow her over the edge.

Thankfully, there are paper towels in the corner, so I quickly clean both of us up while I fight to steady my breathing. I still have another two innings to play, and I can't take the field looking freshly fucked.

Checking my watch, I see I'm on the verge of being late and kiss Lyla hard and fast. "We'll talk after the game, yeah?"

"Of course. Go kick ass, babe. I love you."

My heart speeds up, and a huge grin takes over my mouth. "Love you even more, my girl."

After making sure she's safely in the elevator that will take her to the family boxes, I haul ass back to the dugout only to be greeted with raucous applause and laughter. I flip them off, but even their teasing can't dull my mood. The girl I'm in love with just told me she loves me too in front of millions of people.

Nothing could possibly ruin this day.

Lyla

29

I'm floating on crowd freaking nine the whole way back to the family boxes, my heart full from finally telling Aidan I love him and my thighs still trembling from the epic orgasm he gave me in the storage closet. I've never come that hard or fast, but damn, bossy Aidan is sexy as hell.

The box is full today, but when I enter the room, Wren's eyes immediately snap to mine. Her ocean blue gaze is alight with mirth as she winks at me. Crew is curled up in one of the large reclining seats near the wall of windows that overlooks the field, but when he notices where Wren's attention has gone, he gasps.

"Mommy, you're back!" he squeals, sprinting to tackle me in a hug that would make anyone else think I'd been gone years and not less than an hour. I curl myself around him, holding on as tight as he is and inhaling the watermelon scent of his shampoo that's become as familiar to me as my own.

"See? I told you I'd be right back, Crew-bug. Did you have fun with Auntie?"

He nods against my shoulder but burrows further into my arms. "Yes, but I missed you."

My eyes mist over at the whispered confession, and all I can do is hold him even tighter. "I missed you, too."

When I glance around the room to make sure we're not blocking anyone from the door, I see Wren staring at us in shock. Her mouth is open comically wide, and her eyes are so round that it's a wonder they don't fall straight out of her skull. Crew finally releases me, grabbing my hand to pull me back to his chair.

Wren sits down next to us and slowly reaches out to grasp my free hand in hers, threading our fingers together and squeezing tightly. "Mommy, huh?"

I bite my bottom lip in an effort to control my smile, but it's no use. "It started this morning."

"Does Aidan know? How did he react?"

Pulling out my phone, I show her the messages from earlier, intentionally ignoring her snickers when she sees his contact name. When she actually reads the texts, though, her eyes well with tears.

"Ly..." she chokes. "I'm so happy for you. For all y'all. I can't imagine a more wonderful woman to complete their family." Her eyes dart around the room until they land on Cal in the corner. "Does this have something to do with big and beefy over in the shadows?"

Clearing my throat, I take my phone back and grimace. "That's Cal, our bodyguard. He's hanging out with us until my ex is found and dealt with."

Her eyes widen exponentially. "Until he's *found*? When did he go missing?"

My grimace transforms into a full-blown cringe, and I spend the next fifteen minutes going over the events of the last day in detail, only leaving out the intimate details.

By the time I finish explaining, Wren looks like a fish out of water. "Damn, Lyla-boo. I'm glad you got out when you did because the guy seems like his wheel is still turning, but the hamster's definitely dead."

I raise a brow at her, but she snickers and waves me off. "Crazy. He seems batshit crazy."

Ah.

I open my mouth to reply, but a quick tug at my sleeve steals my attention. "Can we go get a pretzel?"

Ruffling Crew's hair, I nod. "Be right back?" I say to Wren. She smiles and waves us on, so I walk over to let Cal know what we're doing.

He smiles as we approach. "Leaving already?"

I shake my head, but it's Crew who replies. "No, silly! Mommy said we can go get pretzels! I'm getting cheese with mine. Cheese on pretzels is the best. Daddy likes mustard, but that's *so* gross."

Cal chuckles and nods. "I agree. Cheese is the best."

The minute we step into the hallway, the hairs on the back of my neck stand on end, causing me to glance around furtively. Cal sees me pause and tenses, subtly checking our surroundings again. "Did you see something, Miss Taylor?"

The feeling of being watched is thick in the air around us, but a more thorough look around comes up with nothing concerning, so I shake my head slowly at Cal. "I think maybe I'm just anxious because it's getting more crowded with the game about to end.

The Raptors are now leading by six runs at the top of the 9th, meaning the game is practically over and people are starting to leave. Aidan explained to me that baseball games go for nine innings, with each being split into a "top" half, and a "bottom" half. If the home team is leading at the end of the top of the 9th inning, they'll call the game early since the home team bats at the bottom of each inning.

He nods in understanding and hovers a hand over my lower back while I keep Crew's hand locked firmly in mine. "Just stick close, and we'll be back in the box in no time, but maybe we take the stairs instead of the elevator? The less exposed we are, the better."

The hulking man follows our lead to the only stairwell in the vicinity. This area is a little more outdated than the rest of the stadium since it's essentially used as a service entrance, meaning the door is one of those that has a long hinged bar for a handle.

The second I push down on the handle, a gloved hand snarls in my hair, yanking me through the door and slamming it shut before Cal or Crew can follow.

I cry out, falling to my knees at the sting, lifting my head just in time to see Cal ramming his massive shoulder into the door as Sebastian jams it with a metal bat. My stomach sinks like a rock, and my heart races when I realize I'm trapped in this stairwell with the man who almost killed me last year.

"Mommy!" Crew screams. Fat tears drip down his cheeks and soak his light blue shirt as he pounds his tiny fists on the door.

Bas is still wrestling with the door, so I take a moment to assess my surroundings and reassure my boy. "Crew-bug, go find Auntie Wren and stay with her," I yell. "Cal, call the police and find Copeland! I'll be fine!"

Sebastian snarls, whipping around and backhanding me so hard my head hits the metal handrail on the wall, rattling my brain. The deserted stairwell swims around me, and when I reach a hand to the back of my head, it comes away wet with blood. "Oh, shit."

A malevolent chuckle is my only warning before I'm yanked up by my wrists and slammed into the wall. The handrail responsible for the way my skull throbs in time with my rapid heartbeat digs into my lower back as Bas shifts his grip, trapping both of my wrists in one of his big hands. He pulls out a knife with the other, holding it shakily at my neck.

The cool metal of the blade glides up my throat and over my face, tracing my features slowly. "I almost forgot how pretty you look all bruised and bloody, darling. Maybe now that I have you back in my care, Father will stop berating me for letting you get away," he murmurs sweetly, pressing the knife into my neck hard enough to cut. I force the tears back and bite my lip in an effort to stay as silent as possible.

"But you just had to go and be a little fucking *cunt*, didn't you? You just had to go and embarrass me in front of the whole goddamn world, always acting like you're better than everyone else just because your dad is a mediocre actor." He smashes our hands against the wall, and I feel one of my wrists crack, forcing a scream from my throat.

He groans like the sound turns him on. Knowing my ex, it probably does. "Fuck, I missed the sound of your screams, little bunny. It's time to get you back home where you belong. Tied up in my basement where you can't cause any more fucking problems."

His tongue darts out to lick up the side of my neck, making me gag violently. My reaction must piss him off further because he backhands me again. This time, I feel my lip split, but I also feel a warm liquid sliding down my cheek, so I assume his family ring cut me there as well. A pained whimper slips free.

"Come now, bunny. It's time to go." The words come out in a giddy cadence, and he bounces on the balls of his feet like a child excited about a trip to the zoo.

Sebastian drags me down the stairs with him at a pace much too quick for how fast the world is still spinning around me. Every time I stumble over my own feet, he stops to inflict some new form of pain.

By the time we make it to the ground floor service entrance, I feel bruises forming all over my body, and I have cuts on more than just my face from the knife he's wielding.

The back door slams open with force, and whatever Bas sees on the other side has him stilling before he hurriedly pulls me to him by my hair. I cry out as one arm wraps around my shoulder, and the other still holds the knife at my neck just hard enough that I feel the sting of the blade.

"Now, Sebastian, let's not be hasty here. Just let the girl go, and we can forget this ever happened, okay? But I need you to let Lyla go now," a man's voice soothes.

Sebastian growls deeply, the knife digging in even further when I whimper. The man in front of us looks vaguely familiar, but with the way my head pounds, I couldn't place him if I tried.

He definitely looks like he could be a bodyguard of some kind. With his dark jeans, black tee, and coiled earpiece, he would look like an off-duty Secret Service agent if not for the full sleeves of colorful tattoos lining his arms.

"I don't know who the fuck you think you are, but this

is *my* fiancé, and I'll be leaving here with her whether you like it or not."

The knife moves, slicing my throat enough that I feel blood dripping down my neck. I bite my lip so hard blood wells where my teeth pierce the thin skin. The man's eyes widen minutely, and his gaze darts over my right shoulder less than a second before a deafening pop rocks the alley around us.

Bas drops like a rock, only with the way he has me gripped in his arms, he takes me down with him, landing on top of me so we're face to face. I feel a thick, viscous liquid seeping into the front of my shirt and vaguely realize what I just heard had to have been a gunshot.

His weight is quickly ripped off of me, and then Cal's face is hovering over mine, his hands moving over my body like he doesn't know where to start. "Fuck, oh *fuck*, Lyla, I'm so sorry. I didn't— I had to get Crew back to the suite, and I called Ryett in for backup, but it took y'all so long to get downstairs. We didn't want to risk breaching the hallway and him hurting you even worse. Goddamnit, I'm sorry."

Cal's words are a frantic mess of apologies and incoherent mumbling, and if I wasn't in so much pain, I might laugh. As it is, I think I'm in shock because the first thing out of my mouth is, "Who the hell is Ryett?"

He huffs, sounding mildly relieved. "You didn't think the exorbitant price you paid was just to hire little ol' me, did ya? I was just the first one able to be here so last minute this morning. The other men on my team, Ryett, Beau, and Atlas, are all here securing the scene and getting all the different branches of law enforcement up to speed."

The other man, *Ryett* I remind myself, joins us on the

ground, his critical eyes looking me over until they meet mine and soften. "Sorry we had to meet like this, Miss Taylor. My name's Ryett and I'd like to look you over if you don't mind?"

All I can do is nod silently, and it's only when he begins to examine me that I realize I'm trembling intensely. I try to lift my right arm to swipe at the blood dripping into my eye and cry out. Ryett winces. "You'll need x-rays to confirm, but based on visual exam alone, I'm going to say your wrist is broken. Did you hit your head?"

Another nod earns me a shared look of concern between the men in front of me. "Let's get you sitting up, Lyla. The EMTs should be here any minute to get you to the hospital," Cal says gently. They do exactly that, going slow enough that the world doesn't spin this time.

We sit in silence for a moment as I get my bearings, at least until the back door slams open again. Both men in front of me draw their weapons but lower them when they see a shocked Copeland with his hands in the air. "Woah, hey! Wren came and got me. As soon as I was off the field, I ran straight here."

He's telling the truth. He's still in his full uniform, cleats dragging against the concrete as she shifts from side to side. Ryett and Cal separate, having formed a wall of muscle in front of me when they sensed a potential threat.

Cope's eyes land on me and widen. I must have a worse head injury than I thought because I see what looks like tears gathering in his green eyes.

"Tiny," he breathes. In three large strides, he's on his knees in front of me. His large hands skim over my shoulders and down my arms, but he pulls back quickly when he touches my wrist, and I wince.

Fury twists his features into the scariest look I've seen on him yet, and suddenly, he's on his feet and stomping over to where my ex lies, moaning on the pavement. Copeland lands a swift but brutal kick to the asshole's ribs, a loud crack reverberating around the alley walls.

Sebastian screams, his face going purple from both pain and rage. "You motherfucking asshole! I'll sue you for that!"

Cope snorts, swaggering my way. "Good luck provin' I did shit to you, you pathetic prick."

My ex seethes, but the effect of his anger is dulled by the fact that he's face down on the ground with his hands zip-tied behind his back. "There are witnesses," he threatens, spit flying everywhere with each heaved breath.

Some of the shock is finally wearing off, so I look around at the four security guards and my friend. "Did you guys see anything?"

They all shake their heads with large grins.

I shrug delicately, my ribs protesting at the motion. "I must have gotten a good kick in when we were tumbling around in the stairwell."

Bas starts to retort when the alleyway suddenly floods with police and press alike, lights flashing as the officers attempt to clear a path for the ambulance. The door bangs open again, producing the one face I've been dreading seeing.

"Aidan." The word is barely more than a whispered breath, but it's enough to catch his attention. His eyes land on my battered face and fill with tears, but when he notices the blood soaked into the front of my shirt, a hand flies up to cover his mouth as a choked cry escapes.

He hits his knees in front of me and gently, oh so gently, pulls me into his arms. "Angel, *fuck*. When Wren came to find us, I wanted to come right away, but I had to stay and make sure Crew was okay. I came as soon as I could, baby." Aidan's hands move to cup my face, bringing my gaze to meet his red-rimmed eyes, darkened with worry and anger. "I'm so fuckin' sorry I wasn't there."

I shake my head quickly. "No, Aidan, *I'm* sorry!" I cry. The shock has completely worn off now, and harsh sobs wrack my aching body as the pain and reality of what just happened finally registers. "C-Crew w-was there. He s-saw Sebastian take me. I t-tried to reassure him, but h-he was s-so scared!"

Aidan chokes on a sob of his own as he lays the softest kisses all over my sore face, his lips coming away slightly bloody. I cringe, reaching up to wipe it away, but he kisses my finger instead. "My sweet, perfect girl. You did everything right, my love. You did what you could to keep Crew calm, and you kept him safe. But what matters most right now is that you're *alive*. You made it out and came back to me, Lyla. To *us*. Sebastian can never hurt you again, do you hear me? You did that on your own."

I must have a guilty look on my face still because he raises his brows at me and pointedly glances around at the beefy men forming a protective barrier between us and the rest of the world. "Okay, so maybe you had a backup plan. We'll talk about you sneakily hiring security later, by the way. You beat me to it."

He grins briefly before growing serious. "I am so proud of you, angel. You're truly the strongest woman I know, and I can't imagine a better mother for our children."

The EMTs are rushing our way with multiple stretchers, but I keep my focus on Aidan. "Children? Do you know something I don't?"

Even tinged with worry, his grin is flirtatious. "If you think I'm not gonna to tie you to me in every way humanly possible, as soon as possible, you're outta your damn mind, baby."

I don't have time to process his declaration as I'm surrounded by medical personnel and police, each one speaking over the other as they load me into the ambulance. Aidan follows me, but my focus shifts to the scared little boy inside. "Aidan, go be with Crew. He needs you more than I do right now."

He opens his mouth to argue with me, but a tattooed hand lands on his shoulder before he can. Copeland's face is set in stern determination as he settles a glare on his best friend. "Go get Crew and meet us at the hospital. I've got Ly."

Aidan once again starts to argue but is cut off by Cope. "Let her get checked out and cleaned up before Crew sees her, man. He needs one of you with him, and no offense, tiny, but you're looking very *Carrie* right now, and I don't think we need to add anything else to his therapy checklist."

A hoarse laugh escapes, and I think that was his goal because the corner of Copeland's mouth tips up in a small smile. Aidan looks horribly torn, but I smile reassuringly and squeeze his hand. "I'll be okay, Aid. I have Branch here to keep me company while the doctors fix my face and hand."

He snorts, getting my joke right away, but Cope looks confused. I pat him gently on the shoulder. "I know you've seen *Trolls*, pal. The name makes sense."

The big, bad, tattooed grump rolls his eyes, but I swear I see the barest flush hit the tops of his cheekbones.

"Ma'am, we need to leave now," the EMT interrupts us, and Aidan leans in to kiss me hard and fast. "I love you. We'll be there as soon as we can." He looks to his friend. "Take care of her."

Copeland nods seriously, and we're both loaded up. I stare out the small windows at the man I love long after we pull away, thanking every deity I can name that I made it out alive.

30
Aidan

"Where's my mommy? I want my mommy!" Crew's wailing cries echo down the long hallway outside the family boxes, making me pick up my pace. In a few long strides, I'm able to toss open the door, and the second he spots me, he runs into my arms, knocking me to my ass.

"I'm here, raptor. It's okay. Everything's okay now." I maneuver him so he sits sideways on my lap, his light-up sneakers touching the floor and his face buried in my chest as he sobs. Tears flow freely down my cheeks, and I'm so wrapped up in our shared pain that I startle when a heavy arm drapes around my shoulders.

I turn blurry eyes to my right to see Rhodes's solemn face inches from mine. The understanding in his gaze gives me the strength I need to pull myself together for my son.

Several ragged breaths are all it takes to wrestle my emotions back under control. I can fall apart tonight when my girl is safely back in our bed. But for now, Crew needs me to be strong for both of us.

"Raptor, do you want to go to see Lyla?"

His glassy, bloodshot eyes meet mine, snot dribbling down over his lips. Before he can use me as his human tissue, an *actual* tissue appears in front of our faces courtesy of a sullen Wren. I smile in thanks, cleaning up my boy's face. His expression is more serious than I think I've ever seen as he glares at me indignantly. "She's not Lyla anymore, Dad. She's my mommy now. She even said so!"

Before the tears make a repeat appearance, I smooth his hair back from his face. "I know, Crew. I know Lyla is your mommy now. I'm sorry."

Crew nods, relief softening his features now that I've verbally acknowledged Lyla is his mother. I really need to pick up another parenting book. None of the ones I've read talked about how to handle the whole stepparent thing. But is that what Lyla is? Crew's never had a mother, and there's nothing stopping her from legally adopting him when we get married.

Something to think about later.

"Can we go get her now?"

Somehow, in the midst of one of the scariest days of my life, I've gotten everything I ever dreamed of for Crew and me. And I'll never let anything jeopardize it again. With a smile down at *our son*, I say the words I only ever dreamed I would get to say to him.

"Yeah, kiddo. Let's go get your mommy."

"Excuse me, can you tell me what room Lyla Taylor is in?" The bored-looking receptionist glances up, and recognition flares to life in her eyes. In the blink of an eye her annoyed expression shifts to something flirty, and anger has a red haze tinting the edges of my vision.

"Oh, wow! You're Aidan Black. Can I just say I'm a *huge* fan?" Her long red nails touch the top of my hand, but I quickly rip it away, nearly growling at her in anger.

"Lyla Taylor's room number, please?"

Her flirty grin stays fixed firmly in place as her eyelashes bat frantically, the spider-like lashes thick enough that I worry she'll take flight if she doesn't stop.

It's clear I'm not getting any answers here, so I move to the next computer over, where a kind-looking older woman sits hiding a grin behind her hand.

"Hello, ma'am. If you wouldn't mind, I'd like to visit my *wife*, but I don't know what room she's in." I make sure to emphasize the word 'wife' for the other receptionists' benefit, and it makes the one I'm speaking to chuckle.

"She's in room 502. Head to the left and take the second elevator up. The barcode on this pass will get you access to the floor."

I smile at her gratefully. "Thank you." Turning to Crew, I see him with his thumb in his mouth.

Damn it.

It took me until he was almost four years old to get him to stop sucking his thumb, but I guess the trauma of the day is finally catching up to him, and he's reverted to it as a coping mechanism.

My mind is already making a list of things I'll need to do for him, from setting him up with a child psychologist to adjusting our daily routine to allow me some extra time at home to be with him and Lyla.

I follow the kind receptionist's instructions and when room 502 finally comes into view, I let out a breath of relief hearing Lyla's bright giggles echoing into the hallway.

My feet stop involuntarily when we reach the

threshold of the door, and my eyes widen, even as I scramble to grab my phone and hit record while simultaneously holding Crew back with a hand on his shoulder.

"Wait a second, raptor," I murmur. "Let's watch Uncle Cope act a fool for Mommy."

There, in all his scrub-capped, shoe-covered glory, is *the* Copeland Hawthorne, doing his very best rendition of *What Makes You Beautiful* by One Direction.

Lyla is reclined back in a large hospital bed, giggling so hard she's clutching her side and wincing every few breaths. Even with stitches in multiple places on her face and neck, she's still the most gorgeous woman I've ever seen.

As soon as the last notes of the song ring throughout the room, I stop the recording and begin a slow clap that makes my best friend stop dead where he stands, panting. My shit-eating grin is uncontrollable and doesn't fade at all, even when he points a long, tattooed finger at me menacingly. "I did this to make *your* girl happy. I don't want to hear a goddamn word, Preach."

I hold my hands up in surrender and try to tame my grin to a more modest level. Crew finally loses his patience and launches himself at Lyla, his tears starting up all over again as he does. Cope is closer than me and catches him mid-air. "Woah there, big guy. You have to be careful, okay? Lyla's hurtin' real good right now."

Crew's big eyes widen even further, the glossy sheen making them look like true ice chips. "Mommy, you have bruises? My bruises always hurt, too."

Lyla's eyes get misty in response to the tremor in his words, and she reaches her arms out to take him from our friend. Her right arm is covered in a cast that ends below her elbow, the weight making it dip visibly lower than the left.

Copeland just rolls his eyes, knowing she can't support his weight sitting down like that, and gingerly places him at her side before coming to stand at mine.

We watch the two of them in their own little world for a moment before he fills me in. "Doc said she has a mild concussion, broken wrist, bruised ribs, and lots of little cuts and bruises. The cuts on her cheek and neck are the worst. She got fifteen stitches in total, four on the cheek and eleven on the neck, and a fuck ton of butterfly bandages. But your girl is a trooper. She didn't flinch at all when they were stitching her up, and the doctor said he's never seen a reaction like hers before."

He sighs, glancing at Lyla with something that looks like a mix of longing and anger. "Doc also said she has a bunch of healed breaks and fractures all over her body, so my best guess is she's used to dealing with injuries like this. You need to be there for her as much as you can the next few weeks, Aid. I know you likely won't leave her side, but I think it's just as important that she see other friends and family, and especially her therapist."

I nod, already mentally preparing myself for more panic attacks and new triggers we'll need to watch out for. A throat clears behind us, surprising me.

When I turn around, I come face to face with a suspiciously familiar-looking guy with dark auburn hair poorly hidden under a ball cap and huge dark sunglasses.

My brow raises in question as Cope moves so we're shoulder to shoulder and blocking the door. The guy smirks and looks around the empty hallway before removing what's obviously a poor excuse for a disguise, and then I'm staring down one of the biggest movie stars in the world.

Also, you know, *my girlfriend's father*.

I literally know nothing about this man other than he neglected his only child her entire life and then introduced her to the man who almost killed her, so I keep my face stern and cross my arms over my chest, widening my stance to completely block the door.

One eye keeps Colin locked in my periphery while I turn my face to see my girl cuddling our boy. I feel my expression softening but damn it, I can't help it.

"Ly?"

She looks up with a radiant smile on her pretty face. "Yeah, Aid?"

Clearing my throat awkwardly, I nod my head at the door. "Your dad is here."

She chokes on air, launching herself into a coughing fit. "I'm sorry, did you just say my *dad* is here? Colin Kingsley? In this hospital?"

I nod. "Want me to tell him to fuck off?"

Lyla snorts. "Umm... no. It's fine. You can let him in. Will you guys stay, though?"

My smile is wide. "Always, gorgeous." I turn back to her father and slap the meanest scowl I can muster on my face. "If you're here to gaslight my girl into going home with you and back to those Pennington fuckers, or if you hurt her in *any* way, I will personally ruin your face so thoroughly you'll never act again. Are we clear?"

The smirk is absent from his face, replaced with a serious look to match my own. "Crystal."

Copeland stops him with a hand on his surprisingly muscular chest. "You hurt her, and whatever my friend here does to you, I'll make it look like a day at fucking Dollywood. Are *we* clear?"

At the threat, Colin visibly gulps, causing the side of Cope's mouth to twitch into an almost-grin. "Understood."

We move aside to let him into the room, and I know the second he lays eyes on my girl because he lets out a choked gasp. "Lyla..."

Cope and I move to hover on one side of the room, choosing to take a seat on the small couch and drop the intimidation act for now. I'm fairly confident he isn't going to risk fucking things up this time, but only time will tell.

"Honey, I can't tell you how sorry I am that I didn't know what was going on."

She shrugs, playing with Crew's hair. I've noticed playing with hair is a nervous tick of hers. Mine, Crew's, or her own. It doesn't seem to matter either way as long as she has someone's hair to twirl to calm the anxiety. "I didn't tell you. And you weren't around, so I don't see how you could have known."

The guy looks like she just shot an arrow straight at his chest, wincing like the quiet words are a physical blow. "I know, and I've never been more ashamed than I am right now. I'm sorry, Lyla. So dam—" He glances at Crew. "Darn sorry. I know my promises mean less than nothing to you, but I swear from now on, I'm going to do my best to be an active part of your life, in whatever way you'll let me be."

"What about your deal with Mike?"

Colin scoffs, running a hand through his auburn hair. His hair color is what I imagine Lyla's *should* look like, with the red undertones that peek through the brown she has now, but I've never really asked her if she colors her hair. Knowing she's been on the run, it would make sense.

"The entire Pennington family can fuck off to some remote island in the middle of the goddamn ocean for all I care. The minute you called me, I called Pennington Corp and told them to shove their deal up their collective shady ass."

Lyla snorts, still playing with Crew's hair. I don't think I've ever seen my boy this quiet for this long, but he finally breaks the awkward silence with a whispered question that might make things even *more* awkward, if possible. "Mommy, who's that man? Is he a bad man, too?"

Colin's jaw drops as he stares at Crew with a look of confusion and awe. "Mommy?"

I expect her to shy away from the question or change topics, but she smiles proudly down at our son and speaks in a clear, firm voice. "This is Crew, and that's Aidan." She points at me and kisses the top of Crew's head. "Crew is Aidan's son biologically, but mine in every way that matters, and I plan on adopting him as soon as I can. So, I guess... you have a grandson."

His eyes glisten under the harsh hospital lights as he slowly moves toward the bed, crouching beside Lyla. He's next to his daughter, but his gaze is firmly fixated on our son. Reaching a hand out slowly, he introduces himself. "Hi Crew, it's nice to meet you. I'm Lyla's dad, Colin."

Crew stares at his hand skeptically, glancing nervously at Lyla. "He's not a bad man, Crew-bug. I promise."

He nods before slowly reaching out to take Colin's hand. "If Lyly is my mommy, does that mean you're my grandpa now?"

Colin looks at his daughter with wide eyes, but hers are solely focused on me. I smile softly at her, trying to convey with my eyes that I trust her judgment and will go along with whatever she thinks is best. I know she wouldn't risk Crew, so I'm sure she's going to give her dad a thorough ass-chewing about all of this as soon as she's feeling up to it.

"If he wants to be," she says pointedly. The words are for Crew, but she aims them at her father.

His face lights up, reminding me so much of Lyla. It's easy to see where she gets her mega-watt smile from. "I've always wanted to be a grandpa."

The next several hours are filled with talking, laughter, and some tears as the father-daughter duo catch up and Crew asks endless questions about his new grandfather. But then we're discharged, and Colin and Copeland leave so we can head home.

After tucking Crew into the living room fort bed with us, I'm finally alone with my sleeping son and the love of my life.

For the first time in months, I feel completely at peace. I'm not worried about protecting Lyla from some unknown threat or waiting for the day she calls things off because she's scared. I'm breathing without the weight of the world on my shoulders for the first time in my life, and it's so freeing.

Lyla nuzzles further into my chest, her sweet cherry-vanilla perfume filling my nose and easing any residual fear clinging to my soul. "Aidan?" she murmurs.

"Yes, angel?"

Her glassy eyes meet mine, brimming with hope. "Is it really over?"

My chest clenches for my sweet girl who's been

through so much. Pulling her even closer, I kiss the top of her head. "It's really over, baby."

She sighs, staring up at me with love written all over her gorgeous face. "What do we do now?"

My smile is soft but so very real. "Now we start the rest of our lives together. As a *family*."

In baseball, when the catcher calls for a specific pitch, but their pitcher does something totally different, we call it getting Crossed Up. Lyla coming into our lives feels kind of like that. I called the play only for the universe to throw me a pitch I never could have expected, and somehow, it worked out to be everything I barely dared to dream I could have.

Lying here with my girl and our son, I know getting crossed up was the best thing that's ever happened to us. And if I had to do it all over again?

I wouldn't change a single damn pitch.

31

Aidan

Six Months Later

"You look like you're about to hurl, Preach. Do I need to grab the bucket?" Copeland's laughter at my expense is nothing new, but this time, he might be right. I feel like I'm about to throw up or pass out, or hell, maybe both.

The look on my face must warrant some pity because he smiles sympathetically at me. He's doing that more than ever lately, and I know it's because he's finally let go of his relationship hangups and is happy.

"Come on, Aid. You and tiny have been together like eight months, and you've been wanting to propose to her for at *least* seven of those. Why are you so nervous?"

I scoff. "You mean aside from the fact that we're about to play game 7 in the World fucking Series on our home field? What if she hates the ring? What if she hates that I'm asking so publicly? What if I ask her, and then we *lose the fucking series?*"

Cope's face splits into a manic sort of grin. "One, we're going to win. Like those bakery boxes always say, 'manifest that shit.' Two, she's going to love the ring. You literally had it designed based on an old journal you snooped through. Which, by the way, *please* let me be around when she finds out. I would love to see tiny kick your ass. Three, she won't. She's going to love it because it will remind her of your first date."

He grimaces with a shudder. "Well, the good part, anyway. And finally, so fucking what? If you ask Lyla to marry you and we lose the series, you'll still be fucking *engaged*!"

Rhodes startles me when he slaps my shoulder. "I don't say this often, but he's right, you know."

I wave them off and run a hand through my messy hair. I finally got it cut a few months ago, but it's already getting shaggy again.

The opening notes to *Beautiful Soul* by Jesse McCartney play over the field speakers on our side for the third time this season, and the Raptors fans go fucking crazy. "Oh god, I'm going to puke."

Cope hands me the gaudy fake Raptor blue roses and my mitt, shoving me out of the dugout. "No time for vomit, Preach! Go get your girl!"

Coach and all the other guys cheer me on, and I make my way onto the field to sounds of confusion from the fans, especially the ones who saw me do this exact thing seven short months ago. Just like back then, Lyla is in the WAG section behind home plate, and I hop the fence to get to her.

My heart races faster the closer I get, but the second I see her adorably confused smile, the raging storm inside me calms. Her cheeks are ever so slightly sunburned, and the pink stands out on her beautiful skin, making her eyes look even greener than usual.

Stopping in front of her, she grins up at me. "Hey, Aid. Not that I'm, like, complaining or anything, but haven't we done this already?"

My smile is shaky with nerves as I drop to one knee in front of my girl. Gasps ring out all around us, and a glossy sheen quickly coats her eyes even as her pretty pink lips part in surprise.

I hand her the roses and keep my mitt firmly on my hand, gathering both of her hands in the worn leather and covering them with my free one.

"Eight short months ago, you showed up on my porch hoping to interview for a job and flipped my entire world on its axis. I knew the moment my eyes locked with your gorgeous green ones, I was in trouble, and it turns out I was spot on. I fell for you hard and fast for too many reasons to list, and I find new reasons every single day. You gave Crew a mom, and you gave me a partner in life, but most importantly, you gave me a home. My very own safe haven where I don't have to have my shit together all the time. For the first time in my life, I was given a safe space to just be *me*. And as long as I live, I'll never take it for granted."

I stand up and signal to Cope, who throws the box in a perfect curveball that lands in my waiting mitt. Taking the mitt off, I drop back down to one knee and open the box, relishing in the gasp from my angel and the titters from the women around her when they see the 2.5 Carat oval cut pink diamond on a rose gold band.

"Even if we win the World Series today, you will still be the most important catch I've ever made. Every day, I think I couldn't possibly love you more than I did the day before and every day you prove me wrong." I lean forward to nuzzle her nose with mine, making sure the next words are just for us.

"Lyla, angel, my girl. I look forward to a lifetime of you proving me wrong in all the best ways. Marry me?"

Tears are streaming down her cheeks, but her smile is blinding. "YES! Of course, yes, I'll marry you!"

Her lips crash to mine in a frantic kiss that ends all too soon when the crowd goes berserk around us. After one final peck to her delicious cherry lips, I turn around and thrust both hands into the air. "SHE SAID YES!"

The same words flash on the Jumbotron and if I thought the crowd was wild before, it's *nothing* compared to now. The adrenaline from knowing she said yes buzzes through my veins, and I know now that what Copeland said couldn't be more right. I don't give a single fuck if we bring home the Commissioner's Trophy today because I just got the most important win of all.

Then again, I wouldn't say no to winning the World Series.

After all, my future wife is watching.

"I can't believe you guys won the World freaking Series!" Lyla squeals between kisses. I haven't taken my mouth off of her since we got home ten minutes ago, and this gearshift between us is really starting to cramp my style.

Rhodes's parents, bless 'em, took Crew tonight so we could celebrate the win on our own. And I plan on *celebrating* all night long with my soon-to-be wife.

Tearing myself away from the sinful temptation of my girl's mouth is a near impossible feat right now, but somehow, I manage it long enough to exit the truck and jog to the passenger side. I make quick work of tossing her over my shoulder in a fireman's carry and booking it up the stairs to our bedroom.

She winces when I toss her down onto the bed, and the heat roaring through my veins quickly turns to ice. "Angel, are you okay? It is your wrist again?"

Ever since her bastard of an ex broke her wrist, she's been having issues with it, but she shakes her head with a mischievous grin.

"No, I'm just cramping a little bit. I'm fine."

My brow furrows as I quickly run through my mental calendar. "But..."

Her grin widens. "Remember when I said I had an appointment yesterday right after the game, and that's why Wren brought Crew home?"

I nod, my mind spinning with worry and worst-case scenarios.

"I had my IUD taken out."

There's a loud record scratch inside my head, but our room is so quiet you could hear a pin drop. "You... had your IUD removed?"

Lyla bites her lip and nods, barely able to contain a grin.

"We're going to have a baby?"

That gets a hard laugh out of her. "I mean, hopefully. But there's the whole *trying* thing we have to do first."

In the next breath, I'm tackling her to the bed as gently as possible, kissing up the side of her neck to nip at her jaw. "Guess we better try hard then. And as often as possible."

Her responding giggles are cut through with a moan when I pull down one of the cups of her bra and flick her nipple with my tongue. Circling the tight bud, I nip and suck at it until it's a stiff peak before repeating the process with the other one.

Kissing my way down her delectable body, I stop at her belly to rain kisses down on the soft skin, saying a silent thank you to the universe for giving me this perfect woman. "Good goddamn, angel. I can't believe you're gonna make me a dad again. I can't wait to see you pregnant with our baby."

I run a hand across her lower abdomen, my imagination running wild with images of her big and round as she grows a perfect little baby with their mama's stunning green eyes.

My hands skate back up to her pert breast, kneading them in my callused hands. She whimpers as the rough skin scrapes along her sensitive peaks. "Aidan," she moans quietly.

I slap four fingers down on her inner thigh, hard enough to sting. "What's my name, angel?"

Her moans get louder. "Daddy, please!"

"You're so pretty when you beg, my perfect, sweet girl. You need Daddy's cock to fill you up?"

She nods frantically, her eyes wide and glassy with desire.

"Soft and slow tonight, baby. Don't want my girl hurting any more than you already are." With that declaration, I slide into her on one long thrust, our matching groans echoing throughout the room.

Each thrust is slow, and even as I angle myself so the head of my cock rubs directly against her front wall, hitting the perfect spot on every stroke. "You take me so well every time. Like you were made for me."

"I was. I was always meant to be yours, Aid."

I rest my my forehead against hers, my hips picking

up pace until we're both crying out our releases. Knowing she's not on birth control keeps me rock hard inside of her, making me not want to leave her wet heat, so I don't.

I roll us so we're on our sides facing each other and tuck her long auburn hair behind her ear. She finally admitted she'd been dying it after Sebastian was arrested and stripped it back to her natural color shortly after.

She's never looked more beautiful than she does right now. Shiny hair spread out around her head like a halo of color, cheeks flushed pink from exertion and lust, mossy green eyes bright with happiness, and a smile on her face wide enough to rival the one she gave me when I proposed.

I run my fingers through her soft hair with a sigh. "I meant what I said this afternoon, Ly. Every day, I think I can't possibly love you more, and every day, you prove me wrong. I love you with every bit of myself, angel. Down to my very marrow."

Her deceptively strong fingers dig into the mop of messy hair on my head, massaging and relieving some of the soreness from the two-piece mask I wear during games. "Meeting you was never in the plan, but I feel like the luckiest girl in the world because I did. You changed my life in all the best ways, Aidan. I can't wait to be your wife."

My eyes dart up to meet hers, searching for any signs of hesitation. "Then let's not wait."

Perfectly manicured brows dip in confusion at my words, but my grin grows with each passing second. Picking up my phone, I start a group chat and add Lyla, Copeland, his girlfriend, Rhodes, and Wren.

. . .

Aidan Black has changed the chat name

CATCHING BALLS (& FEELINGS)

ME

How fast can y'all have weekend bags packed?

WREN'S STALKER

We kinda had naked plans man, what's up? Also, love the chat name, but the rest of us aren't catchers.

DETECTIVE COPE

And I'm sure as shit not catching feelings

FUTURE MRS. GRAY

Rho, Cope, shut up. Is everything okay, Aidan?

DETECTIVE COPE

I'm about to have a girl spread out on my countertop covered in frosting. Is this conversation absolutely necessary right now?

FUTURE MRS. GRAY

Oh, hmm... Rho?

WREN'S STALKER

I'll swing by the grocery store later, Starling.

ME

Lyla and I are getting married first thing tomorrow in Washington DC. Do you idiots want to be there or not?

ANGEL

We are?

WREN'S STALKER

😂😂😂

FUTURE MRS. GRAY

If that's true we need to leave like, an hour ago. Ly and I need to go shopping.

DETECTIVE COPE

I hate you right now, Preach. You owe me

ME:

> Jesus Christ, enough. I don't need to be nauseous before getting onto this damn plane. Y'all do know this is my wedding, too, right? Like, it wouldn't be happening without me.

ANGEL

Aww poor Aidan. Sounds like someone's sad not to be the favorite anymore

ME

> Y'all have an hour. Meet us at Ravens Run airstrip, I'm calling in a favor. And Cope? Can you pick up a few of those cupcakes Ly loves?

DETECTIVE COPE

Yes, Daddy 🫡

Lyla looks up from her phone with amusement and excitement brimming in her beautiful eyes. "We're really doing this?"

I pull her in for a fierce kiss. "We're really doing this, angel. Let's go get our boy and get to the airport. Pack a bag while I make the arrangements."

As my soon-to-be-wife races around the room, squealing excitedly, all I can do is watch her in awe. In less than twenty-four hours, this precious woman will be my wife, and as soon as she's ready, I'll have the adoption papers drawn up so she can legally adopt Crew.

Our lives have changed so much the last year, but I've never been happier. And I know without a doubt I'll take any curveball life throws my way, as long as I get to do it with her by my side.

*Author's note:
This book contains two epilogues, and both **DO** contain pregnancy, birth, and spoilers for books 3 & 4 in the series. Neither epilogue is necessary to read for the overall plot of the book.

EPILOGUE: PART 1
LYLA

One year later
Please, for the love of all things holy, not now.

An intense wave of nausea falls like a thick veil over my mind as I enter Buttercream Dreams. The harsh scent of tequila fills my nostrils and nearly sends me to my knees. Kennedy notices and rushes to my side, concern etched all over her flushed face.

"Tiny! Are you okay?" The calm cadence of her words is soothing enough that I'm able to suck in several deep breaths and let the wave pass. I was so happy when Copeland met her last year, and now that they're together, she's become one of my best friends. She also owns Buttercream Dreams, so that makes my current situation slightly less awful.

Doing my best to breathe through my mouth, I manage a wobbly smile. "Sorry, I'm alright now. I had a stomach bug a couple of weeks ago, and I've had issues with strong scents ever since."

Her mouth pulls into a grimace. "I'm testing out a

margarita cupcake this week, and working tequila into the frosting is harder than I thought it would be."

I snort and immediately regret it when I get a fresh waft of pungent liquor. Slapping a hand over my mouth, I sprint to the tiny bathroom at the back of the shop and make it just in time to heave over the toilet. The meager contents of my stomach make a reappearance just as a cold rag is placed against my forehead.

Kennedy's lemon and sugar perfume fills the tiny room, masking the scent of alcohol and settling my stomach. "That's it, let it all out. Poor tiny," she coos, patting my head. I would laugh if I weren't still trying to get my gag reflex under control.

Gathering the remaining shreds of my dignity, I sit up and offer my own grimace as I take the cloth from her outstretched hand to wipe my mouth. "I'm okay. God, I'm so embarrassed. This is like the third place I've thrown up that wasn't home this week. Every time I think this damn bug is gone, I get hit with another round."

My friend's critical gaze tracks over my face before trailing pointedly down to my midsection. "Lyla... when was the last time you had your period?"

My brows furrow. "Well, that seems kind of invas... *oh my god.*"

Kennedy watches my eyes widen with barely contained excitement. She knows Aidan and I have been trying to have a baby for over a year now, but she also knows we haven't been successful. Panic fills my chest where air should be, and it must be obvious because her gaze hardens on mine.

She points a stern finger in my direction as her lips set in a determined line. "You march your cute ass across the street and get a few pregnancy tests, and then go home and take them." Her eyes soften as she helps me up off the floor. Without letting go of my hands, Kennedy holds my attention.

"I'm not good at the whole pep talk thing, so I don't have any words of wisdom for you. But I do know you have a husband and a little boy at home who would be nothing short of thrilled if you turn out to be pregnant. And if you aren't, then you'll keep trying."

I take a deep breath, holding it for a count of five, and release it, along with some of the tension in my shoulders.

"Okay. Okay, I'm going."

"*OH*, wait!"

Kennedy runs back out, taking a left into the front of the bakery, and I follow. Curiosity eats at me as she digs around the fridge, sticking things into a box so fast I can't make out what she's found.

She turns around with a triumphant grin, thrusting the small yellow box in my direction. "I did cupcakes for a baby shower yesterday and had tons of leftover decorations. So just in case there's a plus sign..."

My eyes water when I see three different cupcakes nestled inside with tiny words spelled out on top of the frosting. One for each member of my little family.

There's a cappuccino chocolate chip cupcake with espresso frosting, the word "Daddy" spelled out across the top. Next to that is a Fruity Pebbles cupcake with strawberry frosting that says "Big Brother." And the last is a dark chocolate cherry cupcake with the frosting rolled in mini chocolate chips, just the way I like it. The word "Mommy" is spelled out on that one, and it takes a considerable effort to dam the tears back. My eyes lift to meet Kennedy's. "Thanks, Ken."

Her own eyes are glassy, but she waves me off. "Get out of here. And text me later!"

It only takes me ten minutes to secure the tests and make the drive home, only when I reach the end of our street, I see Aidan's truck in the driveway.

Shit.

If Aidan is home, there's no way he won't realize something is up, and I really want to surprise him. I see Copeland's SUV parked in his driveway and send a thank you to the universe. I can take the tests at his house. He's just as nosy as my husband, but at least Cope can keep his mouth shut.

With the tests and cupcakes in hand, I park my SUV and rush next door, texting Aidan a little white lie about dropping something off for Kennedy.

My hands are full, so I use my elbow to hit the doorbell, giggling when the device plays a doorbell version of *What Makes You Beautiful* by One Direction.

Rhodes sneakily installed the song after seeing the video of Copeland dancing for me in the hospital. Cope acts like he hates it, which means we all use it as often as possible.

He opens the door with a scowl on his handsome face, but I meet it with a beaming grin and push past him into the house. "Sorry, need your bathroom!"

I hear his heavy footsteps following me, only stopping when I shut the bathroom door in his confused face. "Are you okay? Are you sick? Do you need ginger ale?"

A smile finds my mouth in spite of my nerves. My grumpy best friend is secretly a little mother hen, and me being sick the last couple of weeks has turned him into a hoverer. "I'm okay, Cope." But now that he's said it, I could go for some ginger ale. "But I wouldn't say no to the soda!"

"You got it, tiny."

The second his footsteps recede I tear open the box and carefully read the instructions on the little pamphlet as if I don't already have them memorized from the last year's worth of negative tests.

After peeing on the test, I flip it upside down and set it off to the side while I wash my hands. All the while, my mind runs like a freight train after midnight. I want the test to be positive so bad, but what if I'm a terrible mother? What if my lack of maternal influence renders me incapable of connecting with this baby?

The timer sounds on my phone, and at the same time, a firm knock lands on the door, startling me out of the panic spiral. I contemplate not opening the door, but I could really use a pep talk right about now, so I open it and come face to face with a worried Copeland.

"Tiny, are you sure you're..." he trails off, his eyes widening when he spots the pregnancy test on his counter. "Holy shit. Is that... are you?"

I shake my head, only mildly surprised when my eyes fill with tears. "I don't know. I've been sick for weeks and thought it was just a bug, but I went to see Kennedy at the shop today, and the smell made me sick again, so she convinced me."

He nods, grimacing in sympathy. "I told her not to use actual tequila, but the stubborn little terror rarely listens to me. So, why are you taking the test in my bathroom and not one of the four you have at home?"

"Kenny gave me some cupcakes to surprise Aidan

with if it was positive, but I just... I don't know if I can handle the disappointment I'll see on his face if it's another negative. I want to know, but I can't find the bravery to look."

Copeland sighs, pulling me into a tight hug. "Tiny, I know how much you and Aidan want this, and I know it's been hard, but you're one of the bravest women I know. How about this? You and I will look together. And then, as soon as you know, you can go home and tell Aid."

Releasing a shaky breath, I nod and pick up the test, keeping it face down.

"Plus," he continues. "If it's positive, I can hold it over his head that I knew about his baby before he did. Payback for the stunt he pulled with Kennedy last year."

That has me giggling. "You had your head so far up your ass you never would've seen the light of day if he didn't set her up on that date, and you know it."

He shrugs. "Don't care."

Boys.

"Okay." Taking a deep breath, I flip the test over. "Oh my god."

"Holy shit, you're gonna have a baby. I'm gonna be an uncle again!"

I'm going to have a baby.

"Crew is going to be a big brother. Oh my god, I'm going to have two kids. I think I might throw up."

A small cup of ginger ale is thrust into my hand, and I sip it gratefully. From the corner of my eye, I see Cope watching me warily, but the excitement in his eyes is impossible to miss. My phone dings with an incoming text on the counter, and I snap into action.

Handing the cup back to my friend, I beam at him. "I've gotta go!"

I barely manage to hear his call of good luck before I'm rushing out the front door, test and cupcakes safely in my bag. One perk about Copeland's new house is that it's literally only steps from ours, so I'm in our garage in under a minute.

The sound of *The Princess and The Frog*, Crew's current movie fixation, greets me as I come through the door into the kitchen. Ignoring the anxiety thrumming through my veins, I grab one of our cute serving trays and carefully set the cupcakes out on the island. When they're all set out, I yell for Aidan.

He strides into the kitchen with a huge grin on his face and immediately sweeps me up into a hug. "Hi, angel. I missed you," he murmurs, planting kisses all over my face.

"I was only gone an hour!"

His grin is charming as always, temporarily distracting me from the reason I called him in here. "An hour is way too long without my girl."

I see the cupcakes out of the corner of my eye, and my heart starts racing. "I got us cupcakes," I blurt.

Aidan raises a single brow but perks up when he sees the treats on the counter. With each step closer to the island, my heart climbs higher in my throat. He's only a few steps away when his whole body freezes. "Lyla Taylor Black, what is this?"

He whips around, and I almost laugh when I see the shock on his face. I can't resist messing with him. Just a little. "They're cupcakes, Aidan Jasper Black. Did you take a ball to the head recently that I don't know about?"

He stalks toward me, backing me into the wall. When my back meets the plaster, one of his big hands curls around my throat just under my jaw, tilting my face up to meet his. "You know damned well that wasn't what I meant, angel. Is this a joke? 'Cause if it is, you're being meaner than a starving cat outside a fishstick factory."

I can't hold back my snicker. I've been in this state for two years, and I'm still not used to all the weird colloquialisms they've got.

Seeing the desperation in his eyes has me sobering up fast, and the earlier tears spring to the surface again as I hold up the test. "It's real, Aid. We're going to have a baby."

His icy blue eyes dart between mine and the test for a full minute before he whoops in glee, picking me up and spinning us both around. "Holy shit, you're having my baby. We're gonna be parents again!"

Crew comes barreling in the kitchen, drawn in by his father's exuberance. "Why are you yelling, Dad?"

Aidan's eyes find mine, a question clear in their depths. When I nod, he beams, turning to our son and dropping to sit in a chair so they're at eye level. "Come here, raptor."

Our boy looks wary but moves to stand in front of his dad.

"You remember when you were asking for a baby brother for your birthday?"

It takes a second to click, but Crew is smart as a whip and immediately catches on, turning to me with a beaming grin. "Am I getting a baby brother, Mom?"

My smile is watery at best. "Well, we don't know if it's a boy or a girl yet, but yeah, Crew-bug. We're gonna have a baby."

He screams, sprinting around the kitchen in excitement and shouting all the things he's going to teach the baby.

Aidan stands up, moving so that he's standing at my back, and wraps me up in his strong arms. "You've been pretty quiet. Are you happy, angel?"

I turn in his arms, landing a kiss on his stupidly perfect mouth. "I'm scared, but I'm also *so* happy."

His smile softens. I've talked about my fears of being a mother with him, and he says the same thing every time. "You're already the best mother in the world, and just because you're making this one from scratch doesn't mean the way you love our babies is going to change."

I release a heavy sigh, the tension from the day draining and leaving me emotionally wrung out. "Love you, Daddy."

He smirks, pulling me in for a chaste kiss so we don't traumatize Crew. "Love you more, angel. Always."

EPILOGUE: PART 2
AIDAN

Eight months later

"And I see you've taken on the role of Crew's mother for two years now, Mrs. Black?" Lyla nods, a nervous grin on her face as one hand cradles her large baby bump.

The timing of this hearing couldn't have been more chaotic, considering Ly is 39 weeks pregnant and literally days away from giving birth to our son, but she refused to push it back. She said she wouldn't be bringing another son of mine into the world until she could legally call the first one hers.

The judge smiles kindly at her before addressing our boy. "Crew Black, are you happy and comfortable living with Lyla as your mother? Do you feel safe, loved, and cared for even with the changes currently happening in your family?"

"Yes, ma'am. Lyla is my mom and the only mom I want. She makes our lives better." He shrugs like it's obvious, and I have to hold a hand over my mouth to stifle the chuckle that wants to escape.

Our presiding judge has no such qualms and snickers

quietly before addressing me. "As his biological father, do you swear that all documentation regarding parentage and termination of rights for the mother and maternal grandparents are true and were obtained legally and ethically?"

"Yes, Your Honor. Crew's biological mother terminated her rights shortly after his birth and has been deceased for six years, and in spite of a lengthy court process to have his maternal grandparent's rights terminated, that paperwork was filed and notarized late last year."

She nods, shuffling the paperwork on the bench. "And have you considered the fact that you'll be sharing your son with your wife for the rest of your lives, regardless of your relationship status? These proceedings will give Lyla equal rights to Crew, no exceptions. For all intents and purposes, Lyla will be as good as his biological mother."

My smile widens. "I understand, and we've never wanted anything more." I reach over to toss an arm over Crew's shoulders. The kid is growing like a weed and looks more like a pre-teen than the eight-year-old he actually is.

Judge Crowder looks over the three of us with a critical eye, and after several tense minutes, she beams. "It's not often I see families in my courtroom that share as much love as the three of you so obviously do, and because of that, it is my absolute honor to sign this adoption decree today."

She signs the paperwork with a flourish, and Lyla begins crying, her hand clutching harder at her belly as she pulls Crew in for a tight hug. "Congratulations, you three. I wish you the very best."

I can't see Crew's face because he has it tucked into Lyla's shoulder, but his back heaves, letting me know he's likely crying too. Our adoption attorney has tears glistening in her eyes as she holds up a camera. "Say, 'Happy Adoption Day!'"

We do, and even though I know it's going to be a disaster of a picture with all of us red-faced and sobbing, I'll be framing it as soon as humanly possible. Our friends and family rush us from the gallery with flowers, balloons, and a million congratulations, but Lyla hangs back slightly, her grip on my arm turning painful as her nails dig in.

"Angel, you okay?"

Her face has gone ghostly pale, but just when I start to panic that there's something wrong, I notice the puddle at our feet. My eyes widen comically and fly to hers, my mouth dropping open. "Oh, shit."

Wren notices where my attention has gone and inhales sharply. "Alright, Mom and Dad need to go." She turns to me. "Do you have the bags packed?"

I nod. "I put them in the car weeks ago. We're ready."

I expect Lyla to still be panicking but turn to find her crouched down and murmuring with our son. Leaning closer, I'm only just able to hear their words over the din of the excited crowd around us. "I'm sorry you have to share your day with the new baby, Crew-bug. I wanted this to be special just for you."

His grin is blinding as he hugs her tightly. "It's okay, Mom. I can't wait to meet my little brother. This is the best day ever!"

She sniffles, tears still running freely down her face. Her cheeks have filled out a bit during her pregnancy, and while she's still sinfully sexy all the time, I can't deny the change makes her look fucking adorable too.

Turning a nervous smile my way, she holds out both hands so I can help her up. If the size of her belly is anything to go by, this baby is going to take after me with his height.

Pulling her into my chest, I kiss her soundly. "You ready to be a Mommy again?"

She smiles nervously, clutching the bottom of her bump. "Let's go give our boy a brother."

———

"Knock, knock," Wren stage whispers from the doorway of our private room. I know she's doing her best to hang back and be polite, but I can see her nose and one eye through the crack in the door.

Chuckling, I head to the door to let them in. Mama brought Crew in earlier this morning so we could have some bonding time as a family, and it's been pure bliss.

Lyla was a trooper and labored without any medication for over twenty hours, but by the end, she was so tired she opted for the epidural just so she could try to regain some strength to go on.

Four hours later, our boy was born. 8 pounds 11 ounces of blond-haired, dark-eyed serenity. Mama and baby are both healthy, and I don't think I've cried so hard since I held Crew for the first time when he was four days old.

Wren, Rhodes, and Cope all make their way into the room with giant smiles on their faces. Wren and Rhodes dart straight for the small bassinet while Copeland makes a beeline for my girl. "Hey tiny, heard you were a warrior last night."

She beams a tired smile his way as he gently runs a hand over her messy hair. Once upon a time their closeness would have me seething with jealousy, but I've grown to be so thankful for their friendship.

Copeland is no less my best friend, but he and Lyla have a special bond that goes beyond just friendship. He treats her like another little sister, and I think both of them need and deserve a relationship like theirs.

"Hey, Uncle Cope." She grips his hand in hers. "You ready to meet your newest nephew?"

He looks nervous but nods. I can count on one hand the number of times he's held a baby, and even, then it's been more than seven years.

I pick up our sleeping son and cautiously hand him to our friend. Cope's face softens immensely with a small smile as he strokes one long, inked finger down the baby's soft cheek.

"What did y'all end up naming him?"

I glance at my wife, raising a brow. I think she'll want to be the one to tell him. She pats the bed next to her so Cope can sit down and leans her head on his broad shoulder. She keeps her eyes trained on our son but raises her voice so everyone can hear. "Everybody, we'd like you to meet Carter Copeland Black."

Cope's jaw drops, and for only the second time in our nine years of friendship, I watch tears fill his eyes as he glances my way. "You named him after me?"

My smile never wavers as I shake my head no. "Ly chose his middle name."

He turns his tear-filled eyes to my girl. "Tiny..."

Her bloodshot eyes get misty, and she tosses an arm

around his waist in a side hug. "You went out of your way to help me before we even knew each other, Cope, and you've continued to do so ever since. The last few years you've become even closer to me than an actual brother would be, and I can't imagine our life without you in it. Carter might not be here if it weren't for you, and I thought it made sense to name him after my best friend."

There isn't a dry eye in the room by the end of Lyla's speech, and as tears drip down Cope's face, I find myself pulling him in for a hug, careful not to squish Carter between us. Lowering my voice so only he can hear, I give him my own version of thanks.

"You've been my best friend for nearly a decade, Cope. You've never hesitated to jump in and help when I needed it, but the way you've been there for my girl has only made my respect for you grow. If you hadn't dove in without question to help with Sebastian three years ago, I might not have a wife and son. For that, I'll always owe you. We love you man, and naming Carter after you was the only choice that made sense."

I lean back and lock eyes with him so he knows how serious I am. "Your place in our life is not dependent on your career with the Raptors. You are a member of this family, whether you come back or not, you got that?"

He nods, clearing his throat. "Got it."

His phone starts ringing, so he hands Carter back, and after their own newborn snuggles, Wren and Rhodes get ready to leave, too. Wren's phone pings loudly, and I watch her eyes widen further as she reads whatever's on the screen.

"Everything alright, Wrenny?" Lyla asks carefully, clearly noticing the change in her demeanor.

She turns wide eyes our way. "Jamie's here."

My eyebrows shoot to my hairline, and I have to work to keep my voice quiet since I'm still holding Carter. "What the fuck? Is he okay?"

Wren glances to her husband nervously, showing him the text. Rhodes visibly pales, glancing to me with a nervous look in his eyes I rarely see.

"He just became a father."

ACKNOWLEDGMENTS

I say this with every new book I write, but Aidan, Lyla and Crew truly own a piece of my soul. Lyla's struggles with panic and anxiety attacks after her trauma is something I pulled directly from my own life and seeing it on page was cathartic in a way, and I have a long list of people to thank for giving me grace during the messy writing process.

First and foremost, Fallon, my angel and biggest supporter, I love you endlessly. Thank you for all the plotting calls and messages and always being willing to listen to me vent about the publishing process. I'm so thankful for you and so proud to call you my friend.

My alpha team! AKA the women who act as my sounding board. Kennedy, Aris, Devin, Sierra, Amber, Sarah, and Vilija thank you for keeping me sane and listening to me rave about not only this book, but all my future books and secret projects. Fan Club Forever.

I once again want to thank my family, for supporting me in all aspects of my life and reading my books even when I beg them not to. It makes our check-in calls so much more fun.

My PS fam, for supporting every book I write and opening the door for so many opportunities I wouldn't have had otherwise.

And last but never least, my readers. Thank you for

taking a chance on Aidan, Lyla, and Crew, I hope you spend as much time crying over them as I did.

ABOUT THE AUTHOR

If you're new here, hi!! I'm Holly. I'm a mid-20's indie author who writes everything from baseball players to broody cowboys (surprise!) and small towns.

After years of character plotting and reading so many incredible books I finally started writing my debut in Summer 2023 and made the leap into publishing not long after. When I'm not writing, I'm chasing my tiny human, answering emails at my day job and watching whatever movie my ADHD is hyper-fixated on that month.

(Currently? The *Hotel Transylvania* trilogy)

Crossed Up is my third published book, with many more to come.

Wanna know what's coming up for me and my publishing journey? Click the link to join my Facebook group below if you're on ebook!

If you're not, find us under *Holly Crawford's Reader Group*

Printed in Great Britain
by Amazon